PRIDE V. PREJUDICE

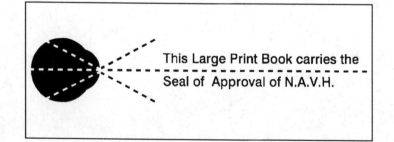

This Large Print Book carries the
Seal of Approval of N.A.V.H.

PRIDE V. PREJUDICE

JOAN HESS

WHEELER PUBLISHING
A part of Gale, Cengage Learning

GALE
CENGAGE Learning·

Farmington Hills, Mich • San Francisco • New York • Waterville, Maine
Meriden, Conn • Mason, Ohio • Chicago

GALE
CENGAGE Learning®

LIBRARY OF CONGRESS CATALOGING-IN-PUBLICATION DATA

Hess, Joan.
    Pride v. prejudice / by Joan Hess. — Large print edition.
        pages cm. — (A Claire Malloy mystery) (Wheeler Publishing large print hardcover)
    ISBN 978-1-4104-8069-9 (hardcover) — ISBN 1-4104-8069-0 (hardcover)
    1. Malloy, Claire (Fictitious character)—Fiction. 2. Booksellers and bookselling—Fiction. 3. Women detectives—Fiction. 4. Large type books.
I. Title. II. Title: Pride versus prejudice.
PS3558.E79785P75 2015b
813'.54—dc23   2015010220

Published in 2015 by arrangement with St. Martin's Press, LLC

Printed in Mexico
1 2 3 4 5 6 7 19 18 17 16 15

To Michael Morton,
who survived twenty-five years in prison
for a crime he did not commit.
In 2013, the prosecutor was found guilty
of failing to provide exculpatory
evidence and survived five days in a
county jail.

1

"You have a better chance of getting on the space shuttle than you have of getting on a jury." Luanne's pronouncement was accompanied by a noticeably snooty smile. She was looking sleek and tan after her annual safari to the beach, but that did not excuse her attitude. Had she not been my best friend, I might have been a wee bit annoyed.

I opted to remain on a more cerebral plane. "Do you suspect I'm non compos mentis? I can assure you that I have all of my marbles in a box somewhere in the attic," I said. We were seated at a scarred picnic table in the beer garden across the street from my cherished Book Depot, working our way through a pitcher of beer on a lovely, lazy afternoon. The sky was blue, the breeze adequate to battle the last gasp of August heat. Students from Farber College were beginning to wander in, but most of the tables were unoccupied. "I've never been convicted of a felony. I don't drool or fall asleep at inopportune moments. Perry Mason would embrace me as a juror."

"Aren't you overlooking the inescapable fact that you're married to the deputy chief of the Farberville Police Department?"

"There is that," I admitted.

"And that you have a reputation for meddling in official investigations?"

"Rumors of my interference have been greatly exaggerated. I was merely assisting the police on those rare occasions when they seemed to be straying in the wrong direction." I may have blushed slightly, as befitted my modest nature.

Luanne laughed until beer dribbled out of her mouth and her eyes watered. She finally gained control of herself and took the napkin I offered her. "Oh, yes, you tiptoe among the suspects, dropping only the slyest comments, hovering unseen in the corner at the fateful moment when the perpetrator falls to his or her knees and bleats, 'I did it!' The detectives scratch their heads and wonder about the identity of that Sherlockian wisp of haze."

"Good afternoon, ladies and gentlemen. I

want to take a moment to thank you again for your willingness to make whatever sacrifices are necessary in order to serve on our jury. It is vital to our system in this great country that citizens such as yourselves participate in the dispensation of justice." Prosecuting attorney Edwin Wessell, as he'd introduced himself to us, leaned forward to emphasize his sincerity. He was short and lean, with petrified dark hair, an expensive suit, and large, somewhat yellowed teeth. Unfortunately, they matched his complexion, which resembled a cheese pizza flanked by two tomato slices for ears. After sucking in a breath, he resumed telling us how we represented all things true and good in the past and present, and would have the honor of doing so in the future.

I suppose I should have been flattered to be epitomized as a flag-waving patriot, but I was mostly hungry. The day had begun well before the unreasonable hour of nine o'clock, when we'd been told to arrive at the courthouse. I'd wasted too much time trying to decide what a dedicated member of a jury would wear to do more than slurp a cup of coffee in the car. The next seven hours had been a series of forays in and out of the courtroom. We'd met Judge Lucille Priestly, a busty middle-aged woman with an emphatic chin and hooded eyes. The assistant prosecutor, a twitchy young woman, had given us a startled look before burying her nose in stacks of folders. The defendant's attorney, a pudgy man with bristly blond hair and rosy cheeks, who might have gone to law school with the assistant prosecutor, seemed even less enthusiastic to acknowledge us, although he had admitted his name was Evan Toffle. The defendant had managed a weak smile. Her name, we'd been told, was Sarah Swift, and she was charged with first degree homicide. She wore a white blouse, and her long gray hair was loosely pinned in a bun. Her expression was more suicidal than homicidal.

Prosecutor Wessell finally ran out of platitudes and consulted briefly with his assistant. "As I'm sure you all know from watching television, the next process is what is called voir dire. I am going to ask you a few questions, after which my colleague will do the same. Juror number seven, I believe you noted on the questionnaire that you were detained for shoplifting."

This perked me up. Number seven was the only one among us who had dressed for tea with the queen. Her very high heels had clattered like a jackhammer on her frequent trips to the ladies' room, and she'd pitched a less than genteel fit when confronted with a stale sandwich for lunch. "It was a mistake," she said coldly. "As I made clear to the police officer, my husband is a doctor and I am on the board of several charities. I merely draped the scarf around my neck to see if I liked it, and then forgot about it. The charges were dropped."

Wessell gazed at her for a moment, his thin lips pursed. "I'm sure it was an oversight. Now, juror number three, may I ask you about encounters with the defendant at the local farmers' market?"

My attention did not wander, but it did meander a bit. Sarah Swift's eyes were closed, and her hands were tightly clenched on the arms of her chair. Her breathing seemed measured. Although I read the newspaper assiduously, I'd missed any articles about her purported crime. We'd been told only the essential nature of her offense: first degree homicide. I wondered whom she was accused of killing — and why.

"Juror number ten, I believe you put down your name as Claire Malloy. I found this curiously misleading. Would you care to tell the court your real name?"

"Claire Malloy," I said in what may have sounded like a gurgle.

" 'Malloy' is the name of your first husband, now deceased. I understand he died under mysterious circumstances."

"He died when his car was hit by a chicken truck on a mountain road, in a heavy snowstorm."

"Where were you at the time?"

I was baffled. "At home, with my child."

"Was this confirmed by the investigating officers?"

Increasingly baffled, not to mention displeased. "Yes, it was. Are you accusing me of something?"

Wessell rubbed his hands together, suggesting this was merely a warm-up volley. "Why would I accuse you of a crime, Mrs. Malloy? Is there something you haven't told us?"

I looked at the judge, who was watching me with a puzzled frown. I had an urge to slam back the ball with a wicked slice of iciness, but I reminded myself of my mild nature and inherent civility. "It was an unfortunate accident. I'm sure there's a report somewhere, Mr. Wessell." I did not say his name with discernible warmth. I had no idea why he was attacking me as if I'd been implicated in Carlton's death. I hadn't. The state police had concluded that it was the result of poor weather conditions. The driver of the chicken truck had been exonerated. I'd been informed, not questioned. "I wasn't driving the truck. I was at home, as I said a minute ago."

"But you have been involved in other homicides, have you not? I believe the police considered you a suspect in the brutal killing of a local writer."

"For approximately thirty seconds. I knew the woman, but I had no reason to harm her. Her husband was found guilty and sent to prison."

"So you say," Wessell said with a minute sneer. "What about the other homicides, Mrs. Malloy? There have been a lot of them in your vicinity. I'd list them, but I hate to waste the court's time. No matter where you go or what you do, someone always ends up dead."

The jurors on either side of me shifted nervously in their chairs. I regret to say that my eyes were so rounded with astonishment that I could feel them. "There have been occasions when I assisted the police in their investigations and subsequently testified in court. But I was never, ever responsible for any homicide."

"Yet innocent parties died. Just how many bodies have you stepped over in your so-called attempts to assist the police?"

"I have no idea," I said flatly. "Why don't

13

you tell me?"x

Wessell rubbed his hands again. "I don't want to upset your fellow jurors. Let's return to the issue of your real name, shall we?"

"My name is Claire Malloy, although that's not what's on my birth certificate. It is on my passport, driver's license, credit cards, Social Security card, utility accounts, voter registration, and library card." I glowered at him. He was lucky that the first row of jury members and a waist-high railing were between us. I am not inclined to violence, but I was ready to wipe the smirk off his face.

He turned back to his assistant for a whispered consultation. I forced myself to breathe deeply and uncurl my fists before my fingernails drew blood. I noticed the defendant was regarding me with a peculiar expression, although I couldn't interpret it. I was fairly certain I'd never met her. Her eyes were a vivid blue, her cheekbones high and predominant, her face lined with threadlike wrinkles. If she'd wandered into the Book Depot, my bookstore on Thurber Street, she'd done so without catching my attention. I occasionally went to the farmers' market at the town square, but I couldn't recall having any conversations

14

with her. When I frowned, she looked away.

"Now then, Mrs. Malloy," Wessell said, "is it true that you remarried several months ago?"

"Yes, but I kept my last name."

"Whom did you marry?"

"Peter Rosen."

"Would that be Deputy Chief Peter Rosen of the Farberville Police Department?"

I clamped down on my lower lip before I blurted out a rude remark about his perspicacity. When I could trust myself, I said, "Yes, but I kept my last name. If this disqualifies me from serving on the jury, okay. Why don't you stop badgering me and send me on my way?"

"I am not badgering you, Mrs. Malloy — or should that be Malloy-Rosen? I am simply trying to determine why you've attempted to hide your identity from the court. Please remember that perjury is a felony."

The fateful straw crushed the camel's back. I'd done my level best, but now I was so furious that I was momentarily overwhelmed by a surge of adrenaline. My jaw quivered. I closed my eyes and willed myself not to leap over the first row and the railing in order to grab Wessell's shoulders and shake him until he begged for mercy. I would show none. I finally opened my eyes, delicately cleared my throat, and said, "I did not attempt to hide my identity. I filled out the jury questionnaire carefully and noted my husband's name and position. I did not change my name when I remarried because of my daughter."

"And your reputation, which is remarkable."

"Thank you." I did not say this with customary gratitude.

"You're welcome, Mrs. Malloy-Rosen."

If there had been a spotlight in the courtroom, it would have been aimed at me. I felt as though I were in a grimy interrogation room, charged with a horrific crime that would lead to the gallows. I gritted my teeth and stared at Wessell, who had clearly taken it upon himself to play the role of Bad Cop. He stared back. I willed myself not to blink. This mute exchange of hostility might have continued all afternoon if the judge had not yawned and said, "Well, Mr. Wessell?"

"I move to strike this juror for cause," he said. "She has personal ties to the local police department and is likely to be prejudiced."

"Juror number ten, you are dismissed," the judge said.

There was a collective sigh of relief as I stood up and edged past the other jurors in the second row. My face was hot and my legs were unsteady, but I maintained my dignity as I headed for the door. As I went past the defendant, she looked up at me with a sympathetic smile. I felt an urge to squeeze her hand and offer a few words of encouragement. Wessell might have ordered the bailiff to shoot me if I did, however, so I continued out the door and down the hall to the exit. Once in my car, I slumped back and replayed the scene. The prosecuting attorney had attacked me as if I were a cockroach scurrying across the courtroom floor, rather than merely pointing out that I was married to a police officer and therefore apt to have a bias — a bias that one would assume was in his favor, not the defendant's.

I considered dropping by the PD to talk to Peter, but he had mentioned an afternoon meeting with some agency that consisted of cryptic letters. Luanne had decided to take a long weekend and had scampered off with her current amour, a professor of botany who was obsessed with ferns.

I needed solitude and sanctuary. I drove through Farberville's version of rush hour and out a county road to my perfect house. It had not been on the market when I first saw it, but a couple of murders and an exposé of illicit activity had not deterred me. As I parked by the porch, I couldn't keep myself from gloating, although in a ladylike fashion. It was an antebellum jewel, with gray shingle gables, gingerbread trim, and ten acres of clover-strewn fields, an apple orchard, and its own indolent stream at the bottom of the hill. The spacious rooms had hardwood floors, high ceilings, and a state-of-the-art kitchen that I had not yet mastered completely. The master suite was on the first floor, with his-and-her walk-in closets, and the bathroom had a dressing table and racks to ensure that the fluffy towels were warm. French doors opened onto a private terrace. The second floor was Caron's domain, along with guest bedrooms.

I peeled off my pantyhose, changed into shorts and a T-shirt, poured myself a drink, and went out to the terrace to ponder ways to humiliate Prosecutor Eric Wessell until he slunk back under his rock. I was certain I'd never met him before, although we could have been at the same ghastly civic banquets. I did have a reputation, but I hadn't been involved with any cases in his jurisdiction. I tried to erase the image of his smirky face and equine teeth, the flakes of dandruff on his bony shoulders, the almost maniacal glint in his beady eyes as he tore into me with the charm of a rabid weasel.

That proved to be impossible, so I went into my playroom, also known as the library, and sat down in front of the computer. I did a search for Sarah Swift and found articles in the local paper, the earliest more than a year old. She was accused of murdering her husband, John Cunningham (proving I wasn't the only woman on the planet who hadn't changed her name after getting married). They lived out in the county on an unfamiliar state highway and owned an organic blueberry farm. I closed my eyes as I visualized myself squashing a blueberry pie in Prosecutor Weasel's face and smiling as the purple goop dripped off his bushy eyebrows, then took a breath and continued reading the screen. According to the sheriff's department, Sarah had been at a book club gathering in Farberville the night of the incident. Alcohol had been consumed. When she returned home, she'd allegedly shot her husband in the chest with a shotgun and left him to bleed to death in the barn. The following morning she'd called the sheriff's department, claiming she'd discovered the body when she went to the barn on her way to feed the chickens. Neighbors had acknowledged hearing a blast at midnight. Based on the sheriff's calculations, Sarah had had adequate time to arrive home by eleven. Wessell had characterized her as a vindictive, cold-blooded killer who had ignored her husband's pleas for help and simply gone to bed. Her fingerprints were on the shotgun, which was found in a hall closet.

"Oh, Sarah," I said as I looked at her grainy mug shot. "Was he that awful?"

"Are you talking to the computer or to yourself?" said Caron, my offspring and occasional bane of my existence. Although we both have red hair and freckles, our dispositions are polar. Had I not personally supervised her overall well-being since birth, I would have suspected dark forces had resided under her crib and guided her stroller. She recently arrived at the heady landmark of legal majority without a felony, but there had been moments. Many moments.

She came into the library and perched on the ladder. "Either way, Mother, it's a symptom of some icky kind of delusion. Had any chats with the potato peeler lately?"

I did not turn around. "The potato peeler made a pithy remark about a bedroom upstairs that is littered with every piece of clothing you own, as well as a goodly amount of mine. The olive tongs murmured something about my sandals and the netherworld beneath your bed. Oh, and you won't believe what the colander —"

"I said I'd clean my room when I got home from school." She repositioned herself on a leather chair and gave me the vastly superior look of an eighteen-year-old Pulitzer Prize–winner who moonlighted as a Parisian runway model and a CEO. "Did you get on the jury?"

"No," I muttered.

"Peter told you they wouldn't let you serve because of him. You should have just called the courthouse and had your name removed from the list."

"I was willing to do my civic duty." I turned off the computer and ushered her out of the library. "Peter may not make it home for dinner. Look in the freezer and find something to eat. I intend to dine on scotch and water, with a glass of wine for dessert."

Caron sat down on a stool next to the marble-topped kitchen island and studied me with what might have been genuine concern. "What's wrong with you?"

I told her about Wessell and the voir dire. She did her best not to snicker, but her efforts were less than successful. I was not yet ready to see the humor in my public embarrassment. I banged open the freezer door and said, "Pizza, microwave entrees, odd things in a freezer bag that may be hot dogs from your last pool party."

"Can I have a party this weekend, like Sunday? Everybody's going to the lake Monday because of Labor Day. We're going to have a humongous picnic for all the cool seniors. Joel's uncle is going to be there with his party barge, and Kyle's got a ski boat."

"As long as you clean up your room, do laundry, and replace my clothes in my closet."

Caron's lower lip shot out in a classic pout. She'd begun working on it in utero and perfected it before she could toddle. By first grade, she was well on the road to high crimes and misdemeanors with her accomplice, Inez Thornton. I'd bailed them out and bawled them out to no avail. Now all I could hope was that they would leave for college free of manacles. Twelve months to go, I reminded myself as I retreated to the terrace.

I must have dozed off because I almost fell off the chaise longue when Caron shook my shoulder and said, "Mother, you need to see this! It's on TV! Hurry!"

I followed her into the living room and stood in front of the TV. The local news was on, and the weather girl was gushing about an expected thunderstorm with the possibility of lightning and thunder. As opposed to what, I did not know. "You want me to watch this?" I asked Caron.

"Wait for it," she replied grimly.

Waiting required us to watch several commercials urging us to buy cars, join the newest health club in Farberville, and take advantage of an amazing sale on mattresses. Finally the two newscasters, Tweedledumb and Tweedledumber, appeared on the screen, their noses powdered and their smiles radiant. The distaff member of the team sobered as she gazed into the camera and said, "Today jury selection began in the trial of Sarah Swift, accused of killing her husband in a domestic confrontation. Let's go live to our courthouse correspondent, Thomas Pomfreet. What's happening, Thomas?"

Thomas seemed startled as his boyish visage filled the screen. He regained his composure and said, "It's been quite a day here at the Stump County courthouse. Prosecutor Wessell and defense attorney Toffle took their time questioning potential jury members. By five o'clock, the jury was finally impaneled. Judge Priestly declared that the trial will not begin until Tuesday because of the three-day holiday weekend." He gave the camera a quirky little smile. "The highlight of the day came when Prosecutor Wessell accused a potential juror of perjury for misrepresenting her legal name. It seems that Farberville's own Miss Marple failed to change her name after marrying a prominent member of the police department. She and Prosecutor Wessell bandied words over her involvement in a large number of local homicides. The woman was excused and left the courtroom in tears."

I dropped onto the sofa. "That's ridiculous! I was too furious to bother with tears. I was trying to think where to buy a weasel trap or a small bazooka."

"He accused you of murder?" Caron said in a squeaky voice. "Never mind about the party. Is it too late to send me to boarding school?"

I decided not to mention that Wessell had as good as accused me of murdering her father. "Get online and find out, dear. I hear there's a charming one in Greenland."

"This is Not Funny!" She stormed upstairs. I doubted she would reappear with a laundry basket anytime soon.

Once Thomas had faded from the screen,

his colleagues moved on to a bungled robbery at a convenience store. I was marginally grateful that they had not decided to produce inane banter about my humiliation. There had been no spectators in the courtroom, which meant someone had briefed the news station. I had a pretty good idea who it might have been. I went into the kitchen and was splashing water on my face when the phone rang. I had no inclination to answer it, so I let the answering machine handle it. As soon as I heard the first word, I recognized the voice of my ESL student, a Russian woman named Yelena. She assured me that she was most furious at the TV report and quite sure I hadn't killed anybody lately. The next call came from a loyal customer, commiserating. As did the next. A professor from the drama department called to dismiss the report as sheer poppycock. It seemed every last person in Farberville had been watching the local news and was currently discussing my innocence or lack thereof.

It was clearly time to return to the terrace. Hawks circled in the sky, ever vigilant for something tasty for dinner. Grasshoppers whirred in the meadow, and butterflies landed on the lush flowers in the beds surrounding the pool. A mockingbird in the orchard ran through its repertoire. Inside the house, the telephone continued ringing with what I suspected were more condolence calls. The only sympathy I wanted was from my handsome husband, who would gaze at me with his molasses-colored eyes and promise to have Wessell's car impounded.

An hour later I was still brooding when said husband came out to the terrace with a bottle of wine and two glasses. He fussed over me for a lovely moment, then sat down and poured the wine.

"Did you see the local news?" I asked.

"I heard about it."

"What is wrong with that dreadful man? You'd think I vandalized his house and stole his law diploma. I can't remember ever having met him, much less offended him." I blinked to hold back tears. "If I did, I hope I drew blood."

Peter leaned forward to kiss me. "I'm the cause of his animosity. He aspires to be a judge and came by the PD to ask for support. The captain locked himself in his office. I told Wessell that I was obligated to take a nonpartisan position but would not have supported him in any case. The guy's a jerk. He has a reputation for going after women and minorities, prosecuting on

26

minimal evidence and demanding harsh sentences. He charged a battered woman with attempted murder after she threw a skillet at her abusive husband. He's sent a large number of black teenagers to prison for possession of pot or alcohol. Rich people are charged with misdemeanors, if charged at all, while the poor are slapped with felonies for the same offense."

"You could have warned me," I said sulkily.

"I didn't realize he's so damn vindictive." Peter held up his hand. "No, I am not going to have him arrested for a parking violation. When jurisdiction is fuzzy, we have to work with the sheriff's department and Wessell."

"What about jaywalking?"

"No, and I don't want you locked up for assault — or stealing his battery. You're going to have to get over it."

"Over his squished body." I leaned back and took a sip of wine. An idea had come to mind while Peter was talking. A very fine idea. Wessell had humiliated me. Now it was time for me to humiliate him. Peter was gazing at me with a squinty, suspicious look, so I smiled and said, "You're right, dear. I need to get over it. Shall I stick a pizza in the oven?"

2

As soon as Peter left for his office the next morning, I took a cup of coffee into the library and settled down in front of the computer to do more research about Sarah Swift's case. Her lawyer, Evan Toffle, had been appointed by the presiding judge minutes before the arraignment. She pled not guilty. Prosecutor Wessell requested that she be remanded because of the heinous nature of her crime. Toffle pointed out that his client owned a farm with livestock that required daily attention. The judge set bail at five thousand dollars and warned her not to leave the jurisdiction. She made bail that day.

I wrote down her address and located it on an online map. I went into my bedroom to dress for the occasion. After a few minutes of indecision, I put on slacks and a T-shirt. I gazed at my reflection in the mirror, and then replaced the T-shirt with a sensible blouse. I took off the slacks and put on a skirt. I reminded myself I wasn't an attorney and switched back to slacks and the T-shirt. I then took off the slacks, put on shorts, and grabbed my purse.

County 107 was lined by pastures, shabby houses, and carcasses of rusted trucks and tractors. I watched for numbers on mailboxes and eventually turned onto an unpaved road, and soon after into her driveway. The house was large, but hardly a showpiece. It might have been impressive fifty years ago, but decades had weathered the white wood siding and peeled shingles off the roof. One of the upstairs windowpanes was patched with silver tape. Efforts had been made, though. The porch had wicker furniture with cheerful print cushions and hanging baskets with bright petunias. The downstairs windows were covered with white sheers that wafted in the faint breeze.

Beyond the house was the reddish-gray barn where John Cunningham had bled to death. Next to it was what I cleverly deduced was a chicken coop, in that the dozen or so chickens seemed to be cooped up inside it. A white pickup truck was parked beneath a large tree. Behind the barn was a field of bushes in neat rows. I was unfamiliar with the fine art of blueberry horticulture, but the bushes appeared to be healthy.

I went up the steps to the front door. A note taped on the glass panel warned me that I was trespassing and should leave the premises immediately. Hoping the note was intended for the media, I knocked and then stepped back, doing my best not to look like a Casual Friday version of Tweedledumber. After a minute, I knocked again. On the cop shows, people are always home and ready to greet detectives at the door. Sarah must have been a PBS viewer.

I went back down the steps and around the corner of the house. A goat looked up without interest. The chickens failed to squawk. I walked through ankle-high grass to the back of the house, hoping Sarah might be hanging laundry or picking okra or whatever storybook farmwives did when they weren't disfiguring mice. A scattering of plants in the vegetable garden had survived the summer heat and were producing produce. There were four aluminum chairs situated around a small redwood table. Dried leaves and twigs on the chair seats and a toppled barbecue grill indicated Sarah had not been hosting garden parties over the summer.

I'd turned to leave when the back door

opened and Sarah came out onto the small porch. "What do you want?" she demanded.

Since she was holding a dish towel, as opposed to a shotgun, I smiled and said, "I'd like to talk to you, but if you tell me to leave, I will. You may not remember me."

"Juror number ten, right? That was quite a show yesterday. Whatever did you do to earn Wessell's animosity?"

"He and my husband had an unpleasant exchange."

"Your husband being the deputy chief of the Farberville Police Department."

Her expression suggested that she wasn't fond of the profession, but I didn't blame her. "Yes," I said, "but your case is out of his jurisdiction. He's actually a very nice person who helps little old ladies cross the street and never litters. He loathes Wessell."

"All admirable qualities," she said, relaxing into a grin. "I don't understand why you're here, but you might as well tell me over coffee. Come on in."

The kitchen was large and sunny, although lacking in modern necessities such as a dishwasher or a microwave. The worn linoleum floor was clean. I sat down at a round table while she took a cup out of a cabinet and filled it with coffee from a pot on the stove. I fiddled with milk and sugar while I tried to decide how to begin. Asking her if she was guilty seemed overly blunt, but the idea of making small talk was ludicrous. "Awkward" was too mild to describe the situation. "How are you doing?" I finally asked, hoping I didn't sound like a social worker.

"Well, I've been accused of murdering my husband, which is kind of a bummer, and will face the jury in four days. I had to bring in the blueberry crop by myself. My friends are all too embarrassed to call or come by, so I've taken to talking to squirrels in the evening. I was waiting tables at a diner in town, but the manager fired me after the arraignment. I had to sell the car, all but one goat, and most of the chickens. I've been living on our savings. In another month, I'm going to have to decide between electricity and gas for the truck. On a brighter note, I have enough blueberries in the freezer to keep me alive through the trial. If I'm found guilty, I won't have to worry about delinquent utility bills."

"Oh," I said cleverly.

"And you want to know if I'm guilty."

I managed not to blurt out the obvious response, but I did nod. "You don't have to tell me anything. I'd like to know, but I'm not going to ask you. I came to see if I could help you, whether or not you're guilty. If you are, I can try to help your attorney present a decent defense. If you aren't, I will do everything I can to vindicate you and humiliate that weasel."

Sarah gazed at me. "So it doesn't matter if I aimed a shotgun at my husband and pulled the trigger? You're that pissed at Wessell?"

"Yes," I answered with a grimace. "He has a long record of bullying women and minorities. Someone has to push him off his flimsy cardboard pedestal. I consider it my civic duty."

"I see," she murmured. "Your civic duty. Wish I had the wherewithal to be concerned with such lofty principles. The problem is that I'm pushing sixty-four. My math skills are limited, but I figure I'll be at least ninety before I come up for parole." She managed a wry smile. "Will I still qualify for Social Security and Medicare?"

I was beginning to feel profoundly arrogant. I'd fancied myself in a white hat, charging in to seek vengeance because I'd been insulted by Wessell's petty attack. Sarah was facing prison. I glanced at the back door, contemplating a muddled apology and a hasty retreat. In three minutes I would be in my car, and in fifteen minutes I would pull into the parking lot next to the Book Depot in hopes the clerk might be pleased to see me (he wouldn't, but that wasn't the point). I would then do something useful, such as dusting the racks of paperbacks.

"I'm not much of a caped crusader," I said ruefully. "I've been known to meddle in police investigations when I'm convinced a suspect is innocent." I did not ask the question that was palpable in the sudden stillness.

"I didn't do it," Sarah said at last, "and, yes, I'd be grateful for any help you can give me."

"Are you sure?"

"I'm real sure I don't want to spend the next twenty-five years in an orange jumpsuit or whatever it is that inmates wear. Wessell is a son of a bitch. I'd love to watch you send him down in flames. I don't know how you can do it, though. Evan seems to think the case against me is daunting. Then again, I imagine Evan lives in his parents' basement and has yet to lose his virginity. He's a sweet guy, the kind you'd let your daughter date. He's been practicing law for less than two years, and I do mean practicing."

"You can't afford a more experienced lawyer?"

"Organic farming isn't exactly lucrative, and neither is waitressing. We were barely getting by as it was. Tuck used to make a little money repairing furniture. I sold vegetables at the farmers' market until the indictment came in and I was told I wasn't welcome. Want to buy some carrots?"

"I'd rather prove that you're innocent," I said. "Tell me what happened that night, but before you do, who's Tuck?"

Her cheeks reddened. "Sorry, that was what I called my so-called victim. An old nickname, going back to our college days. His name was John Cunningham." Flustered, she picked up my coffee cup and took it to the counter to refill it. When she returned, her eyes were wary and her lips tight.

"Okay, we can call him Tuck. You two were together in college? Where did you go?"

"A liberal arts school on the West Coast. We met there and became close. We got married almost forty years ago, on a hillside. I wore a garland of daisies." She pushed a few stray hairs back into her bun. "Forty years is a helluva long time."

The only thing I'd done for forty years was breathe, but that did not merit a comment. "How did you end up here?"

"Tuck had a friend who'd inherited the

property from his grandfather. The friend preferred life in the big city, so he sold it to us for a pittance in the midseventies. It's not what I'd dreamed of, but Tuck was gung ho to go back to the land and all that crap. He was a romantic, not a pragmatist. He had this great vision of how we could do without electricity and plumbing and raise all our own food. He even insisted that I make soap. When I threatened to walk out on him, he relented on the major issues. I should have left anyway, but I stuck it out for forty miserable years. I probably deserve to go to prison for the crime of stupidity. If it's not a felony, it ought to be."

An unhappy marriage would not sit well with the jury, I thought with an inward wince. "There are plenty of people in prison for being stupid," I said. "That's why they got caught. A couple of months ago a guy held up a local bank, but he forgot where he left his getaway car. He was still wearing a ski mask when the police found him in a parking lot. But let's talk about your case. I read articles in the newspaper. You were at your book club?"

She nodded. "There were a dozen women in it, but only six of us that evening. I can't remember what we were supposed to have read, some thick, depressing book about the woes of a war orphan in a refugee camp. Nobody wanted to talk about it, so we settled back with wine and cheese to complain, whine, and bitch about the men in our lives. I don't know why we pretended to be a book club. We were a support group. I couldn't have survived without my monthly catharsis."

"So you shared your discontent with these women?" I envisioned the jury's beady-eyed disapproval as this came out in testimony.

"I do remember I was really pissed off at Tuck that evening," Sarah said. "I'd asked him to do something for me that day, but he blew it off. Instead, he left a long, detailed list of chores for me to do while he was gone, mostly things he should have done himself."

"Do you still have the list?"

She made a vague gesture. "I think I put it in a drawer so I could stuff it down his throat when he got home. At his best, he was difficult to live with. He was self-righteous and condescending. If I screwed up, he'd lecture me in a patient but slightly frustrated voice, like I was a teenager who'd been caught cutting class. There were times that I had to restrain myself from stabbing him in the back with a kitchen knife." She took a swallow of coffee. "Remember I said when he was at his best. At his worst, he would sulk for days, refusing to speak and totally ignoring me."

"Why did you put up with him?"

Her eyes shifted. "Misguided loyalty, no place else to go. Anyway, I went to the book club, drank some wine, and drove home very carefully. Tuck had told me that he was going on a fishing trip with Will Lund, who lives on the next farm, so I didn't expect him to be here. I went to bed. The next morning I went out to the barn to get a bucket of chicken feed and found his body. I went back inside, called nine-one-one, and was waiting on the porch when the sheriff arrived. I was questioned that afternoon and arrested two days later."

I leaned back in the chair while I thought over her story. She'd recited it without any emotion, but for her it was an old, stale story. I hoped she'd shown at least a modicum of distress when questioned by the sheriff at the scene. The jury would not look kindly upon an emotionally detached widow. "What time did your book club break up?" I asked.

"Ten o'clock. We had a rule so that we wouldn't get thoroughly plastered. I stayed for another half hour to help Billie Lou clean up and listen to her brag about her grandchildren. The oldest had started classes at Harvard and was doing well. Another one was an exchange student in Croatia or somewhere like that. My memory's weak after all this time."

"You left at ten thirty, which means you should have arrived here before eleven. The neighbors reported hearing the blast at midnight. It must have been loud."

"I was asleep by then. The detectives didn't believe me, and I can see from your expression that you don't, either."

I didn't. "The barn's next to the house. Maybe if your bedroom's on the opposite side of the house . . ."

"It's not," Sarah said as she picked up my cup and carried it to the sink. She turned around and leaned against the counter, her arms crossed. "What's more, the windows were open because Tuck refused to have a window-unit air conditioner. All I can say is that I was asleep. If I'd been awakened by a loud noise, I would have gone to investigate. There had been some burglaries in the area, usually during the day when people were at work, but a couple of punks broke into Miss Poppoy's house in the middle of the night and tied her up a month before . . . the incident. They got away with her family silver and her precious television set."

"Were they caught?"

"I don't know."

"Maybe the same men were in the barn the night Tuck was killed," I said. "He took the shotgun and went to scare them off."

"And then they put the shotgun away in the hall closet and left without looking around for anything of value?"

"How do the investigators know it was the same shotgun?"

"They can't be sure, but they determined that it was the same cartridge and shell gauge. They even traced the type and size of the shot to the manufacturer. There was a box of shells with that brand on the shelf in the closet." She looked at me, perhaps expecting a brilliant rebuttal. My complete ignorance of the subject precluded any comment, brilliant or otherwise. "Tuck's wallet was on the kitchen table, with eighty dollars in it."

"We need all the potential suspects we can find," I said, although it was challenging to explain why they'd bothered to return the shotgun — and knew where to put it. It seemed more likely that they would have kept it. "I'll try to find out if they were ever apprehended. What about these neighbors? Who are they and how close to they live from here?"

"Will and Juniper Lund. You may have seen their house when you came up the road. They have a much larger organic farm and sell to grocery stores in the surrounding counties. They recently got a contract with some company that markets organic jams and preserves. Not for millions of dollars, but a decent amount of money."

"Will is the one Tuck said he was going with on this fishing trip?"

Sarah grimaced. "That's what Tuck told me. When the detectives questioned Will, he said he didn't know anything about it. Junie backed him up, said they were babysitting their grandson and Will had promised the child that the two of them would go fishing the next day at the river on the far side of their property. I have no idea why Tuck lied to me about it." She hesitated. "Well, I wondered afterwards if maybe he was planning to meet someone and didn't want me to know."

"Another woman, you mean."

"Yeah, that's what I mean, but don't bother to ask me who. I've thought about it for the last year and I can't think of anyone. Tuck abhorred parties. He barely survived the co-op meetings twice a year and refused to attend the picnics. We hung out with Will and Junie. Years ago I invited a couple of my book club friends and their husbands out here for barbecue, and Tuck was so damn rude that I wanted to toss him on the grill."

I wondered if he'd despised her as much as she'd despised him. It couldn't have been much fun for either of them. Every marriage has its own dynamics, but theirs was hard to fathom. "When did he tell you that he was going fishing with Will?"

"That morning before I left for work. They used to go on fishing trips several times a year. Will knew someone who owned a cabin on the Buffalo River. They'd come home with enough trout to stock the freezer. I was surprised when Tuck told me about it. He'd always been kind of a hypochondriac, but over the last ten years he'd gotten way worse. Every bug bite was the onset of Rocky Mountain spotted fever. A headache was a brain tumor, and a slight temperature was malaria. If he cut his finger, he'd go to the emergency room to demand a tetanus shot. Our medical bills were ridiculous. You wouldn't believe what's in our medicine cabinet. I could have taken in wounded from a battlefield and patched them up without making a dent in it." She shook her head and sighed. "Tuck quit going on these trips with Will five years ago because of all the potentially fatal dangers lurking in the wild. He might poke his finger while choosing a lure or stumble on a root and sprain his ankle. He was afraid to feed the chickens because he might catch coccidiosis. We couldn't have pets because their fleas could carry bubonic plague. Tuck was a real pain in the ass."

I could hear the bitterness in her voice. The jury would, too. "Let's operate on the hypothesis that Tuck was involved with another woman, someone off your radar. Could he have met someone online?"

"Maybe. The library has free computers, and he went there sometimes to read the newspapers and check out books. Medical books, mostly. I worked forty hours a week at the diner. I don't know what he did while I was gone. For all I know, he may have had something going with a librarian or one of the nurses from the ER. He wasn't unattractive until you got to know him." Sarah went into the next room and returned with a framed photograph. Handing it to me, she said, "This was taken two years ago. The tall, bald guy is Will, with his arm around Junie. Tuck has that frown because he was worried that Junie's ragweed allergy was actually tuberculosis and she might cough on him."

I examined the trio. Will was indeed tall and bald, maybe in his fifties, with broad shoulders and a thick neck. His nose was asymmetrical, suggesting he'd been in a brawl. I suspect his combatant had not emerged unscathed. Junie was sturdy, her dark hair in a pageboy style more often seen in old yearbooks. Her features were small and compact, as if someone had squeezed them into the center of her face. As Sarah had said, Tuck was not unattractive. He was several inches shorter than his purported fishing buddy. Wavy gray hair hung below his ears and brushed the middle of his neck. Despite the frown, he exuded a degree of ingenuous charm.

"He was carded in bars until he was thirty," Sarah said over my shoulder. "The dimples, I guess. He used to have a really nice smile. Maybe that's what attracted me to him in the first place." She took the photograph from me and put it on the table, facedown. "I was naive when I went off to college. I was going to major in nineteenth-century English lit, with a minor in history. I assumed all conversations would be about philosophy, art, movies with subtitles, the essence of the universe. Turns out I was wrong. I was a freshman in 1971, when the antiwar protesters were stirring up trouble.

44

They were a lot more interested in American aggression than in British imperialism."

A fascinating topic, perhaps, but I needed more timely information. I wished I'd brought a pad to take notes. "Will and Juniper Lund live on the north side of the road, right? Are they still your friends?"

"They say they are, but they're not knocking on my door with casseroles or invitations to dinner. I don't blame them. Will was Tuck's only guy friend. Tuck used to go over there to watch football and drink beer. Junie treated Tuck like he was her baby brother, even though she was younger. She bought into some of his imaginary illnesses and fussed over him until I wanted to scream. She was always bringing over herbal remedies she'd learned about from some hundred-year-old woman living in a shack in the mountains."

"Do you think they'd be willing to talk to me?"

"You'll have to ask them. They're on the list of witnesses for the prosecution, so it may be thorny. Billie Lou's on it, and the other women in the book club. They'll testify that I said a lot of malicious things about Tuck — and not just at that one meeting — and that I drank a lot of wine that particular evening. Billie Lou insisted that I stay late so she could get me to drink some coffee before I drove home. Instead, I finished off the wine. Evan wasn't pleased when I told him about it."

I sat back and studied her for a long moment. She did her best to meet my gaze, but she was struggling. She was not my ideal choice of falsely accused victims. I was familiar with the fine art of omitting details, and I was certain she wasn't telling me everything. About what, I did not know. "Who else is on the witness list?" I asked.

"The deputies who arrived first, detectives, forensics investigators. My old boss, who'll say that sometimes I came in to work in a foul mood after an argument with Tuck. One of the women at the farmers' market, who saw me throw a tomato at him." She wiggled her eyebrows and grinned. "A ripe one, splat in the middle of his face."

"Who else knew how unhappily married you were?"

"Anyone who ever saw us together for more than five minutes."

I did my best not to groan. "Okay, I think I'd better talk to Evan. You need to call him and give him permission to be candid with me. He hasn't gone out of town for the weekend, has he?"

She laughed. "I imagine he's up to his ears

46

in law books, trying to find some obscure case with a ruling in my favor. The poor boy swears that he believes me, but I'm not convinced that he does. Do you want me to call him now?"

"Please," I said, "and ask him if I can go by his office early this afternoon."

I followed her into the living room and glanced around while she made the call. The furniture was shabby and minimal. Two chairs in front of the small TV were separated by a worn trunk that served as a table. The bookcase was made of planks and concrete blocks. The water-stained wallpaper was apt to have been there when Tuck and Sarah had moved in years ago. A macramé hanging on one wall reminded me of a gnarly giant cobweb. Art consisted of a weathered piece of wood that had been decoupaged with a bumper sticker admonishing me to make love, not war. I agreed with the sentiment.

"Evan says he can see you at two," Sarah said as she replaced the receiver. She told me the address of his office, which was near the courthouse.

I looked at the clock on the mantel above a darkened fireplace filled with ashes. "That gives me time to talk to the Lunds before I drive back to town. Do you need to warn

47

them before I knock on their door?"

"They should be at home. Go ahead and surprise them." She came over to me and put her hand on my arm. "I really do appreciate your offer to help, even if nothing comes of it. I want you to know that I didn't kill Tuck, even though I came close plenty of times."

I told her that I would call later, and went outside. I hoped I hadn't made a mistake (which I have been known to do on rare occasions). I wanted to believe that Sarah was innocent and Wessell was railroading her to further his career — and that I was acting out of altruism rather than pique. The jury would have the final word. Although I knew Sarah might be watching, I walked to the barn and pulled open the heavy door. The redolence of moldy hay stopped me in the doorway. My nose twitched and then exploded in a series of sneezes that caused my eyes to water. I rode out the storm, then wiped my eyes and peered into the hazy light. Stalls that had housed horses were filled with rusted junk. Bits of straw were scattered on the warped wood floor. A patch in the middle had been swept clean, giving me a view of a large, dark stain. As I stared, imagining Tuck's body, something rustled nearby. I retreated to my car.

When I reached the road, I saw the Lunds' house and pulled into their driveway. Their house was as large as Sara's, but in much better shape. Flower beds on either side of the brick sidewalk were well tended. A tire swing hung from the branch of a large tree, and toys had been abandoned in the grass. A grandchild had been mentioned, and as I got out of the car, a small person of an appropriate size came running around the corner of the house, waving what I dearly hoped was a toy gun.

When he saw me, he stopped so abruptly that he lost his balance and sprawled onto an overturned tricycle. I approached cautiously. "Hi," I said. "Are you okay?"

"Who are you?" he said as he got to his feet and glowered at me. "Are you a stranger?"

I nodded. "We have not been introduced. My name is Claire Malloy, and I came by to talk to your grandparents. Would you please tell them that I'm here?"

Scowling, he pointed the cap gun at me. "I'm not supposed to talk to strangers."

"Good point. Do you mind if I knock on the front door?"

His gun made a series of sharp bangs, loosing a wisp of smoke and an acrid smell. I remained unscathed, to his dismay.

49

"Grandma!" he howled abruptly, sounding as though I'd grabbed a handful of his hair. "Grandma! Help! There's a stranger out here, and she's bothering me!"

"You're bothering me," I said in a low voice.

His voice rose to a screech. "Grandma, come fast! I need you, Grandma! It's a 'mergency! Help!"

I stayed by my car, hoping Grandma didn't appear on the porch with a more lethal weapon. I was relieved when Junie came out the front door and hurried down the steps to the walk. She gave me a quick look as she scooped up the little boy. "Gracious, Billy, you sound like you've got a squirrel down your britches. You're perfectly fine, okay? Calm down and take a few breaths. Nobody's going to bother you." She waited until he complied and then put him down. Taking sanctuary behind her, he stuck out his tongue at me. "He's excitable," she added. "He just turned four this summer."

"I'm Claire Malloy, and I apologize if I upset your grandson. I just came from Sarah Swift's house. I've offered to help with her defense, and I'd like to talk to you and your husband if you're not too busy."

She bit down on her lip for a long moment. "All I can tell you is what I told that prosecutor. I don't see how that's going to be of any use to her. Will's not here right now. He had to go into town to sign some paperwork at our lawyer's office."

"Do you know when he'll be back?" I tried not to glare at Billy, who'd moved to the other side of his grandmother's legs and was aiming his cap gun at me. Four can be an adorable age. Caron had written her first ransom note at that age, when she kidnapped a neighbor's cat and hid it in her closet. Since she'd demanded "choklate chip cokies" rather than money, the FBI had not been called in. I would not have trusted Billy with anyone's cat.

"Hard to say," she answered, idly swatting at Billy as he clutched her leg. "He and I need to talk about it. Why don't you give me your telephone number?"

"The trial starts Tuesday. I'm convinced Sarah is innocent, but I'm afraid she'll be convicted anyway. She said you're old friends. Don't you want to help her?"

"She'll get a fair trial," Junie said.

"In a perfect world, yes. However, the prosecutor is determined to prove that she's guilty, no matter what may have actually happened that night."

"I think it's obvious what happened that

51

night. I can't count the number of times Sarah threatened to kill Tuck. She might have been joking, but deep down she meant every word of it. She came home drunk, they got into a fight, and she shot him. She may not have meant to do it. For all I know, she doesn't even remember grabbing the shotgun and going to the barn."

"Why would Tuck have been in the barn?"

"Zombies!" Billy shouted, whacking his grandmother's leg for emphasis. "He went to the barn to fight the zombies! They're dead people with rotting skin and gross eyeballs."

She bent down and clutched his wrists. "I am sick and tired of all this nonsense. You go inside and wash your hands so we can bake cookies for Grandpa before he comes home for lunch."

"Then let go of me," he protested, squirming. As soon as she loosened her grip, he darted across the porch and into the house. The door slammed.

Junie shook her head. "I can't believe my daughter lets him watch all those terrible shows. When he stays with us, he's allowed to watch Disney cartoons and *Sesame Street.*"

I was trying to find a way to convince her to talk to me when my cell bleeped. "Sorry,"

I murmured as I pulled it out of my purse. Peter's name was at the top of the screen. "Hello, dear, can I call you back?"

His voice lacked its usual warmth. "Can you meet me for lunch in half an hour? I'll be waiting for you at that silly place on the square that calls itself a bistro." The screen went dark.

I took a crinkled grocery receipt out of my purse and scribbled my telephone number on it, then gave it to Junie. "I do hope you and your husband will agree to talk to me. I'd like to know more details about what you heard that night. I'm not challenging you or implying that you were wrong. I'm just trying to help Sarah."

Junie's mouth sagged. "I feel really bad about having to testify against her, and so does Will. We don't know what happened in the barn. It could have been an accident or self-defense. I'll call you this evening."

"Thanks so much," I said automatically, distracted by Peter's call. I got in my car and drove back toward Farberville, forcing myself not to speed, since a ticket would fall into Wessell's jurisdiction and I might be hanged. Peter had sounded grim, implying something serious had occurred. On the other hand, he hadn't told me to meet him at the ER, so I was fairly sure nothing dreadful had happened to Caron. If she'd done something felonious at school, she would have called me, not Peter — if only because they'd made some sort of secret deal involving her behavior and the model of car he was giving her for graduation.

My stomach twisted as I pictured my perfect house in flames. I decided Peter would have been at the scene shouting encouragement to the firefighters rather than meeting me for lunch. At the faux bistro. When he could get away from the office, he preferred to have a burger. The last time we'd gone to the bistro for lunch was to celebrate his promotion, and that had been at my insistence. He would not suffer quiche to tell me about an assignment in some obscure location. I was more likely to hear about that over a bottle of wine.

As fate would have it, all the parking places on the square were filled. My bloodless fingers gripped the steering wheel as I abandoned all hope and found a place in the municipal lot behind Town Hall. My hands trembled as I stuffed quarters in the parking meter, and I was feeling lightheaded when I finally barged into the bistro and sat down across from my darling husband.

"What?" I gasped, perhaps unattractively.
"My mother is coming."

3

"What does that mean?" I said, gaping at him.

Peter pushed a glass of wine across the table. "It means my mother is coming to visit us. Drink this."

My jaw was too slack to drink anything. I covered my mouth with my hand and mumbled, "Is this a joke?"

"Nope. She called this morning with the news. A friend of hers who has a private jet is flying to Fort Smith on Sunday. My mother looked at a map, realized we're only an hour's drive away, and got herself invited. She wants me to pick her up Monday morning and bring her here."

"Why?" I realized how utterly inane I sounded but was unable to stop myself.

"To see me and meet you."

"Why does she want to meet me?" I took a gulp of wine. It tasted like vinegar, but it was not the sommelier's fault. "It's a long flight, and private jets are unreliable. They're always crashing into mountains or skittering off runways. Why can't she just call me? You can send her a picture and she can look at it while we have a civilized conversation about how wonderful you are and how nice the weather is. She doesn't have to make some grueling, perilous trip across the country."

"It's not as if she's coming on a wagon train." Peter was clearly struggling to keep up the Rosen-boy aplomb, but his chin was quivering. "She wants to meet you in person, and I haven't been up there in three years. She's my mother, not a serial killer with a penchant for disemboweling booksellers."

"You don't know that," I said as I took a more dignified sip of wine. With a splash of olive oil, it could dress the salad. "Besides, you once said she was still on friendly terms with your ex-wife. They could have thought up this nefarious scheme together. You didn't think of that, did you?" I gave him an icy stare. "Your mother already loathes me. She's coming to retrieve you and take you back to your ex-wife, who's booked passage on a three-month cruise to the South Pacific. By the time you reach shore, you won't remember my name, much less my face."

"My ex-wife is happily married to a senator and hosts receptions for foreign dignitaries when she's not competing in tennis tournaments."

"I knew it," I said darkly. "Does she have her own charity that builds hospitals in Mozambique and schools in Angola? Has she been nominated for a Nobel Prize?"

He nodded. "She's won the Peace Prize three years in a row, and she's a tribal chieftain in Nigeria. What's more, she's written a bestselling novel and mastered the art of alchemy. She had to cut back on her hours as the chief of neurosurgery at Johns Hopkins in order to take charge of NASA."

"A brain surgeon and a rocket scientist. Why am I not surprised?"

Peter had the audacity to laugh, although he leaned back in his chair to stay out of range should I fling the contents of the wineglass at him. Which was not unthinkable. "Is it possible you're overreacting, dear? My mother is coming for a couple of days. The two of you may not become best friends, but you'll find a way to get along, if only for my sake. I'll drive her back to Fort Smith, and she'll fly home."

"Of course I'm overreacting, Peter. That's

not the point. Anyway, she can't come on Monday because we're having people over. Tell her we're sorry, but it simply won't work. She wouldn't know anybody, and she'll be bored by all the mundane conversation about the drearier aspects of police work."

"Jorgeson and his wife are very pleasant. They like opera, as does my mother. Chief Panzer and his wife just returned from a trip to Borneo. Luanne can talk to my mother about antique jewelry. Isn't her current boyfriend a botany professor? My mother collects rare orchids. No one is going to discuss surveillance techniques and the inadequacies of the state crime lab."

"You don't know that."

My husband, who was growing less adorable with every breath, leaned forward and put his hand on mine. "Are you afraid of meeting my mother?"

"No," I said firmly, if also mendaciously, "I just don't want her to have a miserable time. It's much hotter here than it is in Newport, and Farberville's not a cultural magnet. She'll feel as if she's been airlifted into a primitive society that has yet to discover anything more advanced than indoor plumbing and cable TV. I'm thinking of her, that's all."

"She's looking forward to meeting you and Caron, not attending a performance by Yo-Yo Ma. All you have to do is be yourself. The two of you will get along just fine." He picked up a menu and with a nearly inaudible grunt said, "I think I'll have the onion quiche and a salad. What would you like?"

"Arsenic, with a side of old lace."

I had some time to squander before my appointment with Evan Toffle, so I parked in the alley behind Secondhand Rose, Luanne's vintage clothing store tucked amid the bars along Thurber Street. The sole customer was a woman trying on hats in front of an Art Deco mirror. She asked my opinion, and I assured her that the lavender was perfect. After she'd paid what I thought was an exorbitant price for a felt cap with a molted feather and departed, I sat down and said, "Peter's mother is coming."

"Here?" Luanne glanced at the door.

"Here as in Farberville, more specifically my house. Monday morning. Three and a half days. I don't even have time to have the interior repainted and the tile regrouted in the guest bathroom. I haven't been upstairs in a week. What if Caron decided to redecorate her room in satanic images?"

"Why would she do that?"

I stood up. "I don't know why I expected any sympathy from you. If I hurry, I can go to the mall to buy new towels and be back in time for my meeting with a lawyer. You need to brush up on opera, orchids, yachts, and Yo-Yo Ma." I froze in midstep and scowled at her. "Don't you dare so much as smile, Luanne Bradshaw! You may think it's all a big joke, but I happen to be taking it seriously — okay? Instead of goggling at me, why don't you find out how I can hire a string quartet for Monday afternoon? It doesn't matter how much they charge. I have a checkbook!"

Luanne caught me before I made it out the door. "Sit," she said, "and put your head between your knees. I think I have pills left over from a prescription for tranquilizers. Let me get you a handful."

"I need to buy towels," I whimpered.

"You need a stiff drink, but it's too early. If you swear you won't leave, I'll pop next door for lattes. Can I trust you?"

When I nodded, she grabbed some bills from the cash register and hurried out to the sidewalk. I obediently sat down, but propped my elbows on my knees and cradled my head in my hands. I had no excuse for my irrational panic. I was not a dewy young bride who'd been tormented by tales of a wicked mother-in-law. I was forty years old. Until I'd married Peter, I'd been doing just fine on my own. I'd supported myself and reared a child who, despite her protests to the contrary, had survived without a closet of overpriced jeans and whimsical flights to Rome. The Book Depot was not considered a serious threat by the chain bookstores, nor was Caron in contention for a summer internship at the White House, but we'd managed.

All I knew about Peter's mother was that she was a wealthy widow with three sons, a mansion, a chauffer, and a household staff slightly smaller than the cast of a Broadway show. She'd been fond of Peter's first wife. I bit down on my lip and refused to allow myself to elaborate on their relationship. I was fond of traditional mystery novels, lemon bars, weepy movies, and my perfect house. This did not preclude potential fondness for whatever else was out there. Like orchids and opera.

When Luanne returned, I accepted the proffered latte and said, "I am not a complete disaster of a human being, you know. I have admirable qualities, like compassion and wit. I have yet to produce an edible soufflé, but my raspberry mousse is divine. Caron complimented me on my ability to retrieve messages on my cell phone. I can type forty words a minute. I have read the complete works of Jane Austen, Mark Twain, Agatha Christie, L. Frank Baum, Charles Dickens, Marcel Proust, and Elizabeth Peters."

"You might want to read the works of Sigmund Freud," she said as she sat down on a stool behind the counter. "Specifically, *Studien über Hysterie.* Need a translation?"

"No," I said grumpily. "Peter sprung this on me an hour ago. If he'd off-handedly mentioned the possibility that she might come for a visit in the next twelve months, I'd have time to assimilate it."

"And buy towels."

"Towels? How about a new wardrobe? I don't own a single item of designer clothing. What will she think when she sees me in jeans and a T-shirt? Her scullery maid probably dresses better than I do. The charity stores in Newport are crammed with last year's hottest fashions. Haute couture in Farberville means all the buttons are sewn on securely."

Luanne let out an exasperated noise, as if I were being unreasonable. I shot her an offended look, which she rudely ignored. "I'm not in the mood to hold your hand while you whine like an egotistical teenager.

63

Peter's mother is not going to stand in the doorway and appraise your clothes, or wince at the lack of rubies and emeralds around your neck when you load the dishwasher. She simply wants to meet you. You married her son. You're part of her family. She may not clutch you to her bosom and tell you to call her Mom, but she will find a way to like you" — she stopped to point her finger at me — "unless you give her a legitimate reason to dislike you. At the moment, you're doing just that. Get over it, Claire."

I deflated. "I've already acknowledged that I'm overreacting. I wish I could shrug off my anxiety, but I can't. If Peter's mother does find me less acceptable than the exwife, she'll have to deal with it. There's nothing short of extraterrestrial interference that can change who I am. I prefer shorts to little black dresses and pearls. I go barefoot in the house. I read mysteries, not fashion magazines. If Coco Chanel showed up on my doorstep tonight, I wouldn't recognize her."

"Nobody would," Luanne commented wryly. "She was buried more than forty years ago."

"Peter's mother was probably at the funeral, snuffling into a lace hankie." I finished my latte and stood up. "Thanks for the session, Ms. Freud. I need to go meddle in the affairs of mere mortals. I'll see you Monday at four." I strolled out the back door with impeccable assurance, but once I was in my car, I was unable to come up with a coherent thought. I'd never seen a photograph of Peter's mother, so it was impossible to visualize with any clarity the dreaded confrontation that would occur Monday at high noon.

I was still sitting there when an employee of the coffee shop came out a back entrance, a cigarette in one hand and a lighter in the other. He gave me a suspicious look, as if I might be planning to dive into the nearest Dumpster. I managed to insert the car key in the ignition, flashed him a smile, and drove past the garbage cans to Thurber Street. I had half an hour before I met with Sarah's lawyer. It was not enough time to buy towels, redecorate the guest bedroom, and take a class in the art of the soufflé. Or any one of them.

I hadn't said anything to Peter about my plot to humiliate Prosecutor Wessell, since he was apt to object in a blustery sort of way. After lunch, he'd mentioned a meeting. It struck me as an opportunity to drop by the PD and see what I could find out about Miss Poppoy's burglars. If they were at large, they could qualify as suspects. Perhaps, I thought as I headed for the PD, they'd left the shotgun in the barn. Sarah had been so shocked by the discovery of Tuck's body that she'd mindlessly carried the shotgun inside. It was conceivable. Or they'd taken the shotgun when they went into the house to search for valuables, and were looking in the closet when they realized that Sarah was home. They'd panicked and fled. Neither was much of a theory, but it was the best I could do.

The desk sergeant informed me that Lieutenant Jorgeson was in his office. I found him in the hall, gazing morosely at the vending machine. Peter had said that Mrs. Jorgeson had dictated a diet that excluded fats, salt, and extraneous carbs, all available for specific combinations of coins. "Ms. Malloy," he said as he spotted me, "how are you today?"

"We're looking forward to having you and your wife out to the house on Monday. Did Peter tell you who else is coming?"

"I believe he did," Jorgeson said uncomfortably. "The captain and his wife, Luanne and a guest, and . . ."

"Peter says she likes opera."

"Mrs. Jorgeson and I truly enjoyed the campus summer production of *Pagliacci.*

The soprano did a superb job. The tenor may need to consider changing majors."

"Farber College can't compete with the Met. I'm hoping you can help me find a little bit of information about an old case. Do you have a few minutes?"

Jorgeson sighed. "What old case interests you, Ms. Malloy?"

"A burglary," I said, aware that he'd heard about my encounter with Wessell and was familiar with my propensity to take an interest in homicides. "A sweet elderly lady lost her family silver. Did the police recover it?"

"Give me the name and I'll look it up." He gestured for me to precede him into his office. He did not sound enthusiastic, but he rarely did. I told him the victim's name was Poppoy and that she lived beyond the city limits. He toyed with his computer for several minutes, then said, "Patience Poppoy, a year ago last June. She told the deputies that two men forced their way inside, bound and gagged her, and ransacked the house for valuables. They made off with a box of silver, a TV, an antique musket, and a platinum wig. None of it made it to the local pawnshops."

"What about the perps?"

"Both white, average height and weight, wearing ski masks, so there wasn't much to go on. There was a similar break-in two months later, over in Hasty. The police there hauled in suspects but couldn't hold them." Jorgeson looked up from the screen. "Is Miss Poppoy a friend of yours, Ms. Malloy?"

"In a way," I said. "Is there anything else in the report?"

"One of her neighbors reported a suspicious van in the area. The description was too vague to be useful."

"What's the neighbor's name?"

"I don't think it matters, Ms. Malloy. The van was described as dark green. The witness said he'd noticed it parked alongside the highway a couple of times. He didn't think anything about it until after the burglary. Nobody else reported seeing it. The deputies wrote it off as teenagers drinking beer or smoking marijuana."

"The name, please." I may have sounded like Oliver Twist asking for a second helping of swill. I hoped Jorgeson was a softer touch than Mr. Bumble.

"I shouldn't do this," he said, gazing at the computer screen. "Deputy Chief Rosen warned me not to encourage you. Wouldn't it be better if you went home and picked flowers for the guest room?"

"That's on the schedule for Monday morning." I made a mental note to start a list as soon as possible. "I'm just trying to help out an old lady who lost her most treasured possessions."

"And her wig."

"She's probably too embarrassed to go to church without it. I cannot bear the idea of her being forced to lead such a lonely, pathetic life. This is no longer a police matter. The case is stone cold. Not even I can interfere in a nonexistent investigation, Jorgeson. All I want to do is find out if this neighbor has remembered anything else about the van or its occupants."

"Zachery Barnard is the name. The address is Pinkie Sheer Road. No telephone number."

"Thank you, Jorgeson. There's no reason to mention this to Peter. He must be very busy with the DEA."

"Not really. Being bureaucrats, they have to follow official guidelines, one of which is to have periodic briefings with area police departments. Things are quiet, at least for the moment. The good citizens of Farberville are refraining from assaulting or murdering each other. Rush starts next week, so there will be a lot of minor-in-possession violations and DWIs."

"Fraternity boys will be boys," I said as I stood up.

"We usually have more trouble with the sororities." Jorgeson came around his desk and opened the door for me. "We'll see you Monday, Ms. Malloy. Mrs. Jorgeson's excited about bringing her potato salad. It's her grandmother's recipe. She's dragging me to the farmers' market in the morning to buy fresh herbs."

I stopped as a metaphorical lightning bolt struck the top of my head, splattering my composure. Peter's mother was more likely to be accustomed to filet mignon with Béarnaise sauce than hamburgers, potato salad, and baked beans. Mrs. Jorgeson might have her grandmother's treasured recipe, but Luanne had informed me that her recipe for baked beans began with a can opener.

"Are you okay?" Jorgeson said, his hand on my arm. "Would you like to sit down for a few minutes?"

"I can't," I croaked. Would all the caterers be booked because of the three-day holiday? There could be dozens of weddings scheduled for Saturday and Sunday. I could learn to make Béarnaise sauce, given time to practice. Peter could grill asparagus along with the steaks. Baked potatoes would be too gauche, but I could find a recipe for mushroom risotto. Would the bakeries be closed on Labor Day? I realized I was on the brink of breaking into a sweat.

Jorgeson tightened his grip as I began to wobble. "I do think you should sit down, Ms. Malloy. The deputy chief's meeting should be over any minute. Why don't you come back into my office while I call him?"

"I don't have time for solicitude. I may alter the menu on Monday, but I'll let Mrs. Jorgeson know tonight so you won't have to waste a trip to the farmers' market."

"Mrs. Rosen butters her toast like the rest of us," he said.

"Unless the butler butters it for her." I patted him on the cheek and returned to my car. For the record, I was not the victim of mother-in-law brutality. Carlton's mother, Miss Jessica, had not been the most likable person, but I'd found her amusingly eccentric in our encounters before she was murdered by a greedy family member. I need not elaborate on who exposed the murderer.

Trying to recall the ingredients in Béarnaise sauce, I drove to the Legal Aid office, located in what had been a bus depot before the city bought and renovated it. As I went inside, I noticed that the original redolence still lingered, a noxious combination of exhaust fumes, bleach, and unwashed bodies.

The receptionist eyed me. "Yes?"

"I have an appointment with Evan Toffle."

"Down the hall, on the right."

Evan was seated behind one of the three desks jammed in the room. Much of the remaining floor space had been dedicated to filing cabinets, wastebaskets, crumpled paper balls, and mismatched chairs for clients. The sole window offered a view of the back of an office building. No one had attempted to nurture a potted plant.

"Hey," he said as I came into the room. "Sit anywhere. My colleagues are gone for the day." He gestured at the pile of folders and open law books on his desk. "This isn't my idea of how to spend Labor Day weekend, but here I am. I, uh, don't quite know how to address you. Wessell made a muddle of the issue."

"Please, call me Claire. Sarah told you that I've offered to try to help her." I sat down on a chair across from him. "I hope that doesn't offend you."

He cleared his throat. "I looked you up online."

"The newspaper articles exaggerate my involvement," I said modestly. "I may have stepped in when the detectives overlooked a clue or two, but my assistance was nominal. Prosecutor Wessell made me sound like a caped avenger. I am simply a concerned citizen."

"Yeah," he said, "and I can use all the help I can get. Wessell has a strong case, as well as thirty years of squashing defendants. I graduated and passed the bar two years ago."

"Why didn't one of the more experienced attorneys take this case?"

"I got stuck with it in mid-August, prime vacation time for those with enough clout to dictate their schedules. I was in the courtroom, waiting for another arraignment, when the judge nailed me. The consensus in the office is that Sarah killed her husband after a domestic blowup, and that she'd accept a plea bargain for manslaughter. No trial, no headlines." He gave me a pained grin. "That would have required her to plead guilty, which she won't. It also would have required Wessell to offer her a deal, which he won't. He has his eye on an upcoming vacancy in the district federal court."

"So I heard," I said. "How strong is his case against Sarah?"

Evan picked up a file, glanced at it, sighed, and tossed it back in the pile. "He's got motive. The ladies from the book club will testify that Sarah was angry at her husband. At the last meeting she said that she wanted to kill him because he'd forgotten to pick up her prescription before he left town. She was joking, of course, but the jury may not share her sense of humor. She —"

"Prescription?" I said. "For what?"

"An antidepressant. She admitted that she's been taking them for twenty years, on and off. I suggested that we consider bringing up the possibility of mental impairment, but she refused to consider it. She said living with her husband would depress anyone." He closed his eyes. "She shared this with her book club ladies. Wessell can't drag in her therapist, but he can emphasize the point that she used drugs. I don't know the name of the particular antidepressant, but I can almost guarantee that it carries a warning not to drink alcohol while taking it — which Sarah did. Wessell will characterize that as recklessness on her part. If I bring up temporary mental incapacity, he'll point out that she should have been familiar with the potential side effects."

"Let's move on, shall we?" I said, trying to hide my discouragement. Evan needed all my positive energy; he looked as though he might lapse into tears at any moment.

Not a good sign in a lawyer. "Sarah told me that she drove home, went to bed, and wasn't awakened by any loud noises. Maybe the combination of the drug and alcohol knocked her out."

"If she'd actually taken any pills. She'd run out several days earlier. That's why she was so annoyed when Tuck didn't pick up the prescription. I asked her if she had more to drink after she got home, but she said no. The only liquor in the house was a dusty bottle of cooking sherry. No empty bottles in the trash or in the truck." He picked up the folder again, and for a moment I thought he was going to fling it at me. I was preparing to duck when he dropped it. "I've never fired any kind of gun. After I was assigned to the case, I went out to a gun club facility and asked for a demonstration. A twelve-gauge shotgun makes a remarkably loud noise. The estimated decibel range is one hundred and sixty-five. To put that in perspective, you're in pain at one hundred and twenty-five decibels, and in danger of permanent hearing damage at one hundred and forty decibels. The neighbors from the next farm heard the blast. Their house is maybe two hundred yards away. Sarah's bedroom is less than a hundred feet away."

"She must be a sound sleeper," I said.

"Very sound."

"Earplugs?"

He shook his head. "No, and the investigators will testify that she had no problem hearing them. One of them called to her while she was upstairs, and she answered him."

This was not going well. I was relieved that Evan Toffle was not a total incompetent, but Sarah might need Johnnie Cochran, F. Lee Bailey, and the rest of the team to avoid a guilty verdict. "Did she tell you about a burglary in the area earlier that summer? Two men broke into a neighbor's house, tied her up, and made off with her silver and other miscellaneous objects."

Evan made a note on a yellow pad. "No, she didn't. I'll request the report from the sheriff's office. Do you think it's relevant?"

"Not especially," I admitted. I related my two hypothetical scenarios that explained how the shotgun had ended up in the closet. When he failed to voice admiration for my ingenuity, I said, "The two men were never caught. It's possible they were skulking in the area and noticed the house was dark."

"If the house was dark, maybe, but it wasn't. Tuck was home. According to what Sarah told me, Tuck had gone on a fishing trip with the guy across the pasture." He opened the folder. "William Lund denied any knowledge of this. One of them lied about it, but that still puts Tuck in the house before midnight."

"All we know is that he was in the barn," I countered. "Was the medical examiner sure about the time of death?"

Evan found another piece of paper. "Within a four-hour period, yes. The Lunds both confirmed hearing the shotgun right about midnight. Based on coagulation, body temperature, seepage, and some scientific jargon, death occurred between midnight and four o'clock. The medical examiner will testify with a high degree of certainty. We can't call in another expert who might have a different opinion because it's not in our budget. I felt like a fool when I asked." Grumbling unhappily, he closed the folder and templed his fingers. "Sarah's story is that she got home before eleven, brushed her teeth, and went to bed. She heard nothing out of the ordinary. The next morning she woke up at seven, had breakfast while she listened to the radio, and went out to the barn. When she saw the body, she knelt down and determined that he was dead. She went into the house, called the sheriff's department, and was sitting on the porch steps when the first deputies arrived twenty minutes later."

"Could he have been shot elsewhere?"

"Not according to the crime scene investigators, who documented the blood splatters. Even if they're wrong, how do you explain the fact that the neighbors heard the shotgun blast?"

"They're lying," I said.

"An interesting idea, granted, but it doesn't explain why Sarah didn't. The head of the CSI and the medical examiner would have to be in on it, too. I don't see how I can discredit both of them — and prove the Lunds lied." I was trying to concoct an explanation when his phone rang. He shrugged an apology as he picked up the receiver. After several minutes of silence, he said, "It's okay. I can be there in half an hour. Don't cry, for pity's sake. Just stay calm and wait for me."

"A client?" I asked as he hung up.

"My mother's dog attacked the postal carrier, who called his supervisor, who is on his way with the police and an ambulance. Whatever you do, don't mess with a federal employee." He took folders and put them in a shiny briefcase. "I have to go, Claire. My mother's in hysterics. I'll give you my cell phone number. If you think of any way to save Sarah Swift, call me." He handed me his card.

I picked up my purse. "Let me ask you something, Evan. Do you believe she's innocent?"

He hesitated. "It doesn't matter if I do or don't. All I can do is present the best defense I can."

I followed him out to the parking lot and watched as he drove off in a subcompact that looked older than he was. As I paused to consider his response, the receptionist came out the front door and locked it. She avoided looking at me as she climbed onto a motorscooter, put on a helmet, and sputtered away to enjoy the long weekend.

I was not destined to enjoy any part of the weekend, I thought as I leaned against the hood of my car. I did have time to dash to the mall to buy towels and then sneak them upstairs before Peter came home. I also had time to swing by the Book Depot and utilize the computer to find a recipe for Béarnaise sauce, as well as Béchamel, Mornay, and Hollandaise, purchase the ingredients, and serve them over whatever I found in the refrigerator. Or I could try to help Sarah and make a fool out of Prosecutor Edwin Wessell (aka the Weasel).

Decisions, decisions.

4

I reached Sarah's turnoff without seeing a sign for Pinkie Sheer Road, so I continued onward, my head swiveling as if I were watching an indolent tennis match. Several unpaved roads disappeared into the woods. I was reluctant to explore any of them, since the last thing on my agenda was a flat tire in the middle of nowhere. I finally saw a yard sale in progress in front of a mobile home and pulled into the driveway. Two women in folding chairs, both with fiercely bleached hair and beer cans in hand, watched me intently as I got out of my car. I acknowledged them with a smile and then studied the array of miscellany on card tables. Having spotted nothing remotely charming, I picked up a chipped saucer with a faintly visible depiction of Old Faithful.

"How much?" I asked as I approached the women.

"Fifty cents," said one of them.

I took out my wallet and found two quarters. "This must be a souvenir of your trip to Yellowstone."

"She bought it at a flea market," said the second woman. "Paid a nickel, if I recall."

The first woman cackled. "Maybe, but it's worth fifty cents now."

"It certainly is," I said as I gave her the coins. "By the way, do you know where Pinkie Sheer Road is?"

"Why you lookin' for it?"

"I'm hoping to find Zachery Barnard. I was told he lives around here."

The second woman finished her beer and crumpled the can with her hand. The snake tattooed on her bicep squirmed. "That old fart? Nobody with a lick of sense wants to find him, not even the census taker. He'd sooner spit in your face as give you the time of day. Did you notice the clothes on the rack over there? I reckon you and me are about the same size."

We would be if I gained fifty pounds. "I'm in kind of a hurry. Can you give me directions to Mr. Barnard's house?"

She stood up and put her hands on her hips. "You sure you don't have time to look at the clothes? You might find some real sweet bargains."

The first woman snorted. "She don't look

like she wears used clothes, Taffy."

"Oh, I do," I said hastily. "My best friend owns a secondhand clothing store in Farberville. Why don't I take a quick look at what's on the rack?"

I ended up with a pair of plaid shorts, a blouse with discolored armpits, a plastic pitcher, a necklace made of seashells, and three well-thumbed issues of *People* magazine. After I'd handed over seven dollars and forty-five cents, the women told me that Pinkie Sheer Road was the next turn on the right. They were taking beers out of a cooler as I pulled onto the county road. The money had been well spent, I thought, since the dirt road lacked a sign. I'd been told Mr. Barnard lived in the first house past a pond. The pond was green and brought to mind images of algae-draped creatures arising from its depths. "House" was a polite term for the ramshackle structure with a swayback roof, broken windows, trash strewn in the weeds, an outbuilding of no discernible use, and a sign that warned me to beware of dogs.

I was losing enthusiasm for my mission as I cut off the engine and listened for barking. There was no indication that the house was currently inhabited, but the two women had assured me "that sumbitch Barnard" rarely ventured out since he was "drunk as a skunk afore noon." An old pickup truck was parked beside the house. Two deflated tires and a bird's nest above the dashboard suggested Mr. Barnard hadn't gone anywhere for some time.

"Hello," I called as I approached the front door. "Anybody home?"

A dog barked, albeit in the distance. Although I might lack the grace of a gazelle, I was prepared to match its speed if the barking grew louder. I knocked on the door and then stepped back in case I needed a head start. "Hello!" I called more loudly. "Mr. Barnard? I'd like to ask you a couple of questions. I'm here on behalf of Sarah Swift."

The only response came from a malevolent blue jay on a fence post. Frowning, I turned around and trudged toward my car, wondering if I might have better luck if Sarah agreed to accompany me. I'd opened the car door when a voice behind me said, "What do ya want to know?"

The speaker was not the surly gnome I'd been led to expect. He was close to six feet tall and lean, with heavily tattooed forearms. Stringy gray hair brushed his shoulders. His stare from behind wire-rimmed glasses seemed sober. He might have purchased the baggy jeans and denim shirt from a thrift shop (or a convenient yard sale), but he wouldn't have been out of place in the pool hall on Thurber Street.

"I'm helping with Sarah's defense," I said. "A year ago, after burglars broke into Miss Poppoy's home, you told an investigator that you'd seen a dark green van in the vicinity."

"And?"

"Do you remember anything else about it? Did you happen to notice the license plate?"

"No."

He was not the most cooperative witness I'd encountered, nor the most verbose. I did my best not to sound impatient. "The two men were never apprehended, so it's possible they were responsible for the shooting. If they saw Sarah drive away, they could have assumed the house was empty."

"The guy was shot in the barn."

"So they decided to steal a tractor. I really don't know. How many times did you notice the van, and where?"

He came toward me, his arms crossed. "I didn't get your name."

"Claire Malloy. I live in Farberville and run a bookstore."

"And you're a friend of Sarah's?"

84

"I'm the only friend she has right now," I said, struggling to keep an edge out of my voice. "Her trial begins Tuesday, and her lawyer's going to have a tough time convincing the jury that she's innocent. It will help if he can throw out some alternative suspects — like the men in the van." I wondered if I could bribe him with a plastic pitcher and old magazines, but I settled for a sigh. "I apologize for dragging you away from whatever you were doing. This has been a waste of time for both of us. Have a pleasant Labor Day weekend."

I'd reached my car when he said, "Sorry I can't help. I just saw the van out of the corner of my eye when I drove by it. Once it was parked by the bridge, another time at the turnoff to a private road. Didn't see the driver, didn't glance at the license plate. You think Sarah will be convicted?"

I looked back. "Yes, I do."

"Damn shame." He took off his glasses and cleaned them on his shirt. " 'When lovely woman stoops to folly, and finds too late that men betray, what charm can soothe her melancholy? What art can wash her guilt away?' "

"It's going to take more than art," I said drily as I got in my car. He stood in the weedy yard and watched me as I backed out

85

to the road. I didn't wave. I could understand why the investigators had dismissed Barnard's vague statement. My best bet was Miss Poppoy, who could have recalled more details after her initial shock had faded. She would have to wait until the next day, since it was late in the afternoon and I needed to go home.

Caron and her best friend, Inez Thornton, were sitting by the pool, both texting. I sank down on a chaise longue and asked the trite parental question: "How was school?"

Caron didn't bother to look up. "Okay, I guess. The principal and the guidance counselor were caught having kinky sex in the library. The librarian would have intervened if she hadn't been taken hostage by the custodian, who was high on crack and toting an assault weapon. The SWAT team took him out by fifth period, which meant I still had to go to my AP calculus class. Luckily, I was able to grab a fire extinguisher and put out the raging inferno before anyone was charred. Oh, and I got a ninety-seven on a pop quiz in my world history class."

"I aced it," Inez said. "How was your day, Ms. Malloy?"

"Nothing but lions and tigers and bears."

I leaned back and closed my eyes. "Did Peter tell you that we're having a houseguest?"

"He's not home yet," Caron said, "so he hasn't told me much of anything. Who's coming? I do hope it's the ambassador of someplace really cool like Monaco or Andorra."

Inez giggled. "I vote for the incredibly handsome son of the French ambassador. *Je t'aime, Jean-Claude.*"

"In your dreams," Caron said with a sniff.

"Je veux t'embrasser," Inez warbled, *"et ce n'est pas tout."*

"Not bad," I said. "Haven't you been taking Latin all these years?"

"Latin is utilitarian, but hardly the language of romance. The library has a French language tutorial with a bunch of CDs. I kept checking it out all summer. I plan to do my junior year at the Sorbonne." Inez had accomplished many other things over the summer. Her once limp brown hair was smartly styled and glistened with highlights. Her thick glasses had been replaced with contacts. New clothes, including the tiny bikini she was wearing, had revealed a rather curvy figure. Caron had always been first violin; now she was struggling not to play second fiddle.

"Bonne chance," I said, amused at Caron's

pinched expression.

Inez stopped texting long enough to push back her hair. "To sleep, perchance to dream of Jean-Claude, *mon amour.*" She looked at me. "Unless you're expecting someone else, of course."

"I'm afraid so. Peter's mother is arriving Monday."

Caron's thumbs froze in midtweet. "Peter's mother?"

Inez looked curiously at her. "Is that a bad thing?"

"No," I said, "it's more of a sudden thing. We've never met her. She was on a lengthy tour of China when we got married last spring. She sent an antique porcelain figurine as a wedding present." I clutched my hand to my mouth. "I haven't seen it since it arrived. We repacked it in the same box so it wouldn't get broken during the move. But we unpacked all the boxes, didn't we? I remember labeling it and putting it in the pile behind the dining table." I tried desperately to visualize the stacked boxes, one adorned with a scrawled *Ming Thing.* "Are there any unopened boxes in the storage room off the garage?"

Caron shook her head. "I went out there last week to look for my old yearbooks. There were a couple of boxes of your books, a scruffy suitcase, a stepladder, and a trunk filled with notebooks and letters."

Notebooks and letters that I'd forgotten to burn. I watched her face for a sign that she'd snooped through the contents of the trunk. Her lower lip had not shot out, nor were her eyebrows lowered. "You're sure the porcelain figurine wasn't there?"

"I opened all the boxes, Mother. I would have noticed if one was stuffed with packing peanuts and wadded-up Chinese newspaper. Right before we moved, you had the thrift store guys haul off a bunch of crap."

"Oh, no," I gurgled.

I was battling to breathe as Peter came out to the terrace. He grinned at the girls and then bent down to kiss the top of my head. "Shall I open a bottle of something to celebrate the onset of the weekend? Chardonnay sound okay?"

Cyanide would have sounded okay. "Yes, dear, that would be lovely," I said as I shot a warning look at Caron and Inez. "There's a wedge of brie in the refrigerator, and a box of crackers in a cabinet. Shall I help?"

"Stay right here," he said as he went into the house. Operating a corkscrew tends to make him feel manly, as if he'd grown, picked, and stomped the grapes himself. I would never dream of disillusioning him.

As soon as I heard the refrigerator door open, I whispered, "What time does the thrift store close?"

Caron's eyebrow rose. "How would I know?"

"It'll be open tomorrow," Inez said.

I felt a tiny twitch of optimism. The figurine was a particularly ugly man with a scowl. One arm was missing, as was a bit of his nose. The glaze had flaked off over the centuries. No one would have given it a second glance, I told myself. I could only trust the thrift store workers hadn't tossed it in the trash. "I need help," I said in a low voice.

Greed flashed across my darling daughter's countenance. "I'm pretty busy. Joel and I are going to a movie tomorrow night, so I have to get ready for that. You told me I could have people over to swim this weekend, remember? About a dozen are coming Sunday afternoon. I was just going to get chips and dip, but . . ."

"Money for pizza?"

"Steaks would be nice," she said.

"Very nice. However, this is contingent on your success. If you don't have any luck, I'll spring for hamburgers. Deal?"

The abacus inside her head clicked as she pondered the likelihood of finding the figurine. "How long do I have to try to find it?"

"Until Sunday at three o'clock. Will you agree to be at the thrift shop at nine tomorrow morning?"

Peter gave us a puzzled look as he came out to the terrace. "What're you going to do at the thrift shop, Caron? Volunteer?"

"Absolutely," Inez said. "Now that school's started, we don't have time to volunteer at the Literacy Council. I need to pad my college applications for maximum impact."

"That's right," Caron added. "I may decide to apply to the Sorbonne. I hear they're real sticklers about volunteerism."

"Bonne chance," I said, trying not to laugh.

Peter poured wine into the glasses and sat on a chaise longue. "This wouldn't have anything to do with my mother's visit, would it?"

Inez's eyes widened. "Did she attend the Sorbonne?"

"Not that I recall," he said. "So, how was school?"

The next morning I found a cereal bowl in the sink, indicating Caron had arisen and departed according to schedule. I started coffee, walked down the driveway to the road to collect the newspaper from its box, and was seated at the kitchen island when Peter emerged from the bedroom. He'd fallen asleep on the sofa shortly after dinner, sparing me any awkward conversations. I wasn't in the mood for any at the moment — or for the next three days.

"Shall we go out to the terrace?" I asked. "I'll bring muffins and jam."

"I'm thinking serious breakfast." He opened the refrigerator and began pulling out the components for what he considered to be his signature omelet. "You getting anywhere with your latest murder investigation?"

"My what?" I said haughtily.

"Jorgeson mentioned that you dropped by the PD yesterday while I was in that damn meeting. I asked him for details. When I accessed the Poppoy file, I noticed the address is less than half a mile from the Swift woman's house. Two burglars, still at large. Have you interviewed her yet?"

"No," I said, "and don't bother to tell me to back off. I am not going to let that dreadful weasel throw Sarah to the judicial wolves so he can get elected to the bench. You yourself said he's bigoted and a male chauvinist. Think how much more damage he'll be able to do if he becomes a judge."

Peter grinned. "I wasn't going to tell you to back off, my dear. I was going to ask if I can help."

"Oh."

"Covertly, of course. I can't do anything that could be perceived as undermining the sheriff's department. We coordinate with them on drug- and alcohol-related cases. The sheriff's Harvey Dorfer. You met him when you got caught up in the pet theft business."

Distasteful memories came back like the miasma of pungent cigar smoke that had emanated from his stubby butts. Sheriff Dorfer had been more than testy when I'd attempted to assist in his so-called investigation, and he'd ordered a deputy to arrest me for a variety of petty missteps, including harboring a fugitive. Peter's intervention and my success in identifying the perp had led to a truce of sorts. "Oh, yes, and we did not hit it off. I remember thinking he was ineffectual."

"He's a politician, so he's careful. Stereotypic good ol' boy, but sharp. He has to be to deal with all the crazies in Stump County. Crime and violence are common in some of those little towns in the backwoods."

"Moonshiners?"

He began to crack eggs into a bowl.

"Morons blowing themselves up while cooking meth in their kitchens. Nobody would care if they went off to shacks to do it, but it's always at home, often with children in the next room. Where's the whisk?"

"In one of those drawers," I said. "Would you ask Sheriff Dorfer if I can meet with him this afternoon?" I told him about Zachery Barnard's purported sighting of a suspicious van parked in the area, and his failure to add any pertinent details. "I've been wondering if Miss Poppoy might be able to better describe the men now that she's recovered from the shock."

He brandished the whisk. "I'll call and see if he's in his office, but it's a holiday weekend and it's likely that a rookie has been left in charge. Do we have any chives?"

As I drove out County 107, I began to regret having indulged in the omelet, the sausage, and an hour of genteel marital shenanigans. This was not the time for complacency; it was the time for assertiveness and hunger for the truth.

I turned at Sarah's road and stopped in front of the house. The pickup truck was gone. Although I'd intended to ask her to accompany me when I questioned Miss

Poppoy, I had no time to waste. I was backing up when I realized I hadn't heard from Juniper Lund. Sarah's trial would begin in less than seventy-two hours. I decided to cast etiquette to the breeze and drop by unannounced.

Emily Post would have been appalled.

There were no occupants in view as I parked beside their house, but I could hear the shrill babble of cartoon voices from within. I knocked on the door and waited, willing myself to be steely.

The door opened. I recognized William Lund from the photo Sarah had shown me. "Good morning," he said. "Can I help you?"

"I'm Claire Malloy. I spoke to your wife yesterday."

"About Sarah's trouble," he said with a nod. "When I asked if I could help you, I was thinking about giving directions or looking under the hood of your car. I don't see how I can say or do anything that's going to help Sarah. We feel bad for her. She was miserable being married to Tuck. He had good spells, when we'd go fishing or watch football. We'd all sit around and drink wine, talking about life, politics, and always blueberries. Tuck spent hours at the library researching hybrids, fertilizers, and organic pest control. He knew more than the accreditation inspectors from the IOIA. He used to confuse them with all the chemistry lingo."

"When he had bad spells?"

William looked over his shoulder. "Let's go out on the porch. Billy doesn't need to hear this. He's got a wild imagination, and keen ears. Junie'd throw a fit if she knew I let him watch all those gory cartoons. We can't protect him from everything. There's a vampire on *Sesame Street,* for chrissake." He gestured for me to sit in one of the wicker chairs. "I grew up on *Gilligan's Island* and *Rin Tin Tin.* On Saturday mornings I watched *Lassie.*" He cupped his hand behind his ear. "What's that, boy? Timmy's fallen down the well and is being eaten alive by zombies?"

"Zombies!" Billy howled as he barged out the door, the cap gun in his grubby hand. "Where are they, Gramps? I'm gonna blow their heads off!"

"I think they all went out behind the barn to help Grandma pick vegetables for dinner. You need to go protect her."

Billy pointed the gun at me. "What do you want, lady?"

Candor would not endear me to his grandfather. "Aren't you missing your show?" I asked sweetly.

"Now it's just a bunch of stupid commercials, and I don't care if the zombies want to pick stupid vegetables." He glared at me. "Nobody makes me eat vegetables. I hate vegetables, 'specially carrots. Carrots are nothing but rotten teeth that fall out of werewolves' mouths. You know what cabbages are? They're scaly dragon balls. My cousin told me, and he's older than me. He said that zucchinis are —"

"That's it, Billy," William said. "The commercials should be done by now. You need to go back inside."

"My mother says she sends me here so I can play outside."

"Either go inside or go help Grandma in the garden."

Billy aimed the cap gun at us, then shrugged and went back into the house. His departure was accompanied by a series of bangs and the same whiff of acrid smoke as at our prior encounter.

"You were telling me about Tuck," I prompted William.

"He could be stingy. A lot of us at the farmers' market donate part of our unsold produce to a food bank, but Tuck collected every stray lettuce leaf and took it home. He was ready to drink my beer but got pissed if I drank his. He yelled at Sarah when she bought new shoes. Tighter than bark on a tree, they say around these parts. He was paranoid, too. One night he got drunk and told me that every cop in the country was out to get him, along with the military and the FBI. Sarah told me that he used to sit on the porch, the shotgun across his lap, waiting for" — he held up his hands in mock terror — "a SWAT team, or maybe aliens."

"He sounds like a real pain," I murmured.

"Sometimes, yeah."

"What can you tell me about the day he was shot?"

"For one thing, I don't know why Sarah told the detectives that Tuck and I had planned to go fishing. We stopped going years ago, when he got obsessed with his health. He had crazy ideas about bears, rabid possums, scorpions, surveillance drones, and snipers perched in trees. I got tired of listening to it. If he told Sarah that he and I were going anywhere together, he was lying through his teeth."

It was too close to the trial date for tact. "Is it possible that he might have had plans with someone else?"

William laughed. "You mean a woman? Only if she'd been tested for every communicable disease known to science. I can't think of anyone right offhand who'd put up with him. No, he was home that night. I noticed a light when I went out to check on the chickens. Something got them all riled up, most likely a stray dog or a fox."

"Did you tell this to the detectives?"

"Did I tell them about a nonexistent fox in the henhouse? Yeah, but they weren't impressed." He rocked back and gazed at the porch ceiling. "I like Sarah, but I'm not going to lie for her. Junie's the same way. We heard the shotgun blast about midnight. She went to see if Billy had been awakened, and I went out the back door to make sure the animals were okay. I didn't see or hear anything, so I wrote it off as drunken kids riding around taking potshots at mailboxes. We have to replace ours every couple of years. I want to pack it with explosives, but Junie won't let me."

That would be between him and the postal authorities. "Are you sure about the time?" I asked.

"Real sure. I was watching a movie that was over at midnight. I'd just gotten up off the sofa when I heard the blast. Fifteen minutes earlier I might have missed it, since the posse had caught up with the outlaws in a canyon and guns were blazing. The rancher and his bride were riding off into the sunset at the end of the movie."

"Can Junie confirm the time, too?"

"Said she looked at the clock on the bedside table when she got up. You can ask her if you want."

It was my turn to gaze at the porch ceiling. "Do you think Sarah's guilty?"

"Yeah, but that doesn't mean I'm happy about it. From what I heard, she'd had too much to drink. I can't explain how the two of them ended up in the barn. For all I know, he could have been crawling on the rafters to search for hidden microphones and cameras." He stood up. I interpreted that as an invitation to leave, so I was surprised when he dug a crumpled cigarette pack from his pocket and sat back down. "Don't tell Junie. She believes I quit three months ago, but there are times when I need a smoke." He took a misshapen cigarette out of the pack and lit it. "Tell Sarah I'm sorry about testifying against her, but we don't have a choice. Junie got snippety with the prosecutor, who threatened to charge her with conspiracy if she didn't say what he wanted to hear. She came damn close to punching him."

"Prosecutor Wessell is not genial," I said, somewhat disappointed that Junie had restrained herself. "What does he want her to say?"

"That Sarah hated Tuck and wanted to escape the marriage, that she threatened to kill him more than once, that a few weeks before he was killed, he was sporting a black eye that he blamed on her." He took a drag on the cigarette and exhaled slowly. "I'm going to have to testify to that crap, and the nonexistent plans, seeing lights on at the house, and the time of the shotgun blast. Perjury is serious business. I have to tell the truth." He pinched out the cigarette between his thumb and forefinger, stuck the butt in his shirt pocket, and once again stood up. "I need to see what Billy's up to and then get busy repairing a fence over by the river. Folks, mostly college kids, like to camp out on what's called Flat Rock, and some of them seem to think it's okay to pick whatever they want from my field, even if they have to push down the fence. The damn cows are so stupid they'll decide to go wading. The last time one got loose, it broke a leg. We filled the freezer with ground beef and steaks. Still got most of it."

"One last question," I said. "In the weeks before the incident, did you happen to notice a dark green van parked alongside the county road?"

He frowned for a moment. "Can't say I did."

"Another last question," I said hastily as he reached for the doorknob. "Can you give me directions to Miss Poppoy's house?"

His frown deepened, cutting furrows on his forehead. "Are you thinking those assholes who broke into her house might have shot Tuck?"

"One of my many theories," I said, although I wasn't precisely overwhelmed with alternative suspects.

He obligingly told me how to find Miss Poppoy's house, wished me luck, and went indoors. I returned to my car, turned around, and headed off on my next fruitless mission to exonerate Sarah Swift.

I could only hope Caron and Inez were having better luck. Peter's mother would expect to see her wedding present on the mantel. Were I a devious person, I could claim it was broken during the move, but Peter had been supervising closely and might contradict me. Admitting I'd sent it to the thrift shop would nail me as incompetent — or malicious. It did not bode well for my future relationship with my mother-in-law.

I stopped the car and took out my cell phone. I was concocting a message when

Caron snapped, "What?"

"Any luck?"

"Yes and no. Can we talk about this later?"

"No and no," I said. "What's going on?"

"The lady in charge remembers unpacking it because it was so repulsive. She was going to dump it in the garbage, but one of the other ladies put it on a shelf with the other repulsive oddities. They receive a lot of them, mostly wedding presents."

"Great! Buy it, no matter the price."

"Wow, Mother, why didn't I think of that? In fact, I was just about to ask how much when I noticed that it wasn't there. Inez noticed, too."

My stomach thumped unhappily. Several Anglo-Saxon expletives came to mind, but I contained myself and said, "Well, I guess that's it. Go home and start packing, dear. We'll have to slink away under cover of darkness. Once we're relocated, we'll both have to get jobs. You can work on your GED and apply for a student loan at whichever community college is closest to our shabby little apartment above a dry cleaner's establishment. It won't be as *très amusant* as the Sorbonne, but —"

"We're trying to track down the buyer, okay? The lady is on her phone calling the other ladies to see if anyone can remember who bought it."

"That's incredibly nice of her," I said, fanning myself with one hand. "Please give her my thanks and tell her that I'll come by with a check next week."

"You need to thank Inez. I told the lady that I was devastated because it was a family heirloom given to me by my great-grandmother, a noted Victorian archaeologist. I even squeezed out a tear. The lady didn't buy it, so Inez told her the truth. The lady started laughing so hard she almost wet her pants. I felt like a Complete Fool."

"You still have a few hours," I said. "Call me when you have that thing in your hand. I'll stop by the bakery on my way home and get celebratory cupcakes."

"I'd prefer éclairs with chocolate ganache or a seven-layer tiramisu cake. Talk to you later."

I turned off my cell phone and dropped it in my purse. I was tempted to drive back to Farberville to join the hunt for the missing Ming Thing, but Sarah's trial would begin Tuesday whether or not I disgraced myself in Peter's mother's eyes.

Following William's directions, I drove a quarter of a mile, crossed a bridge, and turned on Wilbur Road. Miss Poppoy lived in an unassuming brick house. I was pleased to see a car parked in the driveway. I glanced in the rearview mirror to make sure I appeared respectable, walked up the sidewalk, and crossed my fingers as I rang the doorbell.

Miss Poppoy came to the door. She was barely five feet tall, and her white hair was so thin I could see liverish spots on her scalp. She looked up at me with the intensity of a squirrel. "You better not be a missionary. I've belonged to the Baptist church for seventy-nine years and I'm not interested in joining a cult."

"No," I said, "I'm trying to help your neighbor, Sarah Swift."

"The trial starts Tuesday. Aren't you a day late and a dollar short?"

"I hope not. Would you mind talking to me for a few minutes?"

She stepped back and waved me inside. "I don't reckon I can be of much help, but I'll answer your questions. Can I fix you like a cup of tea?"

I followed her through a small living room into the kitchen. Once she'd produced cups of tea and a plate of saltine crackers, I said, "I'd like to ask you about the burglars who broke into your house last year."

"Those shitheels?" She took a sip of tea.

"If they hadn't grabbed me in the hall, I would have pulled out my Glock 19 and blown their damn faces off. I keep it in my bedside drawer, loaded and ready. I'm still kicking myself in the ass for not fetching it before I opened the door."

She said all this in such a sweet voice that I was taken aback. I felt alarm for the next missionary who knocked on her door. Previous ones might well be buried in her backyard under the hydrangeas. "You told the deputies that you couldn't describe them. Have you recalled anything about them since then?"

"You think they shot Tuck Cunningham?"

"I don't know, but it's a possibility. No one told Sarah's lawyer about them."

"Bastards took my television set," she muttered. "I missed all my shows for a month. It finally turned up at a flea market in Hasty. I recognized it right off and told the lady that if she didn't give it to me, I'd report her to the police for possessing stolen property. After some finagling, she let me have it for ten bucks. If I'd had my gun in my handbag, I would have gotten it for a lot less. It was my television set, after all."

"Have you remembered anything else about the two men? Accents, tattoos, scars, something one of them said?"

"One of them said something when I kicked him in the balls," she said as she began to nibble on a cracker. "I don't recollect the exact phrase, but it took the Lord's name in vain. I said I wouldn't tolerate blasphemy in my home. That's when they tied me to a chair and put duct tape over my mouth. Assholes!"

"Neither of them referred to the other by name?"

"One of them did say something to the other one. He called him a jerk-off. I wasn't gonna repeat that to the nice young deputy, who was in my Sunday school class twenty years ago. Now that I think about it, it might have been a name, maybe Jerkin or Jenkin or something like that."

"That may important, Miss Poppoy," I said.

"Call me Poppy. Everybody else does, except for that smart-mouthed girl at the doctor's office. She calls me Ms. Popeye. One of these days I'm gonna slap the snot out of her." Her hand tightened around the cracker, reducing it to crumbs. "And that asshole who calls himself a doctor. He's a foreigner, and his accent is so bad I can't make hide nor hair of half of what he says. When I told him I needed a prescription for medical marijuana on account of my lumbago, he had the nerve to tut-tut at me."

"Medical marijuana isn't available in Arkansas," I said, beginning to feel sympathy for the burglars as well as her medical team.

"Wanna bet?"

I had no intention of contradicting her about anything, including the weather and where the sun was going to rise in the morning. "Do you know Zachery Barnard?"

"What's he got to do with this? Do you think he shot Tuck?"

"No, not at all," I said hastily. "He told the investigators he saw a dark green van parked in the area. He didn't notice the occupants, but I'm wondering if it could have been your intruders."

"Casing the joint?" She snorted. "Zachery isn't what I'd call a reliable witness. He came over here one night, must have been close to midnight, to tell me that he'd seen black helicopters landing out back of his house. The old coot was bleating like a motherless calf. He was so drunk he could barely walk. I told him to get off my porch or I'd blow his sorry ass to smithereens."

It was obvious that Zachery was not popular with his neighbors. The proprietresses of the yard sale, and now Miss Poppoy, had referred to him in decidedly unflattering terms. His credibility was sinking fast, but I wasn't ready to dismiss the reports of the dark green van.

"Then you never saw the van," I said.

"I saw it." She picked up her cup and studied the drowned mint leaves. "Turning on Pinkie Sheer Road, another time parked maybe a hundred feet from Sarah's mailbox. Last month when I was coming home from visiting a friend in the hospital, I came damn close to rear-ending it. It was going all of twenty miles an hour. Speed limit's sixty-five. I swerved at the last second and came near landing in the ditch. I shot that sucker the bird as I whipped past him."

Her statement startled me. Her gesture to the driver was almost predictable, but she'd claimed the incident had taken place a month ago. I'd been focused on the previous summer. "A month ago?" I asked cautiously. "In July?"

"Unless you use another calendar, I reckon so. I don't recollect seeing it around the time those assholes broke in, but that could have been because of my cataracts. I was blinder than a bat with an eye patch. I made a coffee cake with curry instead of cinnamon, and sprinkled flour on my oatmeal. With all the driving I had to do, it was a miracle I didn't kill anybody. I guess Jesus was riding shotgun."

On that disturbing note, I thanked her for the refreshments and asked her to call me if she thought of anything that might help Sarah.

It was time to take a shot at the sheriff.

5

Before I drove back to Farberville for my meeting, I decided to stop at Sarah's house. If Zachery Barnard and Miss Poppoy had seen the green van, it was possible that Sarah had seen it, too. The sheriff might take my theory more seriously if I could offer three witnesses. Miss Poppoy claimed she'd seen the van only a month ago. She'd belittled Zachery's credibility, but by her own admission, she was not in a position to cast the first pebble. Sarah's credibility would be suspect. I would have to rely on my innate charm to convince the sheriff to search for the van.

Luckily, I am well endowed. With charm, anyway.

To my chagrin, Sarah's truck was still gone. I parked in the shade and took out my cell phone. Caron answered on the penultimate ring before the dreaded voice mail message kicked in.

"What?" she said.

"I just called to see if you've made any progress," I said, and then waited to be told that the Ming Thing was forever lost, along with any hopes I had of meeting Peter's mother with a measure of decorum.

"Maybe, but being interrupted every fifteen minutes isn't helping."

"What does that mean?"

Caron growled in frustration. "It means we may be getting somewhere. This is a tiny bit more complicated than being sent to the grocery store for milk and bread, Mother. Inez and I were planning to give each other pedicures this afternoon. Right now my toenails look like I have scurvy. Joel will take one look at them and barf on my feet."

I am not by nature a suspicious person, but my maternal antennae picked up on the evasive ploy. "Did you find out who bought the figurine?"

"We're dealing with it, okay? I really don't have time to make inane conversation. Save it for Peter's mother." The connection went dead.

I did my best not to succumb to outlandish visions involving paramedics, campus police, and the Department of Homeland Security. The figurine became a stunted fiend with a wicked sense of humor, a

Mongol Gingerbread Man.

Chasing down the nasty little bugger was Caron's responsibility, I lectured myself as I gazed at the barn. I had time to revisit the scene of the crime before I went to the sheriff's department, which was located near the county courthouse. Thinking of the building reminded me of my humiliation two days earlier, courtesy of County Prosecutor Edwin Wessell.

The interior of the barn remained uninspiring. Contrary to fictionalized CSI investigations, there was not a taped outline of a body. The jury would be treated to photographs, including close-ups of the bloodied corpse. They would not see the shock and horror on Sarah's face when she discovered her husband — if she had been shocked and horrified. I sat down on a burlap bag of what I supposed was chicken feed, sneezed, and considered the conversation we'd had in her kitchen. There was something wrong with her story, and Wessell would trumpet every blemish to the jury. The shotgun blast had been so loud that it awakened Juniper Lund and sent William outside. Sarah hadn't heard it. Her lawyer could claim that she'd passed out from the excess of alcohol, but that would not impress the jury. Credible witnesses would admit that Sarah had detested Tuck and had threatened to kill him. Tuck's black eye would be attributed to Sarah. Being characterized as an abusive alcoholic would not reflect well on her.

All I had to counter the incriminating testimony was a dark green van that could belong to a real estate agent, an Avon lady, a birdwatcher, or a muddled farmer. The likelihood that Tuck had a lover was dim, based on what I'd been told about his disagreeable nature and mental condition. However, there was truth to the axiom that the spouse is the last to know. I had no idea how to find out what Tuck might have been up to when he was on his own. For that matter, I had no idea what Sarah did when she was on her own. Unhappy marriages do not lead to conversations over dinner about anything more significant than the mundane events and errands of the day.

I heard a soft footstep behind me. Before I could turn around, a petulant voice said, "Stick 'em up!"

I raised my hands. "You caught me red-handed, Billy."

"Your hands aren't red."

I stood up, the better to glare down at him. His cap gun wavered as he stepped back. "Do your grandparents know you're here?" I asked.

"Yeah, Grandma sent me over to invite Miss Sarah to dinner. What are you doing here?" He was dressed in full cowboy regalia, with a felt hat, a filthy bandana around his neck, a holster, and boots.

"I came to talk to Miss Sarah, but she's not home. Maybe she'll be here later."

"Okay." He lowered his weapon. "Is this where she killed Mr. Tuck? I don't see any blood or nothing. I'm sorry she has to go to jail. She makes good sugar cookies. Last year for my birthday she gave me a pair of binoculars so I can watch for dinosaurs and bears in the pasture. I saw zombies one time."

"Really?" I said as I glanced at my watch. I was scheduled to meet with the sheriff after lunch, and I needed to leave myself time to purchase éclairs — assuming Caron and Inez were successful.

Billy's eyes filled with tears. "You don't believe me neither. Grandma and Gramps just laughed, but that mean old deputy got mad and said I'd get in trouble for telling lies. I wasn't lying. I did so see zombies the night Mr. Tuck got killed."

My chin dropped in a most unbecoming manner. "The night Mr. Tuck got killed? What exactly did you see?"

"Zombies, over by the river. Bunches of them."

"Let's go sit down so you can tell me all about it," I said.

He gave me a wide smile as we left the barn and sat on the porch steps. He, like Miss Poppoy, was not the most credible witness, and I had only minute optimism that I would hear anything useful. At the moment, it would have to suffice. Dearly hoping that Sarah's pickup would not pull into the driveway, I said, "Did the loud bang wake you up that night?"

"Yeah, it was like a cannon. I jumped up and looked out the window to see if there was army men in the yard. There was someone sneaking around behind the barn. I figured he was stealing vegetables from Grandma's garden. I hate vegetables. My mom tries to hide them in spaghetti or macaroni and cheese, but I always find them and feed them to Lucky. Lucky's our dog. My dad says he's a mutt, but he's the best dog ever. He sleeps on my bed —"

"You saw a man behind your grand-parents' barn? Could you see what he looked like?"

Billy gave me an exasperated look. "It was dark. I got my binoculars and leaned out the window to see where he was. That's

116

when I saw the zombies way over by the river. They were wrestling with each other. Do zombies like vegetables? Maybe that's why the first one stole some from the garden, and the other zombie wanted them."

"I'll have to do some research and get back to you on that," I said absently. I could understand why the "mean old deputy" had failed to take Billy seriously. The child was obsessed with zombies and whatever other fictional brutes were cluttering up pop culture. My childhood monsters had been Dracula, Frankenstein's creation, ambulatory mummies, aliens from outer space, and psychotic humans with chainsaws.

"I did see them," he said. "I really, really did. Grandma didn't believe me, but they were there. She took away my binoculars and told me to go back to bed. Soon as she closed the door, I got up and went back to the window. One of them had a flashlight." He squeezed my hand as he gave me a beseeching look. "I didn't make it up. I swear."

I was beginning to believe at least part of his story. I'd listened to more than anyone's fair share of fantasies from the nursery school set, but I'd never had a problem sorting out the tidbits of truth intertwined in Caron's fabrications. The mention of a flashlight qualified as a glaring anomaly. Unless, I thought with a sigh, I was completely out of touch with the current zombie mythology. Perhaps they drove Jaguars and wore Armani suits, ate sushi made with gray matter, and texted their friends who had not yet risen from the grave to stalk teenaged babysitters.

"Over by the river, you said," I prompted him.

"Wrestling. I couldn't see them good because Grandma stole my binoculars. I had to eat peas *and* carrots *and* beets before she gave them back."

"Brutal." I realized it was past noon. According to Peter, the sheriff was an affable country boy, but we had parted without any promises to keep in touch or do lunch. Wessell's overtly hostile attack on my character had to be hot gossip in the courthouse mileu. I did not want to keep Sheriff Dorfer waiting for me. "I'd like to talk to you again, Billy. Do you think that will be all right with your grandparents?"

He chewed on his lower lip for a moment. "I don't know. They were kind of sore at me when the deputy told them I lied about seeing zombies. It wasn't fair, because I did see them. I can't help it if they're stupid just like the deputy."

"They're not stupid," I said as I stood up. "Adults have small imaginations. It's too bad they didn't see the zombies, but they didn't."

"Do you have a small imagination?"

"No one has ever accused me of that." I patted his shoulder and told him I'd be back later in the afternoon or the following day. He gave me a twenty-one-cap-gun salute as I drove away.

The parking lot at the county jail was crowded. Suspecting the weekend was prime visiting time, I found a parking spot behind the courthouse and walked a half block to the yellow brick building. A sign informed me that cell phones were not allowed during visitation hours, which began at one o'clock. A woman with conical hair and heavy makeup looked at me from her desk.

"Stop here, honey," she said. "You have to sign in before you can visit. Is it your husband enjoying our hospitality, or maybe a boyfriend?"

"I have an appointment with Sheriff Dorfer."

She tilted her head. "On a Saturday afternoon? You must be thinking of another sheriff. Harve lit out of here two hours ago to spend the weekend fishing with his buddies. They're on the third or fourth case of beer by now. Come back on Tuesday, but wait until after lunch. He can be meaner than a polecat when he has a hangover."

He also had no problem skipping appointments, especially with me. Then again, he was a politician. "He's gone for the entire weekend?"

"Maybe I can help you. My name's LaBelle, and I know most everything about what goes on here. I've been the dispatcher since before Harve won his first election. What's your name, honey?"

"Claire Malloy. My husband spoke to Sheriff Dorfer and made the appointment for me."

LaBelle licked her cerise lips as she studied me. "Oh, yeah, you're the woman who got kicked off the jury. I wish I could have been there. Tyrell's sister heard all about it from the court stenographer, who lives in the same apartment complex. Tyrell's a trustee, so he gets to talk on the phone. The other inmates are too stupid to figure out how to use the pay phone. Years ago when it was a rotary phone, some of them used to keep punching the holes until their fingers swelled up." She centered a pad of paper on her blotter and picked up a pen. "Now why don't you tell me why you're here so I can type a memo for Harve?"

"May I speak to the deputy who's in charge?"

She sat back in her chair and gave me an annoyed look. "You said you wanted to see Sheriff Dorfer. What makes you think a deputy can help you?"

I wondered if salmon felt similar frustration as they battled the current to swim upstream. "I need to discuss an investigation."

"Sarah Swift's, right? I bet you were so pissed after Prosecutor Wessell trashed you that you decided to help her. Well, let me tell you that this department conducted a thorough investigation before charging her with murder. Harve reviewed all the reports very carefully. The prosecutor hisself came over and the two of them went through a whole box of doughnuts that morning, as well as three pots of coffee. There's nothing in the file that ain't squeaky clean."

"I'm sure the investigation was conducted with utmost professionalism," I said, easing back in case mascara flew off her eyelashes. "May I please speak to whoever is in charge today?"

"You think Frankie's got nothing better to do than chat with a civilian? Two days ago we busted a truckload of illegal aliens from one of those Mexican countries, and the immigration service still hasn't picked them up. We've been feeding them tortillas and canned beans day and night, but they keep right on griping. They should be grateful to have a roof over their heads and bunks to sleep in. Did they think they could sneak across the border and order room service at the Holiday Inn?"

"I'll try not to waste too much of Frankie's time."

"You've already wasted too much of mine," she said as she jabbed a button on the phone console. She kept an eye on me as she picked up the receiver and told Frankie that "some woman" was whining about seeing him. After a few seconds, she replaced the receiver and said, "Second door on the right."

I could feel the onset of a headache, but I gave her a bright smile and headed down the hall. From somewhere inside the building I heard loud male voices and the excited yammering of a sports announcer. I wondered if they were watching football or *fútbol.* I knocked on the door and opened it. The man seated behind a desk appeared to be slightly older than Caron. His head was nearly shaven, as if he were a recruit on the first day of boot camp. His upper lip was curled, exposing small, irregular teeth. Powdered sugar on his chin and chest suggested that he'd met his quota of doughnuts for the day.

"Thank you for seeing me," I began. "I was under the impression Sheriff Dorfer would be here."

"Not a snowball's chance in hell he'd be here on a weekend," the deputy said, his expression leery. "He left a note saying I should go ahead and talk to you. I'm Deputy Frank Norton. What can I do for you?"

I sat down and smiled. "My name is Claire Malloy, and I'm looking into the case against Sarah Swift. Her trial begins Tuesday, and there are a few —"

"You're the woman what got booted off the jury! I heard you got so hysterical you had to be restrained and forcibly removed from the courtroom. Good thing your husband's the deputy chief. Judge Priestly's real quick to throw folks in the slammer for contempt of court. She fined some sorry-ass lawyer five hundred dollars when his cell phone rang in the middle of a trial."

"I was not hysterical, and I walked out of the courtroom without an escort," I said with laudable restraint. "Ms. Swift's lawyer has authorized me to speak to the people involved in the investigation. I'd like to know which deputies arrived first at the scene."

Frankie stiffened. "That would be me and Rick Harraldson. We took a look and called Sheriff Dorfer. He sent out the investigators. It's all in the report we wrote for the case file."

"Did you interview Ms. Swift?"

"I talked to her, if that's what you mean. She was sitting on the porch swing when we pulled up. Deputy Harraldson ordered me to stay with her while he went into the barn to have a look. He was pretty shaky when he came out and got in the car to call for backup. He told me later that the black flies buzzing all over the body reminded him of when his dog got killed and he found the body two days later. I took a quick look from the doorway." He closed his eyes for a moment. "It was bad, real bad. It's a cold-hearted bitch that lets her husband bleed all night."

"Sarah keeps her feelings to herself."

"She sure as hell did that morning. I asked her what happened, and she rattled off a story about going to the barn that morning and finding his body. Said she didn't even know he was home on account of him saying that he was going fishing with a friend.

Her voice was calm, like she was reciting a grocery list. You'd think she would have cried, but she was cool as well water."

Frankie was going to make a fine witness for the prosecution. His voice had been far from calm, and his eyes were watery. I didn't know if he was more upset over Tuck's body or Deputy Harraldson's dog. "Then what happened?" I asked, my fingers metaphorically crossed that he wouldn't tell me that Sarah had offered to cook breakfast for them.

"I went inside the house and made sure no one else was there, and then came back out and asked her if she wanted to call a relative. She kind of laughed and said she didn't have family within a thousand miles. I didn't see why it was funny."

"People can behave oddly when they're in shock." Or when confronted with the imminent arrival of a mother-in-law.

"She wasn't too shocked to offer us iced tea while we waited for the backup team," Frankie said. "Sheriff Dorfer would have skinned us alive if he drove up and found us sipping tea with the prime suspect."

"Why was she the prime suspect? Her husband told her that he was going fishing, so she didn't expect him to be home when she arrived late that night. She had no reason to go to the barn. An intruder seems more likely."

"We considered that," he said as if he'd taken charge of the investigation. I doubted that Deputy Harraldson let him drive — or even navigate. He opened a folder and flipped a page. "There'd been a home invasion out that way a couple of months before, but it didn't match the modus operandi. There wasn't anything worth stealing in the barn. What were they going to do with a bunch of old tools and tarps?"

"Perhaps they didn't know there was nothing of value in the barn," I suggested. "They were poking around when Tuck caught them. He'd brought the shotgun, and they got into a struggle. The shotgun went off and they fled."

He glanced at me before he flipped another page and squinted at the print. "We considered that. The woman admits she got home at eleven. The blast was heard at midnight or thereabouts. You care to explain what happened during the hour gap?"

That was a bit of a poser, I had to admit. "They were holding him hostage when Sarah drove up. She went into the house and straight to bed. She was sound asleep when the struggle occurred."

"You interested in buying some beachfront property out by Maggody? My uncle owns a hundred acres. Once this so-called global warming kicks in, the ocean's gonna rise."

I pondered several responses, but none of them would win his heart. "I'll keep your offer in mind, Deputy Norton. Could I have a look at the file on the home invasion?"

"Not relevant. The majority of murders are committed by folks known to the victim. We took a hard look at the most obvious suspect, and when her story turned out to be a crock of lies, we arrested her. The grand jury indicted her, and now she's going to trial. None of this has anything to do with the dumbasses what broke into that old woman's house and stole her property." He closed the folder. "You need to run along, Mizz Malloy. I need to make some calls about a stolen dog."

I switched on the maternal glare. "I rarely run along. Who questioned the neighbors?"

His lower lip quavered but did not protrude. "I'll give you five more minutes, okay?" He reopened the folder, shuffled through pages, and finally put his finger on what I presumed contained the pertinent information. "Deputy Harraldson took statements from Juniper and William Lund. The lawyer has copies, so I don't see any reason to read them to you."

"What about their grandson, a little boy named Billy?"

"There's nothing in here about him."

"He was questioned by a deputy," I persisted. "Would that have been Deputy Harraldson?"

"Like I said, there's nothing in here." He again closed the folder, this time with unnecessary force. "Why don't you come back Tuesday and talk to the sheriff? It's my day off."

"I'd prefer to speak to Deputy Harraldson. Is he on duty today?"

"Not hardly," Frankie said smugly.

I was perilously close to losing my equanimity. "Is it possible that he's at home?"

He hesitated, his lips parted as he thought this over. "I can give you his home address, but I can't promise he'll be any help." He scribbled on a notepad, then tore off the sheet and pushed it across the desk. "I'll tell Sheriff Dorfer you were here, Mizz Malloy. Have a nice day."

I did not stalk out of his office, but my posture was perfect, and I did not glance at LaBelle as I sailed out the main door. Once I was in my car, I looked at the paper. Frankie's penmanship was abysmal but decipherable. Deputy Harraldson purportedly lived on Jicama Drive in Mansfield, a small town in a corner of the county. I would require a map, not an insurmountable problem. The real problem was finding evidence that might lead to a not-guilty verdict, and doing so in a few short days. Since I had no idea how long the trial might last, I decided to swing by Evan Toffle's office and resume our conversation.

I had no problem parking in front of his office, since the only vehicle there was his sad little car. The reception room was dark. I rapped my car key on the glass door. After a minute, Evan came to the doorway, looked at me without enthusiasm, and came across the room to admit me.

"Any luck?" he asked as we walked to his office.

"Maybe." I moved a stack of law books off a chair and sat down. "Do you know about the mysterious green van?"

His expression brightened, although the wattage remained low. "It's not mentioned in the file or the discovery material. What's the deal?"

I told him about Miss Poppoy's burglary and Zachery Barnard's sightings. "The sheriff's department failed to see any connection to Tuck's case, so they didn't make an effort to locate it. I'm unfamiliar with the manual on how to stage home invasions, but I'd suppose one of the hints is to watch the house prior to the main event. Miss Poppoy said she'd seen the van parked near Sarah's mailbox."

Evan thought for a moment. "All right, let's hypothesize that the burglars were preparing to break into the house. Criminals are not especially intelligent, but I think they would prefer the house to be empty. Sarah claims that Tuck had already gone on his nonexistent fishing trip when she left to go to her book club meeting."

I held up my hand. "When did she say he left?"

"She was at the café until six. He was gone when she got home. She changed clothes, ate a sandwich, and left shortly after seven. Our burglars would have seen her drive off. Sometime between then and midnight, Tuck returned from wherever he'd been. By eight thirty, it would have been getting dark. He either went inside and turned on lights, or decided to spend the night in the barn, which has no lights. Help me here, Claire."

"Was the house dark when Sarah came home?"

He opened a folder and took out several pages. After a quick scan, he said, "She turned on a lamp in the living room before she left, so she noticed the house was dark when she got back. If that was true, Tuck was either sitting in the dark inside the house or was already in the barn."

"William Lund told me he saw lights in the house earlier that evening."

"So someone turned them off."

I related my hostage scenario. "When he heard the burglars open the barn door, he took the shotgun out of the closet, turned off the light, and crept across the yard. It could have happened any time after eight. For all we know, they sat around and negotiated until Sarah drove the pickup truck up the driveway."

"So all we have to do is find these two gentlemen and convince them to confess. Wessell won't need more than two days to present his case, so I'll need to have them available to testify by Thursday. Would you prefer to call them, or shall I? Gee, I hope they haven't already made plans for the day."

"I have dealt with sarcasm and mockery for three days in a row. My cup has runneth over, and I'm standing in a damn puddle of derision. It's not as though I don't have plenty of other problems. Your mother's dog may have gone after a postal carrier, but my mother-in-law is coming to visit and I lost her damn wedding present and she will notice. Are you going to find it all that amusing when Sarah is sentenced to life in prison? Saving any tidbits of sarcasm to toss at her when she's dragged away in handcuffs?" I realized I had risen and was poking my finger at him as if he were a hapless rotary dial. I closed my mouth and sat down. "Sorry," I said, although I wasn't.

"Me, too. This is my first murder trial, and I'm feeling the pressure. I should have specialized in wills and trusts. I'd be working sixty-hour weeks in the basement of some big firm, but I wouldn't be responsible for destroying someone's future."

"You're not responsible, Evan. Sarah should have divorced her husband years ago and gone on her merry way."

"No kidding. I asked her why she hung around, and all she said was that she'd been stuck with him for better or worse. I can't think of anything worse than spending your life with someone you loathe. Back when I was assigned to the case, I had a girlfriend. She was dropping hints about getting married, and I was mulling it over. By the time Sarah was indicted by the grand jury, I'd soured on the idea of any kind of permanent relationship. Last month I received a wedding invitation from Debbie. She's marrying one of the senior partners at her law firm."

I wasn't sure whether I should applaud or console him. "There are plenty of happy marriages out there."

"Do they all come with mothers-in-law?"

I took a deep breath. "Let's review what I've found out thus far and come up with a plan to save Sarah, shall we?"

6

Our planning session was brief, since neither of us had much to contribute. We did agree that we needed Sarah's input. Evan phoned her, but she didn't answer. Deputy Harraldson's telephone number was unlisted. The only other person I could think of to call was Caron, but I wasn't in the mood to be berated for interrupting her mission to find and retrieve the holiest of the grails.

I left Evan hunkered behind a stack of law books and drove to Mansfield, courtesy of a map drawn on Legal Aid stationery. Although the town boasted a traffic light, it lacked street signs. After a few aimless forays, I was heading back to the business district (a convenience store) for directions when I saw, with mixed emotions, a yard sale. The house was beyond unpretentious, but most likely safe from condemnation. I parked at the edge of the unpaved street and walked up the gravel driveway. A woman dressed in a muumuu and flip-flops, with massively bushy hair and a faint mustache, lowered her face to peer at me over her sunglasses.

Déjà vu and pay-per-view.

"Hi," I said, trying to appear excited as I gazed at the card tables covered with dishes, jars, plastic kitchen utensils, and costume jewelry. "I'm looking for Jicama Drive. Can you help me?"

"You know somebody that lives there?"

"I don't know Deputy Harraldson, but his partner gave me the address. It's about an old investigation."

"That Frankie Norton is one sick puppy," she said. "He used to date my sister's daughter, a sweet girl and popular at school. She was on the honor roll, too, until she took up with him. He kept her out half the night, sometimes brought her home drunk or high. Her grades went all to hell, and instead of going to college on a scholarship, she works at a church daycare center and takes night classes."

"How sad," I murmured.

"Don't go feeling sorry for her. Everybody in the family, including yours truly, tried to talk some sense into her, but she'd just sit there like a bumpkin on a log. You could see your words go in one ear and float out the other. Kids these days think they can have whatever they want just for the asking."

"Kids," I said, shaking my head. "Now, if you could please tell me how to find Jicama Drive, I'd appreciate it."

"My brother's stepson is a real mess. He's not but fourteen, and he's already been arrested twice for DWI. It's his mama's fault. She feels guilty about the divorce and tries to make it up to him by letting him do as he pleases." The woman pulled off her sunglasses to wipe her eyes. "The boy needs discipline, and I mean with a belt. Poor Houston is afraid to raise his voice, much less his hand."

I'd underestimated the social dynamics of yard sales. Vowing to avoid them in the future, even if it involved risking a limb, I said, "Jicama Drive?"

"Why don't you sit for a spell? We all have problems, and talking about them can help sometimes. When my youngest was born, I got so depressed I stayed in my bed for seventeen weeks. It was all I could do to nurse the baby. You ever been depressed like that? So tired all you want to do is cry yourself to sleep?"

I was heading that way. I gave her my most sympathetic smile and said, "I wish I could stay, but I'm in a dreadful hurry. As soon as

I've spoken to Deputy Harraldson, I need to rush home to take care of my daughter. She has scurvy."

"Scurvy?"

"That's what she told me."

"I didn't think folks got that these days." She sucked on her upper lip, trying to decide if I met her criteria for a sick puppy. A quick glance at the street indicated I was the best she had for the time being. "Then again, who knows what these kids are capable of catching. In my day, all we worried about was diarrhea and gonorrhea." She waited for me to laugh, and after I forced out a chuckle of sorts, gave up on me. "Go back to the highway, turn right, and take the next left. It's just past where the mobile home park used to be before the tornado got it. It was a doozey. Some of its residents are in Oz these days, others at the cemetery. My husband and I got our plots booked in advance. We're going to spend eternity under a persimmon tree, if you can imagine."

"It sounds lovely."

"You wouldn't say that if you knew my husband."

I snatched up a lopsided picture frame lacking glass. "How much?"

"You can have it," the woman said. "Ain't

worth a plug nickel. Neither is my husband. Sumbitch is carrying on with Leon's wife. Everybody in town knows about it, except Leon. He fell off the roof of his house when he was putting up Christmas lights four years ago, and he's been humming 'Jingle Bells' ever since."

I retreated to my car, picture frame in hand, and drove back to the highway. I turned right, and then turned left at a vacant lot strewn with branches and skeletal metal. There was a car in the carport of Deputy Harraldson's house. Trying hard not to look like a missionary, I went to the front door.

The middle-aged woman who answered the door could barely find the energy to raise her eyebrows. "Yes?" she said.

"Is Deputy Harraldson at home? I'd like to speak to him about an old investigation. I was at the sheriff's department earlier this afternoon and was given this address."

"Frankie Norton is way too big for his britches. Yes, my husband is home. No, you can't speak to him. Have a nice day."

I inserted my foot before the door closed. "It will just take a couple of minutes. It concerns the Sarah Swift case. Her trial begins Tuesday."

"Yeah, I remember her. She shot her

husband in the barn, right? There's nothing my husband can tell you that's going to help her or you." She again attempted to close the door.

"Please let me speak to him," I said, although it sounded more like a pathetic bleat than a request. "Sarah may be innocent. If she's found guilty, she'll die in prison."

The woman shrugged. "All right, but it's not going to do any good. Richard was diagnosed with early-onset Alzheimer's at the first of the year, and he's been going downhill like a kid on a sled. Most days he knows who I am, but he drifts in and out. I was hoping you were from Social Services. They said they were sending someone to keep an eye on him so I can have a few hours off. I haven't been to the beauty shop for months."

I wanted to hug her, assure her that her hair looked fine, and offer to spend the afternoon with her husband. I restrained myself and said, "Thank you, Mrs. Harraldson."

"You may not be thanking me after you try to get information out of him. Come on in." She stepped back and gestured for me to follow her.

We went into the living room, where an

unshaven man in a bathrobe was watching a baseball game on the TV. He glanced up at me. "Do I know you?"

"I'm Claire Malloy," I said as I sat down across from him. "I'd like to ask you about the Sarah Swift case."

"Shot her husband in the barn," Mrs. Harraldson inserted. "About a year ago, Richard, when you were still working for Sheriff Dorfer."

"He was a good man," murmured Deputy Harraldson. "He kept a bottle of bourbon in his desk drawer. Many an afternoon we'd sit in his office, drinking and smoking cheap cigars. LaBelle had a fit every time she came into the room, claiming it was what she called a 'hostile work environment.' Damn silly woman."

I leaned forward. "Do you remember anything about the investigation?"

He gave me an annoyed look. "Of course I do. Wife shot her husband in the chest with a twelve-gauge shotgun and then waltzed off to bed."

"You interviewed the neighbors, right?" I said, doing my best to suppress my eagerness. "They had a grandson, Billy, staying with them."

"Yeah, cute kid but a real pest. He followed me out to my car and told me some gobbledy-gook about dead men lurching out in the field. Claimed to have evidence. I made a couple of notes just to shut him up. He wasn't much more than three years old, with a helluva imagination. Maybe he'll grow up to be the next Stephen King."

"You didn't follow up on it?" I asked.

"Are you asking me if I walked across a field on a blazing hot day to search for evidence of zombies?"

Even Mrs. Harraldson had a problem with that scenario. "Well," I said slowly, "the little boy might have seen something."

He clamped his lips together and scowled at the floor. After a minute, Mrs. Harraldson sat down next to him and squeezed his hand. I did not move. Finally, he raised his head and gazed at me.

"Do I know you?"

Once I was in Farberville, I stopped by a café and ordered a sandwich to go. I carried the sack into the Book Depot, where Jacob, my overly conscientious clerk, was seated behind the counter. He acknowledged my appearance with a curt nod and then pointed at the rack of paperback fiction. I assumed he was attempting to convey something of grave significance.

"What's up?" I whispered, willing to play

along for lack of anything better to do. "Am I interrupting a holdup? I don't have time to be taken hostage today."

"A potential shoplifter," Jacob whispered back. "He may be armed and dangerous."

"Have you been reading Dostoevsky? Raskolnikov may have begun his career by stealing a volume of Pushkin's poetry, but I doubt he was into science fiction and fantasy. If so, he deserved punishment for his crime."

Jacob failed to appreciate my wit. "I'm waiting until he steps outside, then I'll grab him while you call the police. I've been going over the ledgers, Ms. Malloy. You lose approximately fourteen percent of your stock to shoplifters."

"We do go through a lot of yellow study guides," I said as I went behind the paperback rack. My scruffy science fiction hippie, who'd taken one too many hallucinogens in the seventies, grinned at me. The pockets of his army jacket bulged, as usual. "Put them back," I said, as usual. "Do you know anything about this current zombie nonsense?"

He retrieved half a dozen books from his pockets and replaced them on the rack. "I prefer to stick to the classics, although I may have flipped through a couple of graphic novels about zombies. You thinking about getting one for a pet? Way cool."

"I haven't considered that," I said. "I'm curious to know how they're portrayed. Are they up on technology?"

"Maybe you ought to get a vampire instead. Of course, feeding either of them would be a problem unless you can find a specialty pet store that carries blood and brains. I don't think there's one in Farberville, but I don't get out to the mall very often."

"Would a zombie be depicted with a flashlight?"

He scratched his beard, freeing crumbs and bits of dried vegetation. "I don't think so. They mostly stumble around in the dark."

"Okay," I said. I took one of the paperbacks off the rack and handed it to him. "This is on the house. You have to buy the other ones."

"You could get a werewolf," he said, his eyes flickering, "but you should make sure it's housebroken."

I caught his arm and escorted him to the door. "Have you ever considered getting books at the library?"

"Yeah, but when I tried, an alarm went off when I went out the door and this Valkyrie came whooping after me. This place is a lot more civilized."

"Librarians can be scary." I watched him amble across the street, oblivious to traffic, and disappear into the beer garden.

Jacob did not look pleased as I came back inside the store. "You shouldn't reinforce his larcenous behavior, Ms. Malloy. He's a menace to all retail establishments."

"And he has deep pockets."

I sat at my desk and ate while I tried to come up with a logical course of action for the next two days. Not that I had two days, I corrected myself glumly. Peter's mother would arrive at noon on Monday. I pictured myself in a sundress and high heels, greeting her on the porch. We would exchange air kisses. I would have to serve lunch. Sandwiches were unthinkably rustic. My attempts at making a soufflé had been abysmal, as in inedible. Chicken salad was safe, I supposed, but uninspired. Curried chicken salad, with almonds, dried cranberries —

"Did you get any help from Sheriff Dorfer?" Peter said from the doorway.

I was pleased to be interrupted. "He went fishing. I had to trample over a dispatcher to talk to a deputy, who's a jerk. The deputy who interviewed the neighbors wasn't able to help. I want to ask Sarah about the green van, but she's disappeared. Her lawyer is already thinking about her appeal." I pushed aside the half-eaten sandwich. "Why don't we go fishing somewhere in Mexico? We have valid passports. Jacob can book the tickets and we can head straight to the airport. I don't care if we go to Los Cabos or Cancún, as long as we leave within the hour."

Peter sat on a corner of the desk. "You're admitting defeat?"

"I'll work on the appeal."

"My mother may be disappointed."

"Oh, I totally forgot that she's coming. Why don't you call and invite her to come next month, or the next. The foliage will be breathtaking."

"She isn't coming for the foliage," my darling husband said. "Are you truly so terrified to meet her? She's a bit eccentric, but she doesn't raise rats in the basement and bats in the attic. The chef does that. The parlor maids make minimum wage, and the footmen have all been screened for criminal records. I never believed there were alligators in the moat, but my pony did disappear under mysterious circumstances."

"Shall I assume you think I'm making a fuss over nothing?"

"I think you're making a fuss over nothing. She's merely my mother."

I teetered on the brink. "And I'm merely your wife?"

He looked at the clock on the wall. "I told the captain I'd swing by and review the latest bulletins from Homeland Security. Would you like to discuss the case before I leave? Up to you."

I considered my options and then eased away from the brink. "I can use your insight. You're merely my husband, but you can be useful." I told him everything I'd heard about the green van from Zachery Barnard and Miss Poppoy. "It may have been spotted a month ago, so whoever is driving it is still in the area. The problem is I have no information about its make, age, or license plate. I doubt the sheriff will issue an APB for it."

"The description's vague," Peter said, his eyes narrowed. "You did say that the police in one of the small towns questioned suspects about the burglaries and the home invasion. I'll lean on the deputy at the sheriff's department to get that report. If one of them owns a green van, we can follow up on it. You need to keep in mind that it's Saturday, and a three-day weekend. It's not going to be easy to get anything from what may well be the only police officer in the particular town. He may have gone fishing, too."

"Or she," I said, being a dedicated supporter of equal opportunity (although any woman willing to take the role of chief of police in the grubby little towns in the county could stand some serious therapy). "Sarah's lawyer pointed out that even if we locate two men in a green van, we have to convince them to confess, which may be tricky."

"After you convince Sheriff Dorfer to take them into custody and interrogate them. There's nothing inherently illegal about owning a green van. They could have been looking for a lost dog or admiring the organic farms. Maybe they're hunters, checking out the area for posted property. Deer season opens in November."

"Or casing the joint. I don't have a lot to work with, Peter, so let me have my demented theories. The only other thing I can think to do is to go on a zombie hunt." His reaction suggested that I needed to expound on the remark. I related what Billy had told me about the zombies battling over carrots across the field. With flashlights. Both of us were relieved when my cell phone beeped.

"I found out where Sarah is," Evan said, bypassing standard pleasantries. "You won't believe it. She's been taken into custody by the FBI. Wessell's called a press conference on the courthouse steps. I'm going there now."

Stunned, I looked at Peter. "The FBI has Sarah. Will they talk to you?"

"If they're in the mood, maybe, but I'll have to make a lot of calls. They're not known to play well with others."

He had a point, as he often did. "Okay," I said as I grabbed my purse, "then call the chauffer and tell him we need to go to the courthouse immediately. I'll explain on the way."

Jacob, who probably had listened to the entire conversation, watched us go past him with nary a smirk. I made a mental note to give him a bonus at Christmas.

The scene on the steps of the courthouse lacked drama. Prosecutor Wessell, flanked by two minions, was addressing a TV camera and crew. Half a dozen pedestrians were watching, but they seemed disinclined to organize themselves into a mob. Thomas Pomfreet, who'd reported (and distorted) my dismissal from the jury, clutched a microphone as if it were the Olympic torch. The analogy was appropriate, since Wessell's chest was puffed up in expectation of a gold medal.

"We intend to cooperate fully with the FBI," he said, "but this atrocious murder took place in Stump County, and justice must be served. After Mrs. Swift — or whatever her real name is — has been found guilty of murder, she will be turned over to face charges of unlawful flight to avoid prosecution, conspiracy to commit murder, destruction of government property, and whatever other charges to be determined by the federal authorities. I will have more information later today."

"Where is she now?" asked Pomfreet.

"Her bond has been revoked, and she will be detained in the county jail for the duration of the trial."

I saw Evan cowering in the doorway of a dress shop and went over to him. "What on earth is going on?"

"I don't know much. Sarah was picked up this morning by FBI agents. She hasn't been allowed to make a telephone call." His face was flushed, and he was sweating copiously. His necktie hung like a limp noose. "I can't get hold of any of the other attorneys from the office. I've never dealt with the FBI."

I squeezed his arm. "You can't fall apart now, Evan. My husband has FBI contacts."

I looked at Peter, who promptly took out his cell phone and moved down the sidewalk. "If Sarah didn't call you, how did you find out about this? Don't tell me Wessell informed you out of professional courtesy, because I'll assume you're having a heatstroke and are in need of immediate medical aid."

"An anonymous tip," he said. "I called you and then came here to find out what the hell's going on. Once Wessell stops pontificating, I'll try to talk to him. This is ridiculous. The trial will have to be postponed, maybe for months."

"The trial," Wessell announced in a thunderous voice, "will commence Tuesday morning as scheduled. The defendant's past crimes in no way mitigate her culpability in the death of her husband, an elderly man in poor health. I have spoken to Judge Priestly, who has made it plain she will not entertain any motions for a continuance. As the county prosecutor of Stump County, I have a sworn duty to demand justice. The FBI agents have requested that I avoid any further explanation until later today, but I will say that Sarah Swift has been on their most-wanted list for forty years. We can all sleep better tonight, knowing that she is no longer an imminent threat to the citizens of

150

Stump County." He posed briefly for the camera and then, ignoring Pomfreet's squeaky pleas, went into the courthouse.

I joined Evan in the doorway and leaned against the wall. "What did she do — attempt to overthrow the government? Did I miss a coup?"

"I wasn't taking notes forty years ago. That would be the early seventies, and Sarah would have been around twenty years old. In college, I guess."

Evan was regarding me as if I'd been enrolled right along with Sarah and had personal knowledge of the era. I took a deep breath and said, "Before my time. It may have something to do with the antiwar movement. She implied that she wasn't involved, but she may have been circumspect. Go see what you can find out from Wessell and his new friends from Quantico."

"Right." He rubbed his temples. "I don't think he's into sharing, and I don't think I'll be allowed access to Sarah, so I should be back at the office within half an hour. I need to get started on a motion for a continuance, even if Judge Priestly has already made up her mind. That will give us grounds for the appeal." He trudged up the steps, paused in front of the door, and then pushed it open as if he had found the courage to enter the lion's den but knew he was on the menu.

Peter returned, looking grim. "Nobody's chatty, but my understanding is that Sarah was part of a campus group called the Student Antiwar Coalition, known to the feds as SAC. There was a protest, and an undercover FBI agent was killed. Sarah and a few other kids escaped and went underground. Sarah has surfaced."

"What about Tuck?"

"He was one of them."

"That explains why they stayed together," I said. "Any bright ideas, Sherlock?"

"I'll go to the PD and make some calls, see if I can get more information about the incident and her status. You may have bet on the wrong horse, Claire. If Wessell doesn't get her, the feds will."

I told Peter that I preferred to walk back to the Book Depot, and we parted without sweet sorrow. The town square was not aflutter with activity, since the farmers' market began to close down shortly after noon. I went into a café and purchased iced tea and a cookie, then sat down on a shady bench. In the past, I may have failed to reveal irrelevant details during my investigations, but Sarah had taken the art of omission to an impressive level. She hadn't tossed out an idle comment about being on the FBI's most-wanted list. She hadn't made passing references to the outstanding charges against her, including conspiracy to commit murder. She'd dropped no wee hints that she and her husband were using false identities to elude the authorities for forty years. It might not have made for an appropriate topic at her book club, but she hadn't shared the information with her lawyer, either.

I nibbled on the cookie as I watched as the parking spaces that had been reserved for the farmers' market pickups begin to be taken by vehicles of a less agronomic nature. A patron from the bookstore waved at me as she entered an art gallery. A professor from the English department glanced at me and hurriedly rounded the corner, perhaps unwilling to be seen in the company of a disgraced nonmember of the jury. Two of Caron's friends stopped texting long enough to gape at me, then resumed updating the world on their current whereabouts and latest philosophical musings. I began to feel like the Notorious Ms. Malloy, a veritable magnet for murder. At least I hadn't shot Carlton in the barn, or even in the chest. According to the Weasel, I was much too devious.

Sarah would not share any enlightenment in the near future. If I believed that she hadn't shot Tuck (or whatever his name was), then someone else had. Most likely, I thought as I sipped tea, not a zombie. Peter, who could be helpful when it suited him, had promised to find out about the green van — if there was anything to be found out.

Images of the Ming Thing began to flit into my consciousness. Doing my best to banish them, I finished my cookie, brushed off the crumbs in my lap, and walked to the Book Depot. The modicum of exercise failed to elevate my spirits. I went through the back door, called to Jacob to let him know I was skulking, and noted that the remains of my sandwich had been neatly wrapped. Like Wessell's case against Sarah. Sarah, who was now a fugitive who'd been on the FBI's most-wanted list for forty years for such minor peccadilloes as conspiring to commit murder. Wessell would not need two days to present his case. Fifteen minutes might suffice. Evan might need ten for the defense.

All I had were zombies. It was time to go hunting.

I drove back out County 107, intending to stop at Miss Poppoy's house to ask her who owned the camping spot William had mentioned. I had reached her road when flashing blue lights appeared in my rearview mirror. I pulled over and watched a sheriff's car race by me, hit the brakes, and turn onto Pinkie Sheer Road. Seconds later an ambulance did the same at a more sedate speed. The two women I'd met the previous day at their yard sale came out to the end of the driveway. When no high drama ensued, they retreated, talking animatedly to each other.

I knew I would not be welcome, but I decided to find out what had happened, albeit from a prudent distance. The official vehicle and the ambulance had stopped by the pond. Deputy Norton and a second deputy were standing in knee-high weeds while medics unloaded a gurney. A large man in bib overalls and a cap beckoned to them from beside the pond. Near his feet was a sodden lump covered with pond slime, but even from where I'd stopped I could see the soles of boots and a splayed arm.

I clung to the steering wheel and stared at a clump of oak trees while I replayed my conversation with Zachery Barnard. He had failed to live up to the decided low expectations of his neighbors; he'd been sober. And he'd quoted Oliver Goldsmith, not a bawdy limerick. I was trying to imagine him on Miss Poppoy's front porch at midnight, ranting about black helicopters, when a rap on the window startled me.

"Mizz Malloy," Deputy Norton drawled, "what the hell do you think you're doing?"

"Waiting to find out what you're doing," I said. "Who's the deceased?"

"Who said anyone is deceased?" he countered with a sneer.

"Just a wild guess, Deputy Norton. The paramedics didn't leap over the fence to rush to his aid, which implies it's a little too late for CPR. You and your colleague don't appear to be doing much of anything. Is it Zachery Barnard?"

"You know him?"

"I spoke to him yesterday. What happened?"

"It ain't none of your business, but I suppose it can't hurt. Yeah, that's Barnard. The guy over there, name of Jeeter Buchanon, said he was driving by and saw something in the pond. Thought it looked like a body, so he went over to investigate. Dragged Barnard out of the water, identified him, and called us."

I am not fond of coincidences. "Cause of death?"

Deputy Norton snorted. "Now how would

we know? The medical examiner's on the way, but it'll take him another half hour to get here. Jeeter said there wasn't any sign of blood but he could smell whiskey. Barnard had a reputation for gettin' drunk and blunderin' around at night. Dumb shit fell in the pond and drowned, if you ask me." He stepped back and gave me a hard look. "I don't want to know why you spoke to Barnard yesterday or any other day, but if you don't get the hell out of here right now, I'll put you in the backseat of my car and take you in for questioning. Do I make myself clear?"

I willed myself not to make a scathing remark, since he was petty enough to follow through with his threat. While he watched, hands on his hips like a belligerent bouncer, I maneuvered the car until I was turned around and then drove back to the highway, hoping he enjoyed a mouthful of dust. I stopped at the edge of the road as a wave of nausea swept over me. I could taste slimy green water. I could feel tentacles of sodden weeds drifting across my face. I managed to open the car door and lean over as everything I'd eaten came spewing out. Once the spasm subsided, I sat back up and found a tissue to wipe my mouth and chin.

Miss Marple would have been aghast.

7

There were two cars parked in front of Miss Poppoy's house. I was reluctant to intrude on what might be a highly spirited religious (and high-caliber) exchange, but the clock was ticking. I knocked on the door and waited.

"You again?" Miss Poppoy said as she threw open the door. To my bemusement, she was wearing a coppery wig, high heels, and a gaping bathrobe that gave me a glimpse of a misshapen rose tattoo that had passed its prime decades earlier.

"I am so sorry to disturb you," I said in a voice that might have sounded a bit shrill. "Do you know who owns the campsite called Flat Rock?"

"Can't think offhand. Let me ask Geronimo." She looked up at me with a coy smile. "Not his real name, of course, but that's what I call him. You want to come in? We're playing mah-jongg."

I was not about to be lured into what might have been strip mah-jongg. "I'll just wait here."

"Suit yourself." She closed the door.

I tried as best I could to keep my imagination from conjuring up any images whatsoever. I was reduced to mentally constructing a crossword puzzle when she returned.

"The property belongs to Larry Lippet. Go north about a half mile and turn left at an abandoned house. They live in a fancy manor with pillars and all kinds of shit. Marie walks around with her nose in the air like she's smelling something nasty. It's a surprise she doesn't trip over one of those plastic flamingos and break her leg." Miss Poppoy let out a raucous cackle that might have been heard in the hinterwoods of the county.

I was reluctant to spoil her jovial mood (and whatever delights she'd planned for the rest of the afternoon), but I took a breath and said, "I'm afraid I have some bad news, Miss Poppoy. Zachery Barnard's body was found a little while ago. He drowned in that pond near his house."

"Yeah, I already heard. Jeeter called his sister, who called everybody she could think of short of God and the governor. Damn shame, but I ain't surprised. Unless you got other business, I need to go. Geronimo turns into a wild man when he has to wait. I got the bruises to prove it."

I fled to my car. Still battling to stifle my imagination, I drove back to the county road and followed her directions. There were a few mobile homes along the unpaved road, but I had no difficulty recognizing the Lippets' extensive flock of flamingos in front of a large two-story house built in a most peculiar style that hinted of Greek-Mexican fusion. Garden gnomes lined the brick sidewalk like small, pudgy guards, and concrete deer grazed in front of a pergola with a terra-cotta tile roof.

I went onto the porch flanked by columns and rang the doorbell. I was beginning to feel foolish as well as grimy, and I would not have been devastated if no one was home.

The door was opened by a rotund man in jeans and a plaid shirt, with glistening black hair pasted across the top of his head like inky lines. He gazed at me for a moment, then said, "Yeah? If you're selling, we're not buying."

"Mr. Lippet, I'm Claire Malloy, and I'm looking for information about Flat Rock. Miss Poppoy told me that you're the owner."

"She did, did she?"

I did not want to elaborate and end up ratting out her confidential informant. "Do you own that property?"

He nodded. "It's been in the family for three generations. Two hundred acres, give or take. This any of your business?"

In for a drachma, in for a peso, I told myself. "I'm trying to find out if there were campers the night that John Cunningham was shot. I know it's been a long time, but I really think it might help Sarah avoid a wrongful conviction."

"It's not wrongful if she shot him," Lippet said.

"True, but there are some unexplained incidents that might support her innocence. One of them involves Flat Rock."

"About a year ago, right?"

"Is there any chance you remember that night?"

"Hell, no. It used to be our private family swimming hole, but then the damn hippies chanced on it and started sneaking out there weekends. Every time I put up a NO TRES-PASSING sign, the jerks knocked it down. They damn near knocked down the fence, too. I gave up and put in stiles and a trash bin. Sunday mornings after church I go pick up all the wine and beer bottles and litter."

"Thanks for your time," I said. I suppose I could have asked him if he'd noticed any zombies staggering across his field, but he might not be amused.

"Marie may know," he said, scratching his chin. "We let certain groups reserve the area, mostly from churches. You want to get rid of hippies, get yourself a bunch of Baptists and tell 'em they have permission from the Almighty to stay there. Instead of thumping Bibles, they thump heads."

"Would you please ask Marie if she remembers who might have reserved Flat Rock that night?"

"Wait here."

I sat down on a porch swing and let my feet brush the floor as I tried not to get overly optimistic. More than a year ago, and during a popular month for swimming, toasting marshmallows, and, for some, getting high by the light of the moon. Or playing flashlight tag.

Lippet came to the porch. "You're in luck, little lady. Marie keeps a notebook so we don't end up with a holy war. She recalled the day Cunningham got killed because it was her birthday. That particular Saturday we let our church's teen choir have the campsite. Well chaperoned, of course. Even then, I had to pluck some condoms out the water downstream. I didn't say anything because the preacher's daughters are in the choir."

"Do you know the names of the chaperones?" I asked, desperate enough to overlook the phrase "little lady."

"The choir director's Grady Nichols, so he would have been one of them. I don't recollect who else was there. You want me to ask Marie?"

"I'd appreciate it."

He went back inside while I considered how to handle this frail tidbit of information. There had been campers at Flat Rock on the pertinent night, but not in close proximity. No one had contacted the sheriff's department to report seeing anything of significance, including the living dead. I had failed to come up with a plan of action when Lippet returned.

"Marie says that Tricia Yates called her to set the date and said she would be accompanying the kids. Fatso Feathers was supposed to go, too, but he ended up spending the weekend in jail over in Hasty. Dumb shit had a lovers' quarrel with Carol Louise Pippins and drove his truck into her living room. She thought it was so romantic that it took three deputies to pull 'em apart."

"Do you have any idea how I might get in

touch with Grady or Tricia?"

"You think Sarah's innocent?"

I cleverly deduced that Mr. Lippet had failed to catch the breaking story on the local TV channel. I realized I was hesitating and, with all the conviction I could muster, said, "Yes, I do. I don't think the campers from your church will have anything to contribute, but I have to follow up on all the possibilities. Sarah says she didn't shoot her husband."

"Sumbitch deserved it," he said with a grimace. "Caught him hiding in the bushes by the rocks, watching hippie chicks skinny-dip. That's not to say there's anything wrong with watching those perky young breasts and fine rumps, but Cunningham tried to tell me they were FBI agents." He gazed over my head, his mind clearly reliving the moment — and the view.

"Grady and Tricia?" I said.

He frowned. "Choir practice is on Saturdays at four. Try the church."

I asked for directions and he obliged. After thanking him, I returned to my car. It was already four thirty. I careened down the road, loosening some neurological screws as well as whatever held the car together, and turned on the county road. As I went past the turnoff for Pinkie Sheer Road, I noticed more official vehicles parked alongside the ditches. The deputies must have been annoyed by having their weekend interrupted, but I was not tempted to meddle. If Prosecutor Wessell heard about my minor involvement, he would be out on the courthouse steps yet again, gleefully slandering me. If and when I sued him for defamation, I would think twice before retaining the services of Evan Toffle.

The Mount Zion Methodist Church was at the edge of Farberville. The white-shingled building had a steeple but lacked the spires and Gothic arches of a cathedral. Gargoyles need not apply. Numerous cars and trucks were parked in the gravel lot. I found a space, gazed sadly at myself in the rearview mirror, and then entered the building.

"No, no, no!" shouted a perturbed male voice. "You sound like a bunch of alley cats! Focus, people!"

The choir appeared to be composed of about a dozen kids, some barely into puberty and others ready for college. Acne abounded. Their director was a man in his late twenties, dressed in trousers, a white short-sleeved shirt, and a bow tie. He would not get past Miss Poppoy's doorstep — even if his name was Cochise.

I walked down the aisle and tapped his shoulder. "Please forgive me for interrupting, but I'd like to speak to you for a few minutes."

"Yeah, why not?" He looked at his charges. "Take five and be ready to hit the right notes when we start up." He gestured at a pew.

Once we were seated, I said, "I know this is a long shot, but I'm looking into what happened the night you took this group camping at Flat Rock. Do you remember anything out of the ordinary?"

"Out of the ordinary for these outstanding young people? I don't recall any earthquakes, bolts of lightning, tidal waves, or nuclear explosions. Rachael had hysterics because Jason sat next to Annie on the bus. Tricia confiscated two bottles of vodka, a switchblade, and a plastic bag of hand-rolled cigarettes. Owners of said contraband were not happy campers. Young Atkins forgot to mention that he doesn't know how to swim until he reached the middle of the river. Carter was found hiding in the girls' tent — twice. Other than that, no."

"No one saw anything in the field across the river?"

Grady's smile vanished. "What do you mean?" he asked in a hard voice.

"There was a report of activity in that area."

"The young people were told not to cross the river, and none of them did. What's this about?"

"Did you hear a shotgun blast?"

"Oh," he said, nodding, "that was the night some woman shot and killed her husband. Who are you?"

"A friend of the accused woman, who has the presumption of innocence until proven otherwise. Do you mind if I speak to your choir members?"

"Good luck with that." He stood up and went through a door next to the platform, apparently unconcerned by the possibility I might be gunned down by the sopranos or trampled by the tenors.

I gazed at the sprawl of teenagers. Some were texting; others were in cozy conversations. They hardly looked outstanding, or upstanding, for that matter, but there might be a future mathematician or surgeon among them. I made my way up the steps and approached a trio of girls. No one showed a flicker of curiosity.

"I'd like to ask you about the camping trip a year ago," I said.

"Really?" said a well-developed brunette in a tight halter. "That was ages ago, like

167

history."

"Bianca can't remember what she had for lunch," inserted a less-developed blonde with dark roots and braces. The third girl whipped out her cell phone and began to text.

I looked at the blonde. "Did you hear a loud noise around midnight?"

"You mean Jessie's fart? It was like an explosion. We all had to scramble out of the tent before we died of asphyxiation. I almost threw up." Her laugh was brittle as she studied her fingernails.

"Anything else?" I asked.

"You ought to ask Miss Yates, the church secretary," the brunette said. "She had some kind of allergy thing and spent the night out on the rock, splashing water on her legs and feet. She went through a whole bottle of calamine lotion." She took out her cell phone to update the world on the current noncrisis.

"How do I find Miss Yates?" I asked the blonde, but a cell phone had appeared in her hand as well and her mind had left the building. Perhaps they should text their Sunday morning choral presentation, I thought as I went back down the steps and followed Grady's path into what proved to be an office.

He was standing next to a desk occupied by an older woman with short silver hair and faded blue eyes. She clutched a wadded tissue in one fist. Although I was not at my best, I was offended by the apprehensive expression on her face. I resisted the urge to check behind me for ghouls or armed men in ski masks.

"Who are you?" she demanded.

Not among ye faithful, I surmised. "Claire Malloy. I live in Farberville and own the Book Depot on Thurber Street. I'm trying to help Sarah Swift before her trial begins on Tuesday." I could have offered a more detailed autobiography, but I felt as though I'd covered the essentials.

"She shot her husband," Grady added helpfully, eliciting a gurgle from the woman, who seemed ready to take refuge under her desk.

"Sarah Swift has been accused of shooting her husband," I corrected him. "I'm here with her lawyer's permission."

"What do you want from me?" the woman asked.

"Are you Tricia Yates?" I waited until she nodded. "You were with the choir at Flat Rock the night it happened. I was wondering if you might have seen or heard anything?"

Grady snickered. "I already ran through the list of high crimes and misdemeanors, including Stanley's vodka and Carter's nocturnal expeditions to visit the girls."

Tricia Yates continued to regard me with anxiety. "I don't understand why you think I know anything. It was a horrible night. I wasn't happy until I got home and took a long hot bath. If you think I had time to wander around that nasty field, then why don't you volunteer to chaperone this group when they go on a retreat in October? Tell me your name again, along with a telephone number."

"Yeah," Grady said.

"Then you didn't hear a shotgun go off about midnight?" I persisted despite the warmth of my reception, which registered thirty-two degrees on the Fahrenheit scale and zero on the Centigrade scale.

Tricia dropped the tissue on her desk. "I heard frogs, birds, and a whole lot of giggling."

"Yeah," Grady said again.

He was beginning to annoy me. "Could I speak to Ms. Yates privately?" I said as I sat down and crossed my legs.

She gestured at him to leave. When he was gone, she said, "I told you that I have nothing to contribute. It was an ordinary campout. We arrived in the middle of the afternoon. Grady supervised the boys while they put up the tents, unloaded the gear, and gathered firewood. I organized the girls for kitchen duty. We ate hot dogs and burned beans for supper, and had a lovely prayer service at sunset. After that, we all sat in a circle around a fire and talked about keeping Jesus in our lives. They were all very earnest, naturally. You'd have thought they were little saints, not jail bait and drug dealers."

"One of the girls mentioned that you developed an allergic reaction," I said with a slathering of sympathy. "What a miserable night."

She shuddered. "Hellish. I must have walked through poison ivy somewhere along the path. I had blisters for two weeks."

"I'm surprised you didn't hear the shotgun."

"Maybe I heard something, but I didn't worry about it." She put the tissue in a wastebasket and picked up a pen. "I need to finish the books for August, so if there's nothing else . . . ?"

There was, but I wasn't sure what it was. "Thanks for your time, Ms. Yates. I hope you don't get roped into chaperoning this retreat."

"Not on my life." She tried to smile, but the result was tepid.

Grady had failed to reorganize his troops and was pacing across the front of the room, his brow creased and his lips tight. I wasn't sure if he was anticipating another round of atonality or more questions from me, but I went out the front door to my car. My visit had caused Tricia Yates's visible disquiet. I didn't understand why, since I'd asked mild questions with low expectations of learning anything of relevance. There was more to their story than they had shared, but I couldn't force them to elaborate. I knew where they and the choir would be the following morning, should I come up with a way to coerce any one of them to spill the truth.

The sun was not yet over the yardarm (or my arm, anyway), so I decided to drive back to the Lippets' road and have a look at Flat Rock. I debated calling Peter, but I didn't need any discouragement. I retraced my route and turned past the bridge. I saw no indications of a path or a stile before the Lippets' house, so I continued. The road grew rougher, and I slowed to a crawl as I gazed at pastures on both sides of me. At last I came to a dirt road with a padlocked gate. I parked, put my cell phone and keys in my pocket, and locked my purse in the trunk of my car.

I walked across the road to a stile next to an overflowing trash bin. This stile did not have railings, but I made my way up the steps, carefully eased over the barbed wire, and came down without a mishap. Giving a modest salute to my vast, unseen audience of avian admirers, I followed a trodden path through a field of cornstalks. My audience was now composed of grasshoppers that buzzed in my face and gnats that swarmed around my head. Crows jabbered as they swooped down to attack the cornstalks. I flapped my hands and muttered rude things until I reached yet another stile. As I ascended it, I saw the river and a large expanse of, well, flat rocks. Eureka.

After a short hike across a weedy expanse, I arrived on an especially fine flat rock that abutted the river. A shift in topography had created a wide pool that looked like a lovely place to swim. The high trees on the far bank made rippled shadows on the still brown water. The avian choir, initially silenced by my arrival, resumed calling for mates. Based on Grady's assessment of his choir members, I hoped they relied on other mating calls (or tweets).

Except for a crushed plastic bottle caught

in weeds on the far bank and some charred wood, I saw no recent signs of human occupancy. Had there been skinny-dipping hippies the previous evening, Lippet had cleaned the area of bodies and litter. He had done so umpteen times since the choir had camped a year ago. However, anything of significance had happened on William Lund's property, which was going to require me to walk on water. Regrettably, that was not among my many talents.

I did what I was sure Sir Henry Morton Stanley had done when he failed to find Dr. Livingstone having tea in a proper tent next to the source of the Nile, which was to throw propriety to the breeze and take a break. Once I'd found a place to sit, I took off my shoes and let my feet dangle in the water. I scooped up water and cleaned my face. The serenity and the solitude were intoxicants. People, including my beloved husband, had been yammering at me for three days.

I was pondering whether or not to call him to find out if the FBI had been more forthcoming when my cell phone buzzed in my back pocket. My hand began to tremble when I saw the call was from Caron, who could be whooping with success or begging for bail.

"What's up, dear?" I asked carefully.

"We think we know where it is, but there's a problem."

"Where is it?" I asked, then froze as an enormous dog bounded into view. Barking hysterically, it flopped across the flat rock, crouched, and growled in a most unsettling fashion. Its fangs were visible. Spittle flew from its mouth as it shifted its weight. Although it was more apt to be a German shepherd than a gray wolf (*Canis lupus*), it appeared to weigh close to a hundred pounds. Or five hundred. Some tormented soul had opened a cage in Satan's kennel.

"What is it, Mother?" Caron shrieked.

"A dog — a nice dog. Nice dog, aren't you? Yes, a good dog." I sounded as convincing as a child miscast in a school play. "Good dog!"

The beast, whose pedigree must have originated with the Baskervilles, did not fall for my ploy. It continued to growl as it moved around me. The hairs on the back of its neck were stiff, making it clear that my mere presence had raised both its hackles and its primal instincts.

"Tell it to go away," said Caron, always helpful.

"I'm not going to tell it to do anything," I said in what I hoped was a steady voice. I scooted to the very edge of the rock and tried to gauge the depth with one leg. My foot did not make contact. The dog made an ominous gurgle as it approached. Clenching my teeth, I eased off the rock. The water was only waist high. That was the good news. The bad news arrived seconds later when the dog loosed a frenzy of barking, interspersed with ill-controlled lunges at my person. I shrank away, felt my feet slide, and fell backward. Despite the brute's volume, I heard my cell phone as it slipped out of my hand, plopped in the water, and sank before my deeply appalled eyes.

"See what you made me do!" I said to the dog in my bad-doggie voice. "Now go away!"

The dog stopped barking and gazed at me with a look that, had I been a fan of anthropomorphism, might be described as wounded. I was preparing a less critical remark when it began to sniff my shoes.

"Don't even think about it, Rover."

The dog didn't pause to think about it, but instead picked up one shoe with its mouth, wagged its tail, and took off in the direction of the cornfield.

"Come back here!" I yelled, adding an uncouth Anglo-Saxon expletive for emphasis. I also commented on its canine parentage via the Old Norse word *bikkja*. I may have said some other things as the seriousness of my dilemma hit me like a splash of cold water. I was soaking wet and semishoeless. My car was parked across an expanse of corn stubble, rocks, and whatever denizens lurked underfoot. I could not call the Mounties. More importantly, I could not call Caron back to learn what she and Inez had uncovered concerning the Ming Thing's whereabouts — or why there was "a problem."

I climbed out of the water. A puddle formed around my feet as I gazed rather sadly at the path the brute had taken. I could hear no barks or an owner's voice. Serenity and solitude became less appealing. Spending the night on a rock was not at all appealing. Caron had no idea where I was, and Peter had left me at the courthouse. When darkness fell and I was missing, he'd call Evan. No help there. I could only hope that my adorable Sherlock might remember Miss Poppoy's name and call her. Could I rely on her to answer the door — and say that I'd asked for directions to Flat Rock?

I reminded myself that I had a couple of hours of daylight to extricate myself from the situation. Since I was already as wet as I could be, I slipped back into the water and swam to the far bank. From a gravel bar, I could see a barbed-wire fence behind a line of scraggly oaks and pines. I made my way across the rocks to the edge of the Lunds' property. The second story of the house and the barn were visible beyond the endless rows of blueberry bushes. Billy could have seen something, I thought as I ventured a few steps farther, feeling oddly furtive. Too many campers had come and gone over the previous year for me to anticipate finding any sort of clue.

As I swam back to the flat rocks, I tried to picture the campsite as constructed under Grady's supervision: a tent for the girls, a tent for the boys, two tents for the chaperones, a primitive kitchen area, and a campfire. Although Grady and Tricia had insinuated that they had restrained their hormonal charges, teenagers were a devious subspecies. Larry Lippet had said he'd found condoms downstream.

The hound from hell had not brought back my shoe. The remaining one was covered with slobber, but I put it on my left foot. Walking across the flat rocks presented no problem. The stile was a good hundred feet away, however, and no one had rolled out a red carpet to cover the rocky ground.

My first step with my bare foot was miscalculated and elicited a yelp. I tottered on my shod foot as I inspected my heel, which was not bleeding profusely or even oozing. The first stile looked very far away; the second stile was a good deal farther. I looked carefully before putting down my unshod foot. At this rate, I would be back at my car by the time the teen choir sang for the Sunday morning congregation. Unless it got dark, as it tended to do every night, in which case I might miss the opening statements at Sarah's trial.

I spotted a piece of wood that might serve as a walking stick and made my way over to it. As I reached for it, a snake slithered onto the edge of the rock. My retreat lacked grace, and I ended up on my derriere in the weeds. I blinked to hold back tears of frustration. The sun was over the yardarm, whatever that was. The shadows from the trees covered the width of the water. The chirps and twitters had lost enthusiasm; the birds had either found mates or called it a day. Before much longer, they would call it a night.

Desperate situations call for ingenuity and immodesty. I took off my shirt and wrapped it around my bare foot, then secured it with strategic tucks. It slid off after one step.

179

Huffing with irritation, I took off my bra and secured my makeshift moccasin. I hobbled toward the first stile. I felt a few stabs of pain, but I forged ahead without pausing to examine the wounds. Bleeding to death was not a concern. Being caught in the dark was at the top of the list, along with snakebites, bats, and other wonders of Mother Nature.

I reached the stile and made it to the top. As I lifted my left foot to step over the barbed wire, I heard a sound that chilled my entrails. The blasted dog came racing down the path, barking its head off. It could not have done so with my shoe in its mouth. I cringed as it stopped at the bottom of the stile and assessed its chances of ripping me to shreds, as it surely had done to my shoe.

"Go away!" I shouted. "I've had enough of you! You're a bad, bad dog!"

The bad, bad dog sat on its haunches and growled.

The only potential weapon I had was my remaining shoe, but it didn't seem wise to sacrifice it. It did not seem wise to retreat down the stile, since the dog wasn't hampered by the fence, nor did it seem wise to continue my minimal progress. I sat down on the top of the stile to try to think of something that seemed even the least bit wise. Nothing came to mind except to out-wait the dog, although its minute canine brain could take eons to determine we were at a stalemate: I wasn't coming down, and if it tried to ascend the steps, I'd bash it on the head with my shoe. Or fist, I amended. When facing severe danger or deprivation, violence has a certain charm.

And so I sat for what seemed like a very long time. The dog had the audacity to relieve itself on the bottom step of the stile, staking out its territory. I watched Venus rise in the western sky. The dog snuffled and then plopped down in the stubble. I stayed on my perch and concocted recipes for such unknown delicacies as German Shepherd's Pie and Hound Hash à la Florentine. This reminded me that I hadn't worked out menus for lunch and dinner on Monday — with Peter's mother. I was considering the possibility of sirloin burgers when I saw a flashlight in the field.

I made it to my feet. "Over here!" I yelled, abruptly aware of how dark it had become. The light bobbled as it came closer. "Be careful! There's a vicious dog at the bottom of the stile!" I waved my arms but then dropped them when I realized the inanity of signaling in the dark. "The stile!" I repeated.

"Hold yer horses!"

To my dismay, I recognized the voice.

8

"This way, Deputy Norton," I called, although I would have been more pleased to be rescued by anyone else in the county, including Billy's mortality-challenged buddies. Had I hackles, they would have been sharper than porcupine quills. The beam of his flashlight hit my face. "It's Claire Malloy," I added as I squinted at the darkness.

"Yeah, I ran the plates on your car," he said. "You're trespassing on private property, so I'm gonna have to take you in. You might want to put on your clothes before we get to the department. Then again, maybe you like parading around half naked."

I abruptly realized I was indeed half naked, since I was wearing my shirt on my right foot. I fumbled to untie my bra as the light moved forward. "Beware of the dog," I said in a pathetic ploy to slow him down. At that moment, I could hear his smirk.

"Get out of here!" he bellowed at the dog, or so I assumed.

I was chagrinned when the dog clumsily got to its feet and trotted away into the night. "Sexist mutt," I said in a low voice as I put on my bra and shirt with all due haste. The phrase also described Deputy Norton, but I didn't want him to take offense and stomp back to his car. I was the princess in the tower, so to speak, and for the distasteful moment, he was the only knight in the neighborhood.

"I'm surprised you're on trespass duty," I said as I came down the stile into the cornfield.

"One of my men saw your car on the highway and reported to me, Mrs. Malloy. Lippet said you'd been at his house, so I decided to follow up. I thought I told you to butt out."

"I did," I said, doing my best to sound dignified as I wobbled on one foot. "I was following a potential lead in Sarah Swift's case. Deputy Harraldson acknowledged that a witness had seen activity near Flat Rock the night of the murder. I confirmed that it was possible, that's all."

"So to celebrate this astounding discovery, you took off your clothes?"

"The dog ran off with one of my shoes.

The ground's rough."

I waited for another sarcastic remark (I could thinks of dozens, if not hundreds), so I was rather flabbergasted when he slipped his arm under mine so I could hang on to his shoulder. Each step with my bare foot felt as if I were traversing a bed of hot coals, but I bit my lip in an admirable display of stoicism and slogged along until we reached the stile by the dirt road.

Deputy Norton waited until I'd scrambled over it and then joined me by my car. "What witness you talking about?" he asked.

"The Lunds' grandson. He was three years old, but —"

"Three years old? Geez, how could we have failed to record his every word? Did he see a cat in a hat, too?"

The truth would not play well with the transformed Deputy Hyde. "He saw some-one with a flashlight on the other side of the river."

"I didn't see anything in the reports."

"No," I said, "because Deputy Harraldson didn't bother to write up the interview. I believe the boy saw someone that night."

"High school and college kids come out here all the time. Lippet can't stop them unless he wants to stand guard twenty-four hours a day — with a shotgun. Damn kids got no respect for the law."

I did my best to look respectful and a tiny bit penitent. "Thank you so much for helping me across the field," I said as I pulled my keys out of my pocket.

"What do you think you're doing, Mrs. Malloy? I told you I have to take you in for trespassing. Get in my car."

"Is this necessary? You can write me a ticket now, or I promise to come by the sheriff's department tomorrow and clear this up. I'd really like to go home and collapse."

"So would I," he said coldly, "but I'm on duty until ten. It's been a helluva day. It began with you barging into my office, so it might as well end with me booking you. What goes around and so on. You can collapse in a holding cell until we can get you transferred to a women's facility. Get in my car."

"Mr. Lippet put up stiles to make it easier for people to get to Flat Rock. Has he ever demanded that these people be arrested?"

Deputy Norton pulled out handcuffs. "You want to wear pretty jewelry?"

I got in his car.

It took Peter over an hour to free me from the holding cell, where I'd met two very drunk sorority girls, a woman covered with tattoos, and a hooker named Angel. We got into his car, and once we were headed out on the highway so I could fetch mine, I said, "I can explain."

"I'm sure you can." He held the steering wheel so tightly his knuckles were little snow-capped peaks. So manly, my husband.

"Or you can sulk."

"I was worried about you. Caron called me with a garbled account of you being attacked by a dog. She had no idea where you were. I finally remembered the lawyer's name and called him, but he said he hadn't seen you since the courthouse scene. I drove by the Book Depot to see if your car was there. It wasn't, and the lights were off. I drove out to Sarah's house on the chance you'd broken in for some crazy reason. No car, no lights."

I politely overlooked his remark about "some crazy reason" and said most reasonably, "Did you try Miss Poppoy's house?"

"You may be familiar with that area, but I haven't spent the last forty-eight hours crawling down back roads. What does she have to do with it?"

I told him every place I'd gone and what I'd learned, which wasn't much of anything. "I think there must have been an incident with the church choir teenagers, but the chaperones aren't talking. Lippet told me that the preacher's daughters are in the group. Maybe they're involved."

"In the murder?" asked Peter skeptically.

"No, the shenanigans on the Lunds' side of the river." I stopped for a minute. "I didn't see any poison ivy."

"And that's a bad thing?"

"I don't know. Tricia Yates claimed to have gotten a rash from it and stayed up all night, feeling sorry for herself. That wouldn't preclude the teenagers from getting into mischief; they simply had to be stealthier than usual."

"Sneaking across the river under the nose of a sentinel can't be any harder than, say, breaking into the biology storeroom at the high school to liberate frozen frogs."

"I would say the latter is more of a challenge," I said. "Caron and Inez had to elude the custodians and any lingering faculty and staff." It seemed like a good time to change the topic. "I need to question the miscreants without the presence of the chaperones, but I don't even know their names, much less how to drag them off to the nearest dungeon for a bout on the rack."

"Let's say a couple of them admit crossing the river to drink, smoke pot, or have sex on what must have been an uncomfortable patch of weeds. One of them had a flashlight. All that proves is that the kid saw them."

"It adds credibility to the rest of his story. He claims he saw a figure by the barn."

"Didn't Lund say he went outside after he heard the shotgun? The kid couldn't recognize him in the dark, so he created an imaginary scenario — unless you believe in zombies. Please don't nod, Claire."

"You didn't clap for Tinker Bell?"

"Yes, but I was five years old. By the time I was six, my brothers had tipped me off about Santa Claus and the Tooth Fairy, thus shattering my innocence." He pulled over beside my car.

I unbuckled my seat belt and leaned over to kiss his cheek. "I'm so sorry you turned into a cynic at such a young age. We can still hunt Easter eggs."

"Laid by a rabbit? I don't think so."

"Maybe he buys the chocolate ones at Walmart," I said. "That's what I told Caron when she questioned the concept."

He waited until I got in my car and started the engine, and then we both headed home. As soon as I arrived, I took a hot shower to wash away any vestiges of dog slobber. When I emerged from the bedroom in dry clothes, I found Peter on the terrace with a plate of sandwiches and a bottle of wine. I thanked him in a mildly lascivious fashion, then settled down to eat, drink, and think. The first two were easier.

"But," I said after I'd polished off the last bite, "if William Lund was out by the barn, why didn't he see whoever was cavorting by the river?"

"You said that you could see the second story of the house. He was at ground level and preoccupied with the animals. He didn't have a reason to walk across the blueberry field."

"Well, he should have," I said as I held out my glass. "Did Caron mention where she and Joel were going tonight?"

"No, just that she was spending the night at Inez's house. I was too concerned about you to demand details."

"I'd better call her and let her know I'm okay."

"I called her after you called me from the county jail. She said she'd see you in the morning. I hate to ask this, but are she and Inez up to something that might not be legal?"

"Double-dating is protected under the Geneva Convention," I said, trying to sound more confident than I felt. "Or the Treaty

190

of Versailles. I often confuse the two." I gazed at the stars for a minute. "What about Sarah?"

"The feds are still tracking down the paperwork. It's been forty years, back when vintage VW Bugs roamed the earth and there were no computers. And, of course, it's a holiday weekend. Her real name is Carol Ann Draper and John Cunningham's was Douglas Tucker. The antiwar protest took place at a liberal arts college in Southern California. I don't have any details. She was questioned all day and is currently at the county jail in a private cell."

"Did Evan talk to her?"

"Tomorrow morning, if he can get past that insufferable dispatcher."

I went inside and returned with a package of cookies I'd hidden in the back of the refrigerator. "Do you think she shot her husband?" I asked.

Peter sighed. "Her story is flimsy. I can understand why Sheriff Dorfer had her arrested. Had this happened in my jurisdiction, I would have done the same thing. I see three scenarios. One, she's a profoundly deep sleeper. Two, she shot him and went to bed. Three, she wasn't there at midnight."

"So where was she?"

"How would I know?" he said. "Why

don't you ask her in the morning?"

"Good idea, Sherlock." I was too tired to think anymore, so I joined him on the chaise longue and let my head rest on his chest. "I'm still going to get the Weasel."

I met Evan at his office and gave him a recap of the previous day's fruitless endeavors as we walked to the county jail. I was wearing a skirt, a jacket, and pantyhose, doing my best to look like a dedicated, altruistic lawyer. It was all for naught, since La-Belle was not at the front desk. A deputy escorted us to an interview room, and five minutes later brought in Sarah. After he had left, we looked at each other for a long time.

"Well?" Evan finally said.

Sarah winced. "I guess I omitted a few things. It all happened so long ago that I didn't think it mattered. I was a different person then, and so was Tuck. We were so confident that we were going to spread peace and love."

"The dawning of the Age of Aquarius?" I said.

"Basically."

Evan seemed bewildered. "What does astrology have to do with it?"

"I'll explain when you're older," I said. I turned to Sarah. "What took place at this protest that brought the feds down on you like a pack of feral dogs?"

"There were about ten of us in the group, and we were earnest. We picketed the ROTC Department, handed out pamphlets, and drew peace signs on the sidewalks with chalk. Tuck stood on the front steps of the library and read the names of those who'd been killed in that senseless war. I wore flowers in my hair. One guy climbed a tree in front of the student union and announced that he wasn't coming down until the American troops were pulled out. We thought it was silly, but the frat boys showed up with golf clubs and baseball bats. The campus cops had to protect us all night while we sang 'Blowin' in the Wind.' It would have been more impressive if we'd known all the lyrics."

Evan was beyond bewilderment. "And that put you on the FBI's most-wanted list?"

"No," Sarah said with a frown, "I was just giving you some background. A new guy, Roderick, joined our group. He'd been a student at Berkeley until he was expelled for vandalism, trespassing, and pissing off the president of the university. He came up with the idea of a protest at the student union on the day the military recruiters had reserved the ballroom. We chained and padlocked the front doors and then sat down and chanted, 'Hell, no, we won't go.' The campus cops arrived, along with the local police. We were accused of holding the people inside hostage." She chuckled. "There were three other doors into the ballroom."

"But someone was killed," Ethan said.

"The cops tried to drag us away from the door. Roderick threatened them with a knife. A cop pulled his gun. The students watching the show panicked. Another recent addition to our group, Abel, tackled Roderick. All of a sudden it was pandemonium, with people screaming and pushing each other. That's when Tuck grabbed my wrist and yanked me through the cafeteria and out to the street. We heard later that Roderick had wrested the gun from the campus cop and hell broke loose. The other cops took out their guns and started firing. Roderick was finally thrown to the floor and handcuffed. Abel was dead at the scene. Turned out he was an undercover FBI agent. Roderick was charged with murder, and the rest of us as co-conspirators and therefore equally guilty. Tuck and I fled to a commune in Oregon. Someone there knew how to establish false identities."

I leaned forward, thinking it might be useful information if I disgraced myself in front of Peter's mother. "How?"

"It wasn't hard back then. We searched cemeteries until we found the headstones of children, ordered birth certificates from the state authority, and applied for Social Security numbers. I've been Sarah Swift longer than I was Carol Ann Draper. Poor Carol Ann would have bought the Brooklyn Bridge if anyone had offered her a deal. Well, the Golden Gate Bridge."

Evan was staring at a legal pad. "Wessell told me that he'd received an anonymous tip concerning you and Cunningham. Do you have any idea who might have made the connection?" She shook her head.

"Did he say when he received the tip?" I asked Evan.

"He said something about it taking a long time to verify the information and deal with the FBI. I didn't pin him down because it didn't seem relevant. I have an appointment tomorrow with the head of the investigation. I don't think he'll tell me anything. The first thing I'll do Tuesday is file a motion for a continuance, but if Wessell was telling the truth, Judge Priestly will deny it." He gazed at Sarah. "Have you reconsidered a plea bargain, assuming Wessell will go along?"

"I didn't kill Tuck," she said coldly, "and I'm not changing my story. The feds may have a hard time finding witnesses to the shooting at the student union after all this time. No one can claim that I had anything to do with the violence. Tuck and I were outside when we heard the first shot."

She might have been in denial, but I wasn't. I said, "What happened to the others in your group? Were they all arrested and sent to prison?"

"Roderick and six others were sentenced to twenty-five years to life for felony murder. Three others got away and went underground, too. Jamie and Justine showed up at the commune, put together false identities, and were last seen headed for Georgia in the back of a moving van. Laura vanished."

"Did you keep in touch with any of them?" I asked.

"God, no. I didn't want to know where they were any more than I wanted them to know where Tuck and I were. That way, no one could use the knowledge to cut a deal with the feds."

Evan made a note. "Is there anything else you forgot to mention? You know, minor stuff like armed robbery or grand theft auto."

Her eyes narrowed. "I jaywalked once, but I got off with a scolding. What about you? Defended any pedophiles?"

"No, and this is my first murder trial. Unless you're completely candid with me, I'm going to lose it."

"Candor has nothing to do with competency," Sarah retorted angrily.

I intervened before the combatants in the sandbox began hurling plastic buckets and shovels at each other. "Calm down, damn it. Sarah, we need to figure out what Tuck did that day. Do you have any ideas?"

She sat back and sighed. "I told you that I didn't think he was having an affair, but he had been acting peculiar for several weeks. Once I saw him parked across the road when I got off work at the café. There were a lot of times when he got home fifteen minutes after I did. When I asked him what he'd been doing, he offered lame explanations."

"Do you believe he was watching you?" I asked.

"It crossed my mind."

"Because he thought you were having an affair?"

"It could have been paranoia," she said. "His, not mine. He saw feds below every bridge and behind every tree. He was convinced he was under surveillance around the clock, and it was only a matter of time before they stormed the house with tear gas and automatic weapons." She held up her palms. "I know that doesn't make much sense, but he could have decided that if they weren't following him, they were following me."

Evan appeared to have regained his composure, but his face was still rosy. "We need to know what Tuck was up to that day. He made up the story about going on a fishing trip with the neighbor. Could it have been to give you a false sense of security?"

"To meet the feds or my lover?" she said. "I presumed the feds would have scooped us up if they knew where we were — and I didn't have a lover. I was relieved I didn't have to deal with Tuck that evening, that's all. If he was tailing me, he did a good job because I never noticed him. He may have been non compos mentis, but he was competent."

Evan bristled. "And I'm not?"

Once again, I intervened. "Did Tuck ever mention the name of anyone he might have encountered outside of your circle? A clerk at the co-op, a vendor at the farmers' market?"

"I know he went to the library several

times a week to use the computers. He was always coming up with obscure diseases and their symptoms, which he developed on the way home. His other obsession was organic farming. He could cite every banned substance more quickly than he could run through the alphabet. He joined online groups that pester organizations like the International Federation of Organic Agriculture Movements and the National Organic Program Standards Office. He talked about getting certified as an inspector. He was a zealot."

"The library is open this afternoon." I said. "I'll swing by and see if anybody on the staff knew Tuck."

Evan made a note on the legal pad. "I need to work on motions for a continuance and a change of venue. Neither will be granted, but we can use it on appeal."

"Your confidence underwhelms me," Sarah said. "Why bother to prepare for the trial? In fact, why bother to show up at all?"

"Because I'll be arrested for contempt unless I have a note from an emergency room doctor." His face was redder, and I feared for the future of the pencil he held.

"Slug it out, kids," I said as I stood up. "I'm going to church."

■ ■ ■ ■

As soon as I was in my car, I called Caron for the third or fourth time that morning. For the third or fourth time that morning, my call went to voice mail. I didn't bother to leave another message. A clock hovered over my head like the sword of Damocles, its alarm set for noon the next day. Telling myself that Caron and Inez were sleeping late to celebrate their success, I drove out to the church. The parking lot was crowded with equal numbers of cars, SUVs, and trucks. A hound growled at me from the bed of a pickup. I stared at it until it began to whimper.

I found a seat in the back pew and gave vague smiles to those who glanced at me. A tall, bony man stood on the platform, droning on about piety, which seemed to be within the grasp of those who tithed on a weekly basis and bequeathed a chunk of their estates to the church. I noticed a flat wooden bowl being passed down the row. Although my goal was less than pious, I found a dollar and dropped it in the bowl.

"In honor of Labor Day," the man said, "our teen choir will present 'Bringing in the Sheaves,' under the direction of our youth coordinator, Grady Nichols, and accompanied by Miss Norma Louise Ferncuff on the organ. Look upon their youthful faces with warmth and compassion, for they are the hope of the future."

The teenagers filed in, followed by Grady. When he turned to acknowledge the congregation, I discovered the necessity of lowering my face to hunt through my purse for a tissue. I didn't expect to be moved to tears, based on his scathing remarks the previous day, but if he spotted me, he would be suspicious. Once the hope of the future began to sing, I glanced around for Tricia Yates. Unlike fictional sleuths, I was unable to recognize the back of her head.

The choir was doing its best, and I'd heard worse nasal atonality from the CDs Caron played in her room. An elderly woman seated next to me put her hand on my arm and whispered, "Aren't they wonderful?"

"Unbelievable," I whispered back.

"That's my granddaughter at the end of the second row, in a blue sweater."

I zeroed in on a girl with glasses and flaccid hair. I hadn't noticed her at the rehearsal, and wouldn't have as she sang if her devoted grandmother had not prompted me. "A lovely girl. What's her name?"

"Mariah. I was disappointed when her parents didn't name her after me. I was named after my grandmother, and I named my daughter after her grandmother, Jessabel. My name is Loybeth."

The woman in the pew in front of us turned around with a menacing glare. "Hush up, Lobbie!"

I resisted the temptation to inquire about her hobby and looked down. I had a name, which was a start. The choir was bringing in the last of the sheaves with enthusiasm, which meant they would soon depart the platform. I patted Lobbie on the shoulder, smiled, and made my way to the end of the pew without causing any overt damage. I slipped out the front door and went around to the back of the building. There was a small playground, with swings, a slide, a picnic table, and a teeter-totter. As I'd anticipated, the teenagers came out a back door, half of them lighting cigarettes. One upstanding young lad was draining a plastic flask while his friends badgered him to share. They pretty much froze when they saw me.

"I'm a talent scout for a gospel music syndicate in Memphis," I said gaily. "I'd like to speak to a couple of you in private, if that's cool."

"You were here yesterday," said the blond girl with dark roots.

"Yes, I was. After a discussion with Grady, I decided to come back to hear you in action. A promising presentation." I looked them over, noting the varied degrees of skepticism on their faces. It did not seem prudent to point out that I hadn't said what their presentation had promised. Queasiness came to mind. "Mariah, I'd like to speak to you in private, if that's okay."

Dark Roots gaped at me. "Her? She sounds like a cat trapped in a toilet."

"Or being shoved down a garbage disposal," suggested a boy who was smoking a hand-rolled cigarette with a pungent aroma. He guffawed as he lost his balance and fell onto a pint-sized picnic table.

"You are not funny," my victim squeaked.

I gestured for her to join me in a corner of the playground. I waited until we were out of earshot and then said, "I want to know what happened at the campout last year at Flat Rock."

"What does that have to do with gospel music and Memphis?"

"We'll get to that in a minute. I know something happened, and I'm going to be very disappointed if you lie about it."

Mariah scrunched up her face. "Nothing

happened. We got there about three and set up camp. Some kids went swimming. We ate hot dogs, had a campfire, and went to bed. I was terrified a water moccasin would slither into our tent, so I stayed awake and kept my flashlight within reach. We had granola bars and orange juice for breakfast, and went back to the church so our parents could collect us."

"That's the best you can do?"

"I told you everything," she said, then clamped down on her lower lip.

"I'll say this for you, Mariah — you're a poor liar. Please don't force me to have a talk with your grandmother. Lobbie assured me that you're honest."

Tears began to dribble down her cheeks. I felt like the infamous Cruella De Vil kicking a puppy, but I had little time to waste. I turned on the full-wattage maternal look and waited. She glanced at the kids milling around the door, took a breath, and said, "I am honest, but I swore on the Bible not to say anything. I'm not going to end up in hell because of some gospel music thing. I probably do sound like a cat in a toilet when I sing. I'm going to medical school after college. The only reason I'm in this stupid choir is because of my mother. Grandma made her join, so she made me."

Reminding myself that the end justified being mean, I shook my head. "I'm sorry you feel this way. Do you realize that you'll have to take an oath on the Bible when you testify in court?"

Her eyes grew round, as if she were a deer caught in the headlights of a freight train. "Testify in court? I didn't do anything wrong."

"Perjury is a felony. You're going to have to tell the truth sooner or later. I may be able to spare you from a humiliating ordeal in court if you talk to me."

"I can't," she said piteously.

"As you wish. The only thing I see to do is have a word with Lobbie and your mother, Jessabel. Don't blame me if you get into trouble." I turned around and took a step, expecting her to stop me. She didn't. I wasn't optimistic that I could do any better with the other members of the choir. I'd culled what I thought was the weakest of the pack, and she'd turned out to be obstinate. My threat to speak to her mother and grandmother would remain hollow until I had a sliver of evidence about misdeeds at the campout.

Tick, tock.

9

I was seated in my car, debating the wisdom of leaving another slightly hysterical message on Caron's phone, when Dark Roots slipped into the passenger's seat. I hastily stowed Peter's cell phone in my purse.

"Are you really a music scout?" she demanded.

"No," I said.

"You lied to us?"

"Yes."

She frowned, perplexed by the concept of adults who lied with an element of integrity. After mulling it over for a moment, she said, "Why do you want to know about the campout last year?"

"It may help keep a woman out of prison for a crime she didn't commit. Are you willing to talk about it?"

"Why should I believe you?"

"You have no reason to believe me, dear. In your position, I wouldn't believe me either. The woman lives across the field from Flat Rock. The police arrested her for killing her husband with a shotgun. I think other people were involved."

She gave me a shocked look. "One of us?"

"No, but someone saw or heard something. Mariah told me that she had to swear on the Bible not to talk about it. Did you swear, too?"

"Sort of. I mean, like, we didn't have a choice, what with Grady and Mizz Yates standing there. Every last one of us swore we'd never say anything about it. I just got my learner's permit last month. If my pa finds out about it, he'll never let me get my license." She shuddered. "I hate riding on the school bus. I have to be at the bus stop at seven o'clock every morning. It's awful in the winter."

"I'm sure it is," I said, "but it can't be as awful as going to prison for the rest of your life. You won't, of course, but an innocent woman will. Do you want that on your conscience?"

"I don't guess so," she said without conviction, no doubt envisioning the horrors of the daily ride on a yellow bus. "But I did swear on the Bible, and I don't want to be struck dead or end up in hell for all eternity. You'll have to ask Mizz Yates and Grady."

She got out of the car and trotted toward the playground behind the church.

From what I'd heard (and hadn't heard), it was obvious that malfeasance had taken place during the camping trip, and I would have bet my accountant's life that it had happened around midnight. Unless the church was a great deal more peculiar than I'd realized, the oath had not required a denial of the existence of zombies. Tricia Yates had been alarmed when I'd entered her office. I hadn't been wearing a badge or a jacket emblazoned with the insignia of the FBI. It was true that I hadn't resembled a mild-mannered bookseller, unless the job description included a stained shirt and disheveled hair. If anyone should have been unnerved by my appearance, it was the delightful Deputy Frank Norton when he saw me crouched indelicately on the top of the stile.

A dubious claim to fame.

I finally decided my best chance lay with Tricia Yates. She was apt to be inside the church building. The service would end in five minutes, assuming the congregation had been inspired to beat the Baptists and Episcopalians to the local cafeterias and restaurants for Sunday dinner. Competition was stiff. If Tricia was among the pack, I had no hope of detaining her for a quiet chat.

I walked to the church playground. The teenagers had vanished, although a redolence of smoke hung in the air. I went through the back door. Sunday school classrooms lined the exterior side of a hallway, all dimly lit and unoccupied. I heard a resonating hymn being belted out by the congregation, followed by silence and then the rumble of footsteps and voices. When I reached the end of the hallway, I stopped to assess the situation before I turned the corner.

It was a wise move.

"They weren't that bad," Tricia Yates said from no more than ten feet away.

Grady grunted. "Compared to what? A line of homeless people required to sing for their supper? Half the kids don't even know the lyrics. Slackers!"

"You have three months until the Thanksgiving performance. They'll settle down once they're back in school."

"Yeah, and I'll be able to walk on water. The pope will call to invite me to the Vatican for brunch. He'll serve eggs Benedict and virgin Bloody Marys."

"Don't be a drama queen, Grady," Tricia said coolly. "By the way, that woman who was here yesterday was at the service this morning. I was so flabbergasted that I dropped my hymnal. Mr. Vanyonder harrumphed like a bullfrog as he picked it up for me. I didn't know whether to laugh or cry. Who is she? Why is she hounding me?"

"She might be hounding me. I'm not bad-looking, you know."

"This is not about you, damn it!"

A door slammed. I peeked around the corner and saw Grady headed in my direction. I dashed into the nearest classroom and flattened myself against the wall. I held my breath until I heard another door slam. I was fairly certain it was the door that led to the playground. When I heard nothing more ominous than noises from the sanctuary, I went back into the hallway. Grady might have departed, or he might have stepped outside for a minute. Damocles's clock continued to tick and tock. I had no time for caution.

I walked to the office and tapped on the door. I interpreted a gurgle from within as an invitation to enter the room. Tricia Yates was holding a bottle of whiskey in one hand and a glass in the other. When she saw me, she began to tremble so wildly that I hurried across the room and grabbed the bottle before it slipped. "Why don't you sit down?"

I suggested.

"Who *are* you?"

I placed the bottle on her desk. "We covered that yesterday. I know that something happened on the camping trip. If you refuse to tell me, the police will pick up all the members of the choir at their homes and take them in for questioning." Yeah, and I'd be able to keep up with Grady while we strolled across the Tiber on our way to brunch.

"If you're a police officer, show me your badge."

I sat down. "I'm acting in an advisory capacity." It sounded good, but I sensed she wasn't buying it. I toyed with the idea of tossing out Peter's name, rank, and serial number, then dismissed it. One must retain some standards. "Sarah Swift's trial starts in less than forty-eight hours. Did you watch the news last evening?"

She poured two inches of bourbon into the glass and gulped it down with the practiced ease of a cinematic cowboy bellied up to a bar. "I don't know how she got away with it as long as she did. She must have been terrified someone would recognize her."

"She said Tuck was paranoid," I commented, hoping she'd continue.

"I would be, too, if the FBI was after me."

"Then you knew Tuck and Sarah."

"Why would you say that?" she asked as she poured more bourbon into her glass. "I read the newspaper and watch the news. I paid some attention to the story because many members of our congregation live out that way. Not that any of them were involved, mind you."

I folded my arms. "I read the articles, too. None of them mentioned that John Cunningham's nickname was Tuck. Not many people called him that."

"Well, I must have met him somewhere." Tricia may have been in a slight fog, but her look was calculating as she took a more discreet swallow. "I might have bought blueberries from him at the farmers' market. I really don't remember."

"There was no mention of the farmers' market in the newspapers," I said, not at all sure this was true. Her eyelids began to flutter, and her lips were quivering. I went in for the kill. "You and Tuck were friends, weren't you? Did you meet him at the library?"

"What difference does it make? I can assure you that whatever happened at the campout had nothing to do with that horrible murder. There was misbehavior of a trivial sort. Teenagers can be worse than animals. No sense of proper decorum or respect." She put her elbows on the desk and leaned forward, giving me an iota of optimism that she was about to divulge the dirty details. "For them, it's all about sex, drugs, and alcohol. Give 'em an inch and they'll take a hundred miles. I wanted to spank every one of them and send them to bed without supper."

"Why didn't you?"

"They'd already eaten, for one thing, and Grady thought it was better to just forget what happened."

"What happened?"

She waggled her finger at me. "That would be telling, wouldn't it?"

Indeed it would, but that was the point of the conversation. Rather than saying as much, I tried a different approach. "How long have you lived in Farberville, Tricia?"

"Long enough to be sick of it. There are times when I want to go out onto my balcony and scream. The apartment complex is jammed with noisy, ill-mannered college kids who party all night and drive as if they're blind. Last week I was almost run down by a motorcycle while I was taking my trash to the bin. The seniors in the church have square dances and clubs for knitters and quilters. No one reads books or goes to concerts. If I could afford it, I'd move to a city, even if it meant living in a dinky studio apartment." She stared at me as she took a swig from the bottle. "Do you know what they pay me here? Minimum wage, that's what. I work thirty hours a week so they don't have to provide health insurance. Every Christmas I receive a hundred-dollar bonus and a stack of fruit-cakes."

"Surely you could find another job," I murmured.

"I don't have a college degree, and I'm too old to clean houses. I never for a minute believed I'd end up like this, counting pennies to pay the rent and conversing with my houseplants."

"Why did you move here?"

Her eyes slitted. "It's complicated. Why don't you run along and pester somebody else? I need to count the offering and put it in the safe before I can leave. This job doesn't pay overtime."

I did need to run along, although I wasn't sure whom I would pester next. Many candidates came to mind. "I will, but I need to know when and where you met Tuck. If I have to sit here all afternoon, then so be it." I leaned back in the chair and gave her an inscrutable smile. It might have been on the smug side.

Hers was on the manic side. "Maybe the library. I go several times a week to use the computer, read magazines, and check out books. Perhaps I bumped into him there and he mentioned his name. It's uncommon enough that it lingered in my subconscious. Yes, I'm quite sure we chatted while we were browsing in the stacks. I'm addicted to historical fiction and biographies."

Tuck wasn't, based on what I'd heard. I doubted Tricia was interested in obscure diseases and organic blueberries any more than I was. Short of torture, I could see no way to get more information out of her. I had no standing with the Farberville PD, much less the FBI. I wished her a pleasant afternoon and returned to my car. There were no messages from Caron on the cell phone. I opted to call my husband, who was most likely settled in to watch whichever sports dominated the channels.

"Any luck?" he asked in the voice of a male stretched out on the sofa, within reach of a beer and pretzels. And the remote control, of course.

"No," I said sourly. "Can you have someone run a background check on Tricia, maybe Patricia Yates?"

"Why?"

"If I knew, I wouldn't have to ask. Is Caron home?"

"Haven't seen her or heard from her. Damn!"

"Is something wrong?"

"The Pirates scored on an error."

I had yet to encounter any pirates in the investigation. "I'm sure they'll work things out," I said. "The background check may not lead anywhere, but Tricia is hiding something. I'll call you in an hour."

He agreed, albeit with less enthusiasm than I would have preferred. I was digging for my keys when I spotted Juniper Lund and Billy come out the front door of the church. Juniper glanced at me, and then looked away as they headed for an SUV.

I caught up with them before they could get into the vehicle. "Juniper," I said, "can we talk for a few minutes?"

"I don't know any more than I did on Friday."

"I really need your help. Did you watch the news yesterday?"

Billy aimed his toy gun and shot me on the spot. When I failed to crumple to the ground, he tugged on his grandmother's dress. "Can we go? I'm hungry and you said I could have ice cream for dessert if I didn't wiggle in church. I want chocolate ice cream with sprinkles."

Juniper ignored him. "Yes, and William and I were shocked. To think we lived within spitting distance of criminals all these years."

"What's a criminal?" asked Billy.

"Why don't we go to the playground?" I suggested.

"All right," she said, "but I do have to go home to see to Sunday dinner. This is Billy's last full day with us, and I'd like it to be a happy one."

The three of us went behind the church. Billy ran to the swing set, while Juniper and I sat down at a picnic table. After a moment, I said, "It must be dreadful to find out your old friends were wanted by the FBI for a crime they committed forty years ago."

"I don't recall precisely when they moved into their house, but it must have been more than thirty years ago. My boys were in grade school, and I was pregnant. Sarah was so kind after Addie was born. She brought over casseroles and homemade bread several times a week, and babysat whenever I needed her. Now that I think about it, we never really made a connection. She was vague about her background. I guess I would have been, too, if I carried a load of

217

guilt. Do you know any more details about what happened?"

"Sara told me that she and Tuck fled before the shooting began. They were indicted as co-conspirators because they were members of the group."

"I remember seeing those antiwar protestors on television with their long hair, bare feet, and shabby clothes. They could afford to waste time staging demonstrations and sit-ins because their parents paid their college tuition and living expenses. The day after I graduated from high school I started full-time at a shipping company. Two years later, I was married with a baby. Working and taking care of my family took all of my time. I never got more than six hours of sleep at night."

"My husband died when my daughter was very young," I said. "Sleep was a rare pleasure."

"William helped out as much as he could, but farming is a hard job. We both still wake up with the rooster. I'd like to wring his neck, but William will just get another one. Got to keep the hens happy."

I chuckled despite the images that crossed my mind. "I've been trying to figure out what Tuck did the day he was killed. Could he have suspected that Sarah was seeing another man?"

Juniper shrugged. "I was raised not to speak ill of the dead, but Tuck had some mental problems that made him real unhappy. He used to come over to the house late in the afternoon, while William was tending to the farm and Sarah was still at the diner. After a couple of beers, he'd get all upset and claim that she had a string of lovers and was hoarding money so she could buy them fancy things. He admitted that he followed her sometimes, but he never caught her doing anything out of the ordinary."

"Did he have any friends besides you and William?"

"I don't reckon so. He was prickly and hard to be around when he got into one of his moods."

"Tricia Yates told me that she met him at the library."

"What's that supposed to mean?" she snapped.

I detected a trace of jealousy in her voice. "Nothing at all. You seem to have known Tuck better than anyone else. I'm trying to help Sarah, not belittle him."

"If you think they were having an affair, you need to see a shrink. Tuck took his promises seriously. That's why he was so screwed up the summer before Sarah killed him. He'd sworn to take care of her as long as they lived. I felt so sorry for him, but it was his decision to make." She turned her attention on Billy. "You put that nasty thing down right now, young man! How many times have I told you not to pick up dead critters? You march yourself into the church and wash your hands this minute!"

I waited until Billy went into the building. "What was the decision he had to make?"

"You don't want to know. I feel bad about having to testify against Sarah. I don't want to make it any worse for her. If she's not found guilty of Tuck's murder, the FBI will go after her like a flock of Canada geese. Nobody messes with them."

I had never messed with Canada geese, but my experiences with the FBI had included hostile honking and the flapping of bureaucratic wings. "I need to know everything if I'm going to help her," I said. "Please tell me what you meant. If it's irrelevant or aids the prosecution, I won't say a word."

Juniper clasped her hands together and closed her eyes. In a flat voice, she said, "I don't want to tell you, but I suppose I will. Two years ago Tuck confessed everything to me — the demonstration at the college that led to the shooting, their escape, and their

220

false identities. After he finished, he cried like a baby. I wanted to hold him in my lap and kiss away his grief, but all I could do was make sympathetic noises. I promised him that I wouldn't tell William or anybody else. I've betrayed him. Maybe he wasn't paranoid, since he never should have trusted any of us."

"It doesn't much matter now," I pointed out. "Tell me about this decision of his."

"That came later, about halfway through the summer. He became convinced he had a deadly blood disease, even though the medical tests were negative. He got to where he couldn't eat or sleep. Occasionally when I got up in the middle of the night to go to the bathroom, I'd see him walking around his yard. He wanted to see his family before he died, and the only way that would happen was if he turned himself in to the FBI. He said he couldn't bear to die without knowing if his parents were still alive. They'd be allowed to visit him in prison, along with his brother and sisters."

"But turning himself in would implicate Sarah," I said.

"That's why he felt so awful. He never loved her, but he said the two of them were outcasts and had vowed to stick together. I told him that he had to talk to Sarah before he did anything rash. A month later, he was dead."

It was my turn to close my eyes. Up until that moment, I hadn't believed that Sarah had much of a motive to shoot Tuck. They'd survived forty years of a miserable marriage and managed not go after each other with knives. The option to leave was always within reach. When Tuck had told her that he was content to die in prison, she might not have been amenable to doing the same. "Did he tell her?" I asked, crossing my fingers and toes that her response would be negative.

"I only saw him once after our conversation, when he and Sarah came over for supper. We didn't have a chance to talk in private." She stood up. "I better go see what Billy's up to. His idea of washing his hands is to turn the water faucet on and off, and then wipe his dirty hands on a towel."

"Thank you for telling me," I said as she went toward the back door. She did not respond.

Once I was in my car, I rested my forehead on the steering wheel and resisted the urge to howl. I'd been on the case for nearly three days, and all I'd accomplished could be written on the head of a pin. If I believed Sarah was innocent, I was obliged to believe she'd lied to me. Were I a lawyer, I would not be pleased with my client. Evan's duty was to present the best defense possible, to force the prosecution to prove her guilty beyond a reasonable doubt. To do so, he needed an alternative theory or two. I had not yet determined if the green van was significant, and I wasn't especially sanguine that it was. There had been some sort of misbehavior on the part of the church choir, but I could barely justify pursuing it. I felt as if I were following a trail of inconsequential breadcrumbs that would lead me nowhere, all because Prosecutor Wessell had ridiculed me in the courtroom.

I was in an abysmal pit of self-pity when the cell phone blipped. I straightened up and took a deep breath before I answered it. "Well?"

Peter seemed a tad disconcerted as he said, "Am I disturbing you?"

"A dinosaur sitting on my car would not disturb me. What did you find out about Tricia Yates?"

"A couple of traffic tickets. She owns an old white Toyota and is not on the voter registration list. She is not involved in any civil litigation. According to the information on her driver's license, she's sixty-three years old and has blue eyes. Were you hoping for something more dramatic?"

"Not really," I admitted. "She'd be a likely candidate for a liaison with Tuck — if anyone believed he was capable of such a thing. No one does. She declined to confide in me, despite my winsome charm, and I can't make her. She may be pilfering from the collection plate, but that's irrelevant." I went on to relate what Juniper Lund had told me about Tuck's intention to turn himself in to the FBI. We agreed that it did not help Sarah's case. Caron had not appeared, even though she was having a party in a few hours. Mrs. Jorgeson had called to confirm that she was bringing potato salad. Rather than demanding to know his mother's preference in potato salads, I told my handsome husband that I would be home later and ended the call.

Juniper's SUV had left the parking lot during the conversation. A white Toyota was parked in the shade of a clump of trees. As I sat, metaphorically twiddling my thumbs, Dark Roots and the man who'd advocated tithing came out of the church and walked toward a pale blue Mercedes. A second girl trailed after them. I cleverly deduced the trio was composed of the preacher and his daughters.

I finally decided to go to Evan Toffle's office to share my pathetic progress and find out what, if anything, he'd learned from Wessell and the FBI. As I prepared to pull onto the street, a green van sailed by, headed out of town. It was not a remarkably green van, or a uniquely green van, or even an oddly green van. Most likely, it was an ordinary green van owned by a law-abiding couple on their way home from church. I jammed down my foot on the gas pedal and whipped out in front of a pickup truck. A horn blared as I grasped the steering wheel more tightly, my jaw thrust forward and my brow creased.

Other vehicles had inveigled their way into the gap between my quarry and me. I passed a station wagon, and made it back with inches to spare as a laden chicken truck bore down on me. The driver made an impertinent gesture, but I politely overlooked it while I tried to figure out how to get around an RV plastered with bumper stickers. I was still behind it when we came to a stoplight. I made small, irritated noises until the traffic began to move, and then eased to the left as far as I dared to try to catch sight of the van. The RV was as broad as a billboard and disinclined to cooperate.

As we continued away from Farberville on County 107, the traffic began to thin out. I spotted the green van far in the distance, making much better time than the behemoth that waddled along in front of me. Seconds before I was reduced to sputtering obscenities, the RV pulled into a convenience store. I swallowed a particularly vulgar word and hit the gas pedal as if the road were paved with yellow bricks and I could see emerald towers in the distance. Ten seconds later I was stuck behind a thready line of cars and trucks, their drivers blissfully ignorant of everything and everyone. I passed when I could, and ground my teeth when I couldn't. I still caught glimpses of the green van, which grew smaller as it sped on its merry way.

I didn't glance at Sarah's house as I went past, nor did I wave at Miss Poppoy's mailbox. On the far side of the bridge was a slight incline. When I crested it, I realized the green van was no longer visible at the head of the caravan. The particularly vulgar word popped out as I strained to spot it on the side of the road or parked in a driveway. Unless it was a well-disguised race car with an engine more suitable to a large aircraft, it had vanished. I pulled over and stopped. Pounding my head on the steering wheel would result only in an unsightly lump, I told myself as I seethed. I forced myself to uncurl my bloodless fingers and sit back. Had I been a science fiction fan, I would have looked upward for the mother ship. Had I been a reader of fantasy fiction, I might have considered the likelihood that the van had been snatched up by a stealthy pterodactyl and carried away to a medieval fortress in the mountains. ✗

The burst of frustration finally began to ebb. I took several deep breaths and tried to think. I was on the stretch of highway that I'd been over (and over) for the last forty-eight hours. I felt as though I knew every pothole, every battered speed sign, every mailbox. My windshield was splattered with its insect life, my fenders dusted with its unpaved roads. The turnoff to Pinkie Sheer Road was ahead on my right, the turnoff to Flat Rock farther and to my left.

Neither one beckoned to me. I finally pulled back out and turned on the road that went past Zachery Barnard's house and whatever lay beyond it. I averted my eyes as I drove by the loathsome pond where his body had been discovered. His house seemed lost amid the weeds and debris. The road curled this way and that, with no signs of civilization, until I came to a padlocked gate. A sign warned me not to trespass on county property and to beware of high voltage lines. I was not tempted. If the van had taken this route, it had long since vanished into the wilderness.

I turned around and drove back toward the highway, keeping an eye out for any semblance of a turnoff on either side. The ditches were undisturbed. I passed the shack and pond, and then stopped when I reached the highway. The remaining option was the road that led to Larry Lippet's house and property. My memories were not nostalgic, to put it mildly. I'd been menaced, harassed, and embarrassed. I'd also been threatened with legal complications if I were to trespass in the future.

I do not handle intimidation with grace. I turned onto the highway, and minutes later onto the road to Flat Rock. No vans of any sort were parked near the trailers and mean little houses. When I arrived at the Lippets' house, the laird himself was in the front yard, apparently watching the grass grow while he drank a soda. I braked and put down the window. "Hello," I called, plastering on an amiable smile. "Did you see a green van drive by here a few minutes ago?"

He hitched up his pants as he came over to my car. "Heard you had a little problem yesterday evening. I wouldn't have thought you'd be afraid of a dumbass dog like Duke.

228

He's scared of squirrels, and the blue jays downright terrify him." Lippet guffawed, exposing spotted teeth. "Marie asked me if you was daft. Said I didn't think so, but you can't never tell."

"The dog tried to attack me," I said primly. "About the van?"

"No one's come along in the last half hour, except for Wade. Said he was going fishing on such a fine afternoon. I could smell the liquor on his breath from ten feet away. Rumor has it he has a marijuana patch somewhere behind the old schoolhouse, but nobody cares enough to look for it. I sure as hell don't."

"Have you ever seen a green van out this way?"

"Driven by little green men with squashed heads? I seem to recollect seeing a whole bevy of them one night after Wade and I finished a quart of vile moonshine." He rewarded me with another guffaw. "You want to hear about the pink elephants?"

"Another time, Mr. Lippet." I pulled into his driveway, turned around, and drove away before he could leap into my car and entertain me with more of his hilarious remarks. Once I was safely out of his sight, I slowed down. I was certain that I'd seen a green van, but I was less certain that it was

229

noteworthy. Regrettably, it was all I had on my depleted list of alternate suspects. The Weasel would ride his victory to the bench, where he could continue to terrorize the unfortunate souls who lacked money for a high-priced lawyer (and a contribution to his campaign).

I headed back toward Farberville, reviewing every last conversation I'd had since Friday morning. Billy's story was gaining credence, although he had to be docked a few points for embellishment. I was not unfamiliar with the youthful impulse to toss in extraneous details for added drama. In her prepubescent days, Caron had been certain she was being stalked by celebrities (Elvis was one of the culprits) and denied her rightful position in the British royal family by the gypsies who'd made the dastardly switch in the hospital nursery.

I was almost smiling as I came to the turnoff for Sarah's house. The smile evaporated as I saw movement in one of the second-story bedrooms. I slammed on the brakes and skidded onto the gravel road in a fine spray of dust. Sarah had not been released unless something bizarre had taken place, and Peter or Evan would have called me if it had. If she'd found a way to escape from the county jail, she would not have gone home to pack a suitcase. A truck and the SUV were parked outside the Lunds' farmhouse. Prudence suggested I drive there, alert them, and call the police from their living room. Whoever had broken into the house would have ample time to steal or destroy evidence before waltzing into the maze of back roads.

I parked my car as close to the ditch as I dared, grabbed my purse, and started walking. I could see no vehicle except for Sarah's car. The barn door was slightly ajar, however, and I had no view of the side or back yard. As I came to the driveway, I saw a hazy figure behind the sheer curtains in the front room. Everybody in the county who was old enough to watch the news knew that Sarah was in jail and the house was empty. I sidled behind a tree while I considered my minor adventure with the green van. It had been ahead of me when I drove by Sarah's house, but then it had vanished. The perps might have been casing the joint to make sure the police and FBI agents were not there. They'd made a minor detour and returned while I was investigating other possibilities.

I could hear Peter's voice telling me to back away and call for help. His lovely brown eyes were squinting with intensity and his jaw was tight. What would his mother say if she was told that I'd been kidnapped by surly, hirsute brutes in camouflage jackets? Her nostrils might flare with disdain at the vulgar nature of the criminals and the brashness of their hostage. If I'd underestimated my opponents, would she lower herself to attend my funeral? Could I trust Caron to handle the role of hostess after the internment? Would the mourners be appalled by chips and pizza?

It was time to find out, I told myself as I walked toward the house.

10

Rather than storm the ramparts, I went to the barn door and squeezed through the narrow gap. The vehicle in no way resembled a green van. Had it been in better condition, it might have qualified as a vintage pickup truck, but its primary color was a combination of mud and rust, with a decorative splatter of roadkill. I looked in the passenger's window at an unholy mess of beer cans, liquor bottles, dirty clothes, and fast food debris. Vintage fast food debris, based on the blue mold and the maggots. The bed of the truck held a collection of more beer cans, leaves, a sneaker, rubber snakes, rusty tools, a bald tire, and what I initially took to be a furry animal, deceased. A second look confirmed it to be of the species *Wigus platinus*. The gun rack supported a rifle. I was somewhat relieved that it was in the truck instead of in the hands of the burglars.

I slipped out of the barn and darted to the side of the house. The windows were too high to give me a view of the interior. I went around to the back porch and took a quick peek through the glass panel of the door. There were plates and a coffee cup on the kitchen table, as though Sarah had been having lunch when the FBI took her into custody the previous day. The door was not locked. I eased it open and braced myself for a shout of surprise. I was a bit disappointed when I heard a low rumble of voices from the front of the house, thus giving me no excuse to flee in a most cowardly fashion. I assured myself that once I had a glimpse of the intruders, I would retreat with all due haste to my car and call the sheriff's department from the sanctuary of the Lunds' driveway. A most reasonable plan.

I tiptoed across the kitchen. The hallway was empty. I could hear two voices, one gravelly and the other higher pitched and nervous. The TV set was by the front door, and next to it was a wooden crate filled with record albums. The thieves must have been disappointed with their booty — no computer, silver, jewelry, guns, Tiffany vases, or even a platinum wig. I was lamenting the paucity of the household treasures when a man stepped into the hallway and saw me.

234

"Who in blazes are you?" he croaked.

I assessed my chances. He was no taller than five foot six and was wearing baggy jeans, a dirty T-shirt, and a cap. I doubted he was old enough to buy beer or vote. "I am affiliated with the Farberville Police Department," I said in a chilly voice. "Who are you and why are you here?"

He pulled off his cap. "I asked you first, ma'am."

His cohort, also a teenager, joined him. He was bigger and therefore more alarming, but he seemed equally befuddled. "What the hell?" he said eloquently.

I stepped into the doorway, my arms crossed. "I have already called for backup, and I anticipate the arrival of several squad cars within minutes. My partner is outside, and let me assure you that he's armed and dangerous. He's been cited for excessive violence. If either of you moves one inch from that spot, you will require the services of the coroner and a funeral director. Any more stupid questions?" I stared at them until they shook their heads. "I need your names and addresses."

The bigger one actually shuffled his feet. If he'd had a forelock, he would have tugged it. "My name's Bubba, and this here is Benedict. We just dropped by to see if the woman who lives here is home. Thought she might need help with the harvest next month."

"Oh, really?" I said with all the sarcasm I could muster. "Do you honestly think I'm going to believe that? It looks as though you're applying for a job that requires heavy lifting and relocation. Did you fail to notice that she's not home?"

Benedict snuffled. "No, ma'am, so maybe we ought to be on our way."

"To Miss Poppoy's house? No, you've already stolen what you could from her. Do you realize what would have happened if she'd died during your intrusion? You'd have been tried as adults and be spending the next forty years in prison with very rude inmates."

"My cousin shot his pa and only got ten years," said Benedict.

Bubba whacked him on the shoulder. "Your cousin was eleven years old, you moron! Remember Bo Bridges Buchanon? He offed those guys at a liquor store and he got life without parole. He weren't but fifteen when it happened."

I cleared my throat. "Miss Poppoy survived despite your despicable behavior. What would your mothers say if they learned about that? I'm sure they've done the best they could to raise you with proper respect for your elders, and then you two go and pull some boneheaded robberies." I gave them a moment to think it over, and then said, "So which of you owns a green van?"

Benedict shook his head. "My pickup's in the barn. Bubba drove his GTO into the lake a month ago. He had a boat hitched to it and was backing down the ramp when he hit the gas instead of the brake. Sunk the boat, too. Funniest damn thing I've ever seen, except for maybe when his grandpa dropped his pants in court and waved his dingaling at the judge."

"Have you ever been on this property before today?" I asked, struggling to remain stern. "A year ago, for instance?"

"Don't reckon so," Bubba said. "Last night some of the guys at the bar was talking about the lady that lives here, how she was a terrorist and a murderer. We figured that if she was in jail, the house was empty. It seemed neighborly to keep an eye on things, make sure nobody had broken in or anything."

"So you broke in to see if someone had broken in?" I said.

"Yeah," Benedict said, "that's why we're here."

"Is that why the TV set is by the door?"

Benedict looked at Bubba, who blinked and said, "Just being neighborly, ma'am. We best be on our way."

I was too tired of them to demand their last names. I'd memorized the license plate and would share the information with Sheriff Dorfer when he resurfaced after the long weekend. Their fingerprints would be on the TV set. "Then go," I said, gesturing at the door, "and don't even think about coming back here. This house will be under surveillance twenty-four hours a day."

Both of them glanced at the pile of loot and then ambled out the front door. I held my breath until I saw the pickup truck drive across the yard and onto the road. As I exhaled, I tried not to imagine Peter's reaction when I related the story. He might feel obligated to explain exactly how foolhardy I'd been, along with other adjectives that would not reflect well on me. Clearly, the story required editing for his sake. I didn't want him to be agitated when his mother arrived in less than twenty-four hours. Tomorrow. It was only a day away.

I deleted two suspects from the list, since neither Bubba nor Benedict had flinched when I'd asked the pertinent question. The green van was out there somewhere. I had no idea if it was still significant. On that less than optimistic note, I decided to search the house. There were three bedrooms upstairs and an antiquated bathroom with a stained bathtub. I wasn't surprised that Sarah and Tuck had separate bedrooms. Juniper had told me that the marriage was based solely on their oath to remain underground together, like witless rodents in the same burrow. Forty years was a very long time to brood about the past and worry about the future.

I went into Sarah's room. A tattered quilt served as a bedspread, and a bookcase held an eclectic array of fiction and poetry, some in French. On the nightstand was a small framed photograph of two adults and a child, all beaming at the camera. I studied it for a moment, wondering if Sarah had found a way to get in touch with her parents. The FBI's fondness for tapping phone lines would have made a call too risky. Mail would have been routinely waylaid so the postmark could be examined. I replaced the photo and opened the closet door. Her clothes were plain and inexpensive. She'd enrolled in a pricey liberal arts college, and I visualized her pulling up to a dorm in a sleek car packed with suitcases of designer outfits. It had been a hard fall from grace.

I pulled down the boxes on the top shelf and found worn purses and shoes, sweaters, long-sleeved shirts, and a scarf. I continued to search the room without chancing on a diary, journal, scrapbook, or a cache of newspaper clippings and letters. Sarah had kept her secrets without leaving any sort of paper trail.

Tuck's bedroom was a hodgepodge of boxes, duffel bags, stacks of paperwork concerning organic gardening regulations and inspections, and a boggling quantity of medicine for obscure ailments ranging from toenail fungus to excessive ear wax. He'd been prepared to tackle malaria and ring-worms, warts and hangnails. I had no problem believing he had reached mastery in hypochondria before being killed in a less esoteric fashion. Sarah had not bothered to deal with his closet. His basic wardrobe had consisted of threadbare jeans, flannel shirts, one sadly dated black suit, T-shirts, and a single navy necktie. Goodwill would not have whooped with delight had it all been donated.

I pulled a box out of the corner and sat down. Tuck had saved — or hoarded — every utility bill, credit card bill, tax receipt, and income tax form over a four-decade span. I put aside the credit card statements for additional scrutiny and tackled another box. It proved to be more of the same, so I moved along to the next. After I'd sneezed my way through the dust of the remaining boxes, I dragged a duffel bag to the middle of the room and unzipped it. Tuck's dedication to organic farming was profound, based on the number of manuals and brochures regarding the use of pesticides and fertilizers. A thick folder of correspondence indicated he'd communicated often with government agencies. A chemist might have found the information worthy of mild interest, but I'd eked my way through freshman chemistry without grasping the essence of multisyllabic compounds.

I rezipped the bag and dragged it out of the way. What was curious, I thought as I sat on the edge of the bed and gazed morosely around the room, was that Tuck had left no personal papers of any kind. There was no shredder in the house. He wouldn't have sent anything to the landfill or recycling center, where it might fall into the wrong hands and in some obscure way expose his identity. I went back to the hall and looked up for both inspiration and access to the attic. The latter was directly overhead. I grabbed a gray cord and pulled it until the panel came down and I could reach the folded ladder.

I was not enthusiastic about encountering any creature that scuttled or flapped its wings. As I ascended, I called out several warnings to the probable inhabitants so that none of us would be surprised. My hands were damp when I reached the middle step and poked my head through the opening. The attic was partially floored with plywood, the rafters draped with cobwebs. The dust was abysmally thick, and the temperature so high that my skin seemed to shrink. I continued up until I could stand, and then waited until my eyes adjusted to the musky darkness.

I was pleased to see a lightbulb dangling from the ceiling, but distinctly less pleased when I flipped a switch and nothing happened. A blanket had been hung over a window. I moved cautiously toward it, positioning each foot before transferring my weight. I reached it without putting my leg through the floor, and yanked at the blanket until it relented and fell in a heap. Dust enveloped me, setting off a paroxysm of sneezes and wheezes. This did not happen to amateur sleuths in mystery novels, I told myself as I gasped for breath. They were much too genteel for a primitive display of bodily dysfunction. Lord Peter never excused himself to go to the loo.

Once I'd blotted my eyes, I surveyed the attic. There were battered suitcases, lampshades, a pile of drapes and blankets, discarded furniture, a box marked *X-mas ornaments,* a sewing machine that might have been used by Betsy Ross's great-granddaughter, and a large trunk with a padlock. I focused on the trunk. Tuck hadn't trusted Sarah, so it seemed credible that he would stash his treasures in a safe container.

I yanked at the padlock until I accepted that it wasn't going to cooperate with the likes of me. I considered dragging the trunk to the opening and giving it a shove. It would damage the hall floor, but Sarah wasn't coming home anytime soon, and Tuck was in no position to complain. After a series of huffs and puffs, I realized that I couldn't budge the trunk. However, where there was a lock, there was a key. I crawled down the ladder and returned to Tuck's bedroom. I'd already rifled the bedside table drawers, but I'd been looking for letters and photographs. This time I needed a key. My determination began to wane after I'd yanked out the drawers and made sure the key was not taped on a back slat.

The third bedroom had only a bed and a rocking chair. I felt along the top shelf in the closet but encountered nothing except dust and a few yellowed scraps of newsprint. Tuck would not have hidden the key in Sarah's room. I went down to the kitchen and dug through a junk drawer. All the keys were labeled, including one for the basement. I was not in the mood for subterranean exploration, so I took a hammer from the drawer and returned to the attic.

I was pounding on the padlock and muttering under my breath when I heard a male voice shout, "Who's there?"

It was too hot to swoon, so I went to the opening and looked down at Will Lund, who seemed a tad perplexed. "It's Claire," I said. "I'm just checking on the house."

"In the attic?"

"Basements can be clammy."

"Uh, need any help?"

I made a decision based on my aversion to sweat. "Yes, I do. Will you please come up here and help me with this pesky padlock? I've already wasted a lot of time on it, and although I've made a dent in it, it's stubborn." I stepped back as he climbed up the ladder and stood up, nearly bumping his head. I handed him the hammer. "I couldn't find the key, and I am not an expert lock picker."

He grinned. "Neither am I, but I'll try."

He bent down and began to beat on the padlock with admirable ferocity. After a dozen blows, the padlock fell to the floor. I moved closer as he opened the trunk. "Bunch of stuff," he murmured. "Were you expecting to find jewels and gold doubloons?"

"Tuck's personal papers," I said as I took out shirt boxes and a thick pile of manila folders. "I know he had secrets."

Will sat down on the edge of a chair lacking a seat and studied me as if I might have been more at home in a belfry. "Like being a fugitive from the FBI? Like being accused of murder? Yeah, he had secrets. I assumed it was paranoia, but sometimes they really are out to get you. How's Sarah doing?"

"Sticking to her story that she didn't shoot Tuck. The trial starts Tuesday, and her lawyer is scrabbling to come up with a semi-credible defense. Let's take all this downstairs." I emphasized my request with another round of explosive sneezes.

When we arrived in the kitchen, I moved the plates and coffee cup to the sink and gulped a glass of water before sitting down at the table. From the way Will was looking at me, I was fairly sure I no longer resembled an efficient legal assistant. I plucked cobwebs from my blouse and brushed ineffectually at my skirt. "I know Tuck was your friend," I began as I reached for a box, "but if you know anything that might help Sarah, this is the time to say so."

"I wish I could. After Junie and I saw the news yesterday, she told me that Tuck had already confessed to her. I asked her why she didn't confide in me, but she got up and went outside." He looked inside a cigar box, then set it aside. "Maybe it's better that she didn't."

"Can you think of anyone else he may have taken into his confidence?"

He glanced up at me. "Like who?"

I took a stack of letters out of another cigar box and removed the rubber band that bound them. "I don't know. Someone he met at church?"

"Sarah and Tuck never went to church that I know. They were stuck in the hippie mentality, all that spiritual jargon about horoscopes and crystals. Tuck relied on an almanac for his weather forecasts. Wait a minute, are you talking about Tricia Yates?"

"She admitted that she knew him. Did he ever mention her?"

"No," he said slowly, "but I thought I saw them together last summer, maybe June, outside a coffee shop near the campus. They were going in, and I didn't get a good luck.

I said something to Tuck later. He blew me off, claimed he was in Oklahoma at a solar energy symposium."

"You believed him?" I asked.

Will shrugged. "Didn't have a reason not to. He'd been talking about solar and wind power since the technology emerged. He devoted an entire notebook to the amount of money he'd save if he invested in a couple of windmills to generate electricity to run the irrigation system. Columns and columns of numbers and figures."

"What can you tell me about Tricia Yates?"

He glanced at the clock on the wall. "I got to go in a minute, Claire. Junie's making a special Sunday dinner for Billy, and she can get testy if I don't show up on time. Afterwards, I'm going to take the kid fishing one last time. Our daughter and her husband are coming tomorrow at noon to take him home."

"Tricia Yates?" I prompted him. "I'm desperate, Will."

"She started working at the church about three years ago. I'm a deacon, so I was on the committee that interviewed her. She had experience in bookkeeping and office management, which is what we were looking for. Everybody likes her, and we've never had any complaints." He stopped and frowned.

I stayed mute and resisted any sudden urges to grab him by the shoulders and shake more information out of him. He finally looked at me and said, "Except for right after Tuck died. She missed church and didn't show up the next couple of days. One of the other deacons went to her apartment and pounded on the door. Then there she was at the Wednesday evening service, acting as if nothing was wrong. Dismissed her absence as a bout of stomach flu."

"Or a reaction to Tuck's death."

"I don't know," Will said, "but I do know that I don't want to piss off Junie. Good luck with all this junk. Maybe you'll find a stack of death threats, signed and dated." He gave me a crooked smile as he went out the back door.

I spread out the envelopes and studied them. "Oh, Tuck," I murmured, "you were a sly dog, weren't you?"

11

As I'd anticipated, Tuck had been unable to destroy his correspondence, addressed to a variety of aliases at post office boxes in unfamiliar towns in Oklahoma and Missouri. I was vaguely put out when I had to walk down the long driveway to collect my mail; Tuck had driven hours for his. There were no return addresses, and the postal marks were difficult to decipher. The earliest letters had arrived five years ago; the most recent, fourteen months ago.

I gave myself a moment to bask in my success, however minor, and then removed the letter from the oldest envelope. It began with a cheerful salutation and a mention that the writer had come across an allusion to him on something called Facebook and, through mutual acquaintances, had tracked down his PO address. It was a curiously guarded message: If he were indeed the person who had worked in a taco food truck on Venice Beach in 1968 and remembered the name of his co-worker, he could refer to it on Facebook and the writer would send another letter. The letter ended with a peace sign drawn in purple ink

Apparently, Tuck had obliged. The writer had imparted leftist opinions about the political climate, news of a career in hand-made textiles (macramé and tie-dye), and inquiries about Tuck's health and well-being. Purple peace sign. The next letter offered advice about herbal supplements. Purple peace sign. I skimmed several more with the same gist. I was about to admit defeat when I came across a letter that referred to the incident at the campus. Did he regret his decision to flee? Did he feel remorse about the slain undercover officer? Why hadn't he stayed to help the other members of the group? Purple peace sign.

I felt as if I were eavesdropping on a private conversation. I put down the letter and went to the refrigerator to find something to eat. It all looked suspiciously vegan. I settled on a box of gluten-free crackers and a jar of organic almond butter, refilled my glass with water, and sat back down. I would have scrutinized the handwriting with laser eyes had it been handwritten. It wasn't, although the FBI could have nailed the brand of the printer and, with all its stealth capacity unleashed, the day of the week it was sold. I tried to imagine Peter, Jorgeson, or even my late husband selecting a purple marker to sign his letters. The writer was female — and she knew what had taken place during the fateful demonstration. Whether her knowledge was firsthand or based on something as innocuous as a newspaper article was difficult to discern.

I dived back into Tuck's clandestine correspondence. The writer had bombarded him with questions about both the past and his current situation. As I continued to read, I began to feel that a level of intimacy had intensified. A reference to a night on the beach in San Diego. Warm memories of a camping trip in the desert. Nothing overt, mind you, but a middle school kid would have no problem spotting the implicit sexual references. Luanne would have taken to her bed with a cool compress. I opted for a damp paper towel.

The last dozen letters made it clear that the author was residing in Farberville and was no longer reticent about her desires. The prose was more purple than the peace signs. She and Tuck had found places to meet and do more than greet. My eyes widened at the increasingly graphic reminiscences of afternoons spent in lascivious behavior. Tuck's wife and best friends had seriously underestimated his capacity for physical intimacy. My face was warm when I opened the last letter, dated a week before his death. I paid little attention to the description of their last tryst, which had taken place on a picnic blanket. I blushed at the improbability of what had occurred, scolded myself for being a prude, and arrived at the last line. "Same place and time, my lustful lover. Wait for me." Purple peace sign.

Tricia Yates was the obvious suspect. From what Will had said, she'd disappeared immediately after his death and stayed out of sight for most of a week. Was she mourning, or was she overcome with guilt? I spread almond butter on a cracker and nibbled pensively. If she was one of the members of the Student Antiwar Coalition, she'd gone to prison or gone underground. I peered more closely at the postal marks, and finally detected postal abbreviations from the Midwest. Before coming to Farberville, the writer had lived in states laden with vowels. I took out the cell phone to call Peter, but then reluctantly put it down. The darling man would want to know where I was and what I was doing. These were top-

ics best left alone until I concocted a truth-
ful if carefully edited response that would
not cause him undue distress. He had so
much on his plate, what with his mother
coming for a visit and his wife going bon-
kers.

A dusty shirt box caught my attention. I
moved the folders to a chair and opened
the box. It was crammed with newspaper
and magazine clippings, more than enough
to wallpaper the kitchen. Most of the newspaper articles were yellowed and brittle.
Tuck had written the dates in the margins
in print the size of ant tracks. I shuffled
through them until I found a photo that
depicted police tape across a pair of double
doors. FBI AGENT KILLED BY STUDENT
DEMONSTRATORS. It was dated March 1,
1970, and contained little hard information.
A second article, dated the following day,
had a photo of the demonstrators lounging
against the same doors. A heavy chain
prevented the doors from opening. The
demonstrators were dressed in jeans and
sandals, and all of them had long hair and
defiant grins. I looked for Sarah, but the
photo was grainy and faded and it took me
several minutes before I recognized her.
She'd been a beautiful young woman.

I went into the living room and fetched

the photo of Tuck with the Lunds. He was harder to locate, because most of the men sported facial hair, but I finally decided that he was in the middle, his face lowered as he lit a cigarette. There were no women with short silver hair. If Tricia Yates was among the group, she was as elusive as Waldo. A subsequent article identified the demonstrators in custody by name, as well as the slain agent, Abel Reddy. The national press had picked up the story with zealous glee, as had the news magazines. The chief of police had acknowledged that at least five of the demonstrators had eluded capture, but his detectives were working day and night to locate them. When asked if he knew their names, he'd declined to answer.

I picked up the newspaper photo of the group and counted heads. Some were seated, and others leaned against the doors. It was hard to be sure exactly how many had participated, since several of their peers had pressed in to be captured for posterity. If the incident had occurred recently, all of them would have been holding up cell phones.

The next batch of articles, held together with a corroded paper clip, concerned the trial. The FBI had opted to allow the state of California to take its best shot at the six defendants. Four were men, two women, and all of them were in their twenties; three were from California, the others from Wyoming, Ohio (a young man with muttonchop sideburns), and Connecticut. Sarah had told Evan and me that a guy named Roderick, a more practiced antiwar activist, had joined their group. Roderick James, originally from San Jose and more recently, Berkeley. The judge had refused to sever defenses. Their attorneys, no doubt the best money could buy, tried to claim that the undercover agent had instigated the demonstration and provoked the violence, but the jury didn't buy it. The defendants were found guilty of first degree murder during the commission of two other felonies: the murder of a law enforcement agent and kidnapping. The demonstrators had been incarcerated in California federal prisons. I had no idea if federal prisoners became eligible for early release or parole, but those who'd gone to trial had received forty-year sentences, with a minimum of twenty-five years to be served. Fifteen years ago they would have served their time and, presuming they'd behaved with adequate decorum, been sent out into a techno-crazy world with bus tickets, minimal funds, and impending cultural shock.

I went through more articles about appeals (unsuccessful). The media lost interest and moved on, but Tuck had remained ever vigilant. A short article related that one of the women prisoners had developed terminal cancer and was released for humanitarian reasons. Years later, one of the men had been killed in a gang-related riot. I riffled the stack, focusing on the dates that Tuck had conveniently provided. Finally, after twenty years, the Student Antiwar Coalition stumbled back into the news. Roderick James, deemed the mastermind, had escaped from Folsom Prison after he acquired a hacksaw, cut through a fence, fled into a storm drain, and later crawled through a pitch-black sewer to a raft awaiting him on the bank of the American River. Johnny Cash would have been proud.

Nowhere in Tuck's clippings was an announcement that either the escapee or his confederate had been captured. I wondered if Sarah knew any of it. What I did know, however, was that Tuck had been having an affair with a local woman. I spread almond butter on another cracker and leaned back to gaze at the ceiling. Tuck had told Sarah that he would be gone overnight. It was a rather arrogant lie, since Will had not been prepped. There were two possible reasons for the story. Either Tuck had planned to spend the night with his paramour at the "same place, same time," or he'd intended to catch Sarah in bed with her paramour. She claimed she didn't have one, but her credibility had bottomed out several days ago.

Something was gnawing at me, and the organic almond butter was not the culprit. I clasped my hands together and leaned my chin on them. I'd found Tuck and Sarah in the photo. I hadn't found Tricia, but I hadn't ruled her out. By the age of sixty, faces began to sag. Chins softened, wrinkles distorted mouths, eyelids drooped. I shuffled the articles until I located the photo of the demonstrators. It bothered me. One of the articles about the trial had contained a courtroom sketch of Roderick James. He sported the mustache of an old-fashioned bandito and heavy stubble. The artist had depicted him with glowering eyes and a menacing scowl.

I was staring at it when Deputy Frank Norton, who was not at the top of my list of dear friends, came into the kitchen. His uniform looked as though he'd slept in it, perhaps cuddled up with a teddy bear in a matching outfit.

"Mrs. Malloy," he said with a sigh, "what

the hell are you doing here? I told you to butt out, but every time I turn around, I see you. Are you like a serial trespasser?"

"I have Sarah's permission to be here."

"The FBI says it's off-limits until they've completed a thorough search."

"How am I supposed to know that, Deputy Norton? Did they notify Sarah's attorney? Shall I call him?" I realized it was not wise to bait the man with the badge. "I was driving by and stopped when I saw movement inside the house. Two men were here, intending to cart off any valuables they could find. I have their first names and the license plate of their truck. They're the ones who broke into Miss Poppoy's house and tied her up. Teenagers, not very bright. I ran them off, and then decided to see if I could find any relevant material about the death of John Cunningham."

His initial belligerence diminished a tad. "You sure about that?"

"You want their names?"

He took a pad and a pencil out of his back pocket. "Yeah, go ahead. I'll call it in. I got a grandma, just like everybody else."

I cheerfully threw Bubba and Benedict under the prison van, and then sat impatiently while Norton made a call to the sheriff's office. His language would not have pleased his grandma. After he finished, he put away his cell phone and frowned at the mess on the table. "You find anything?"

"Did you know Zachery Barnard?" I asked.

"Nasty sumbitch. I busted him a couple of times for DWI and pestering folks. He'd do thirty days and then go off to the nearest liquor store. I wasn't surprised that he got so drunk he fell in his own pond. Ain't no one going to claim his body, so the county'll have to bury him."

"I think," I said cautiously, "that he's in this photo." I handed him the clipping. "Second man on the left, in an army surplus jacket."

Deputy Norton stared at the photo. "That guy?" he said as he jabbed his finger.

"He looked so familiar. It's been a long time, granted, but the facial bones are right. I'm almost sure that's Barnard."

"The hell it is," he said with a snort. "There's no way that's Zachery Barnard, Mrs. Malloy. You may be desperate to save that woman, but that's not an excuse for concocting baloney." His frown deepened as he read the article. "You think Barnard went to a fancy college in California? I'd be surprised if he ever left Stump County. He could barely read and write. College? Did they offer a scholarship in moonshining?"

"Look at this drawing." I wanted to tell him to use a little imagination, but I wasn't sure he would find my remark endearing. Our relationship was as fragile as almond brittle. It wouldn't help to mention that Zachery had quoted Oliver Goldsmith.

"Not Barnard," Norton said firmly. "Why are you so damn devoted to unraveling the case against Sarah Swift, or whatever her name is? She and her friends killed a law enforcement agent. That doesn't bother you?"

"She didn't. She and Tuck — that's what she called him — ran out of the building before the situation turned violent." I picked up the article he'd dropped on the table and shoved it at him. "This is Roderick James. He escaped from prison twenty years ago. He came here and changed his name."

"How many times do I have to tell you that this isn't Zachery Barnard?"

I sensed frustration in his voice. "In the police reports, there was a notation that he'd seen a green van in the area. I drove out to his house on Friday and asked him about it. He wasn't helpful."

"Did you get pissed and push him into the pond?" Norton asked, edging away from the table.

"Of course not. I went back yesterday to try again and realized I was too late." I hesitated for a moment. "I'm not a fan of coincidences, Deputy Norton. I questioned him about the green van, and his body was discovered less than twenty-four hours later. Maybe he thought I'd recognized him and couldn't bear the idea of being sent back to prison for a very long time. Did you find an empty whiskey bottle by the pond?"

"The medical examiner ruled it an accident. Now you're saying it was suicide. You know something, Mrs. Malloy? I don't give a rat's ass if he fell into the pond or decided to go for a swim. It has nothing to do with Cunningham's murder. We built a solid case against the Swift woman. There were no other suspects. She'd threatened to kill him, and she did. You need to keep your nose out of this and go on about your business." He made a curt gesture. "I'm going to walk you to your car and watch you drive away. If you got a problem with that, we can talk some more at the department."

I had no desire to make new friends in the holding cell. "Fine, Deputy Norton. Let me put all this back in the boxes so the FBI won't find papers scattered on the floor. You might want to inventory the items that the burglars piled by the front door."

He gave me a well-deserved suspicious look and then went back down the hall. I stuffed the letters and articles about the trial in my purse, dumped everything else back in the box, and joined Norton at the front door. He was squatting next to the TV set, copying down the make and model. I told him I was going back to Farberville and wished him luck corralling Bubba and Benedict. He told me that I would have to make a statement in the next day or two.

I kept my chin high as I walked to my car. I was frantic to call Peter, but I dared not linger. I drove into town and parked in front of Evan's office. His car was where it had been hours earlier, when we'd walked to the county jail. I rapped my keys on the door. He emerged from the depths of the building, his shoulders slumped and his face expressionless.

"How was church?" he asked as he unlocked the door.

"Enlightening. I'll fill you in, but first I need to call my husband." I sat down behind the receptionist's desk and took out my cell phone. Evan shuffled away with the alacrity of a zombie on tranquilizers. I waited until he was out of earshot before I picked up the office telephone and dialed home.

"Yeah?" Peter answered succinctly.

"Can you get me in the morgue?"

"You don't need a reservation. Is someone pointing a gun at you?"

"It's too convoluted to explain right now. Do I need official clearance to view a body in the morgue?"

The consequent silence suggested that no one had ever asked him that, especially not his devoted wife. "I have no idea. Go there, knock on the door, and make your request. If that doesn't work, call me. Exactly how convoluted is whatever's going on? Give me the short version."

"I need to see the body of Zachery Barnard, the man who drowned yesterday. I think he was one of the SAC demonstrators." I told him about finding Tuck's cache of clippings in the attic. Bubba and Benedict did not merit mention, at least for the moment. "The only way I can be sure is to compare his face to the one in the photo and sketch."

"I would never dream of interfering with your planned assault on the morgue," Peter said. The poor man may have lacked sincerity, but he was aware that I rarely allowed myself to be sidetracked by technicalities. "I know where Caron and Inez are. I got a call from the department, and I was on the way

263

out the door when you called. They're being held for breaking and entering, trespassing, and vandalism."

My mouth went numb, my lips parted in
an unbecoming manner. "Breaking and
entering what?"

"The Farberville Community Theater.
That's all I know, except that the officer
who arrested them does not want to waste
the rest of the long weekend with paperwork
and is willing to release them into my custody."

"Why would they . . . ?"

"I'll ask them that in about half an hour,
unless you'd like to chat a little longer. Did
I tell you that my mother is allergic to
strawberries?"

"Update me when you know more," I
said, and ended the call without slithering
to the floor. I closed my eyes and forced
myself to breathe slowly. The girls had followed the trail of the Ming Thing from the
thrift shop to the theater. They'd returned
to retrieve it, which was a more civilized
term than "steal it." How they'd gotten into
the building was immaterial. If they'd gone
to Kentucky, I would have expected a call
from Fort Knox. Ditto the Kremlin. I didn't
want to know when and how they'd been
caught. The only significant issue was the

Ming Thing. Did they have it, and how could they could come up with an explanation that Peter might accept?

Evan appeared in the doorway. "You okay, Claire? Do you want a bottle of water?"

I shook my head with undue vehemence. "I'm fine, thank you. Do you want to come with me to the morgue?"

"Why would I want to do that?"

"Consider it a field trip. I'll explain in the car." I grabbed my bulging purse and headed for the door.

"I'm coming," Evan said plaintively, "but I have to lock up."

I sat in my car, stewing about the Ming Thing, until he got into the passenger's seat. "Brace yourself, grasshopper. It's convoluted, speculative, and based on nothing more than an artist's depiction."

"Be still my heart."

I overlooked his attitude and launched into my theories about who was who and who wasn't. At a stoplight, I took the letters out of my purse and thrust them at him. At a stop sign, I showed him the photo and the sketch. By the time I parked at the hospital, I'd covered almost everything. "So all I need to do is ascertain if the body in the morgue is Roderick James. Deputy Norton couldn't see the resemblance, but he has tunnel vision."

"Did you ask him how long he knew Barnard?"

"Twenty years ago the deputy was in kindergarten, busting his fellow students for breaking crayons. It's a lead, for pity's sake. Try to show a little enthusiasm."

We went through the lobby and took the elevator to the basement. It was very quiet. We followed signs to the door of the morgue. I didn't know the protocol, but I was afraid Evan might bolt if I showed any sign of indecision. "Stop fidgeting," I whispered to him as I opened the door. "We're not breaking any laws."

"Yet," he said in a surly voice.

The anteroom had a desk, unoccupied, and standard waiting room decor. The plastic plants were dusty, the magazines on the end table years old. A wire rack held brochures from funeral homes. The predominant odor was a combination of pine trees and bleach. The temperature was low enough to evoke a shiver down my spine.

"Hello?" I called.

"Guess they're closed on Sundays," Evan said, tugging on my arm. "I'll request that the medical examiner send the autopsy results to my office."

"I need to see the face." I knocked on a door with a sign that forbade entry without permission. Evan's grip on my arm tightened and he began to hiss. I was trying to disengage his hand when the door opened and a black man in pale green scrubs looked down at us from a height of well over six and a half feet.

"Help you?" he said.

"Do you have visiting hours?" I asked.

His forehead crinkled as he stared at me. "Not really. You looking for anybody in particular?"

Evan gurgled. I stepped hard on his foot before he blurted out something unhelpful, and smiled at the man. His ID badge was partially covered by a towel draped over his shoulder. I couldn't tell if he was the head pathologist or an orderly — or a fugitive from a professional basketball team. I held out my hand. "I'm Claire Malloy, and I'm a consultant with the Farberville Police Department. I need to confirm the identity of Zachery Barnard." I pointed my thumb at Evan. "He's my assistant, Evan Toffle. Is there any way we might take a quick look at the body?"

"Why not?" The man stood back and motioned for us to enter.

The actual morgue was not as impressive

as the ones I'd seen on TV shows. Farberville lacks the level of crime that keeps city
morgues well stocked. Most of the deceased
went from bed to funeral home without
autopsies. There were two bodies on tables,
both covered with sheets.

"Zachery Barnard was brought here yesterday," I said. "He drowned in a pond on
his property."

The man picked up a clipboard. "Yes, he's
here. You sure you want to see him?"

"Please," I said before Evan could respond
in a less affirmative fashion. He was breathing heavily, and his face was red. I hoped he
wouldn't collapse when a drawer was slid
open. "You can wait outside," I said to him.
"No one will ever know."

He did not take offense at the implication
he was behaving like a timid bunny rabbit.
"Good idea," he said. "I'll wait for you in
the parking lot." He scampered out the
door.

"He's new," I said as I followed the man
to a drawer. He reconfirmed the number
with the list on his clipboard, glanced at
me, and pulled out the drawer. I found
myself staring at the face of a semitoothless
troll with a half-dozen strands of white hair
and a flat, misshapen nose. "Are you sure
this is Zachery Barnard?"

The man reached down to flip over a toe tag. "Yes. He's not scheduled for an autopsy. We're just babysitting until the county decides what to do with him."

"No autopsy?"

"The alcohol level in his blood was sky-high. No extraordinary bruising or wounds. He drowned, or died from a heart attack or liver failure. Could have been all three, but not in that order. We only conduct autopsies when there's uncertainty about the cause of death." He closed the drawer. "We cleaned up the poor bugger, and we're holding him until we get the paperwork. He may be going to med school."

I wasn't quite ready to give up. "Were any other bodies brought in yesterday?"

"A five-hundred-pound woman from the ICU. The funeral dudes are collecting her this afternoon. Sorry if I ruined your day."

"I guess I was wrong," I said, thanked him, and went out to the hall. Evan was not waiting with a penitent look on his face, prepared to apologize for his cowardly behavior. I found him perched on the back of my car. "You make a lousy assistant," I said as I unlocked the car. "What if I'd fainted and fallen on the floor?"

"You were in a hospital. I can't think of a better place to be injured."

269

I bit back the response that came to mind. "The body I saw was that of Zachery Barnard, according to the records. Unless there's a vast conspiracy that includes the sheriff's department and the staff at the morgue, the man I spoke to on Friday was someone else."

"Roderick James?"

"I wish I could get another look at him." I pulled onto the street and drove back toward Evan's office. "If the man was James, then he's probably long gone. It would be too dangerous for him to hang around and risk being arrested."

"Did he murder Barnard?" Evan asked with a gulp.

"How would I know? Barnard was drunk; he could have stumbled into the pond and been unable to get out. His body was coated with slime and weeds, indicating he thrashed around in the water."

"While someone held him down."

I didn't have time to add another murder to my list. "I need to talk to Sarah. Do you want to go with me?"

"I'm not in the mood for another field trip. I need to write a compelling motion for a continuance. Judge Priestly does not care to be overturned in appellate court, and she's aware this trial is going to attract the media. What's more newsworthy than a woman who's been on the FBI's most-wanted list for decades now being tried for murder? Besides, Sarah and I did not part on harmonious terms. You'll do better without me present."

I turned into his office parking lot. "Did she tell you anything?"

"Same old story." He got out of the car. "I'll call the sheriff's department and let them know you're on your way. Come back after you've talked to her."

"Of course," I said with no intention of doing so anytime soon. Mysteries are not solved by burying one's face in a law book. My nose tingled at the thought of book mold.

Evan let himself into the office. I walked to the jail and went into the front room. The deputy who'd been there earlier led me to the same room and said he'd bring the prisoner. I took the packet of clippings out of my purse and arranged them neatly on the table. My identification of Roderick James was tentative. The man with whom I had spoken on Friday was not Zachery Barnard. I decided to call him Oliver Goldsmith until I was more confident.

Sarah came into the room and froze when she saw the array of newspaper clippings.

I'd made sure the headlines were visible, and I was pleased that I'd rattled her. "Sit down," I said, "and have a look at these."

She sat, her shoulders hunched, regarding the rectangles of paper as if they were writhing leeches. "Where did you find them?"

"In a trunk in your attic. Tuck must have been saving them to make a scrapbook. The earliest ones concern the SAC demonstration, arrests, and information about those in custody. The ones in the middle cover the trial. The final few have to do with Roderick James's escape from Folsom Prison twenty years ago." I could see that she was struggling not to react. "Where would you like to start?"

"Tuck hid them in the attic?"

"In a heavy trunk with a padlock."

"I don't believe you." Her voice was flat, but she was visibly agitated.

"I gather he didn't share with you," I said. "Weren't you concerned about your friends?"

"There was nothing I could do. Turning myself in wasn't going to help them, and neither was brooding. I decided that I had to put it all behind me and get on with my life. Tuck agreed. We never spoke about it again."

They'd cohabited with a two-ton elephant

in the room. No wonder their furnishings were sparse. "He may have agreed, but he'd been clipping articles since the day after the demonstration."

She gave me a mulish glare. "That's not true."

"This isn't the time for denial, Sarah. Here's the proof, from your attic. It must have fanned his paranoia, especially when the others were sentenced to twenty-five to forty years in prison." I slid the article with the sketch of Roderick James across the table. "Did you know about his escape?"

"I might have seen something. People at the diner left newspapers on the counter when they finished with them. I used to glance through them."

"But you never heard from Roderick?"

"Why would we? He had no idea where to find us. Even if he had, he wouldn't have risked it."

"But he did," I said mildly. "I spoke to him two days ago. He pretended he was Zachery Barnard."

Sarah looked down. "I heard Zach drowned in his pond. He wasn't as bad as everybody made him out to be. I used to take him homemade bread, goat milk, and blueberries. He kept trying to give me kittens, but I couldn't take one because of

Tuck's imaginary allergies."

"I'd rather talk about Roderick."

"Talk all you want, Claire. I have nothing to say."

I did not stick out my tongue and chant, "Liar, liar, pants on fire." For that smidgeon of self-restraint, I awarded myself a gold star.

"You might want to ask Roderick about the joys of prison life," I said.

12

Sarah brushed the newspaper articles to the end of the table, stood up, and leaned against the ubiquitous green wall, watching me warily. "I don't know how to get in touch with Roderick. Fugitives are not birds of a feather, eager to flock together. We were as dangerous to him as he would have been to us. The FBI had our fingerprints and photos. Tuck and I were very careful not to get so much as a speeding ticket."

"Sit down," I said again, making no effort to conceal my irritation. "If you don't, I'll write off my efforts to help you as a misguided and foolish waste of my time. Wessell will continue to persecute powerless defendants, and eventually I will find a way to expose him. He'll be sorry he tangled with me."

"So this is all about you? He wounded your pride. You want revenge, not justice."

I felt as though my blood pressure had

shot into outer space. I counted to ten, exhaling with each number. I repeated the process in French, and then made it to five (*funf*) in my limited German before I dared to open my mouth. "What I want is the truth, and there's not a damn thing I can do to help you if you insist on lying to me — and to your lawyer. He can't defend you properly if you refuse to help him. So what's it going to be?"

Sarah plopped down in the chair. "I don't know where Roderick is or how to get in contact with him. That's the truth."

"Okay." I didn't believe her, but I have been known to be overly skeptical. "Do you honestly believe that Tuck wasn't having an affair?"

"That's absurd. Who could stand to put up with him and his obsessions?"

I gave her the packet of letters. "Read these." I retreated to a corner of the room and called Peter. Voice mail, suggesting he was occupied arranging to take custody of two wily criminals. I hoped the process was brief, since the red-haired wily criminal was hosting a party in an hour. Chips and dip would have to suffice, since I had no intention of dashing to the grocery store to purchase steaks and potatoes. Or the bakery for tiramisu with chocolate ganache. *Très gauche, le ganache.*

"Oh my gawd," Sarah gasped, her cheeks flushed and her breath wheezy. "This is insane! Who wrote these letters?" She yanked the folded paper out of another envelope and skimmed it. "This is ludicrous!"

I returned to the table before she hyperventilated and I lost my visiting privileges. "I'm not sure, but I have a suspect in mind. Have you ever met a woman named Tricia Yates?" She shook her head. "Will told me that he saw her with Tuck one afternoon at a local coffee shop. Tuck denied it."

"Who is she?"

"The secretary at a local church, in her sixties. I encountered her while I was looking into a church-sponsored teen campout at Flat Rock the night Tuck was murdered."

"I can't believe he was having an affair with anyone," she said. "More power to him if he was. We hadn't slept together for decades. I've never heard that name, and we never went to any church. 'Religion is the opiate of the people,' Tuck used to say in a goofy Russian accent. He was a fan of Karl Marx. I preferred Harpo." She rocked back in the chair and chewed on her lower lip. "Tuck could have had an affair with that woman. I was at the diner all day, and we never owned cell phones. He was adamant that they cause brain tumors. He did the farm work, ran errands, and went to the library between visits to the ER. That's what he said, anyway."

"Any out-of-town trips?"

"Yes, but not with me. One of us had to stay home to take care of the animals. Once or twice a year I traveled with friends from the book club. We went to Little Rock to see the Clinton Library, and to the horse races in Hot Springs. We even went to Memphis to tour Graceland. Tuck attended conferences sponsored by organic farming groups and to alternative energy symposiums. He hated motel rooms because he was terrified of bedbugs." She gestured at the letters. "That's what he told me, anyway. From what I just read, he found distractions. I still can't believe it. Did you find a copy of the *Kama Sutra* in the trunk?"

"I didn't have a chance to go through everything," I said. I saw no reason to tell her about the burglars or Deputy Norton. "The writer was familiar with what took place at the demonstration, and she knew that he worked at a taco truck in Venice Beach. She had some sort of past connection. When the two of you fled to Oregon, did Tuck leave behind a girlfriend?"

Sarah scowled as she thought. "It's hard to remember. There was a lot of sleeping around in those days. 'Make love, not war.' I spent a couple of lusty weekends with Tuck, but then we drifted on, amiably. He was involved with a woman from UCLA the autumn before the demonstration. He broke it off when he found out she was married to a biker."

"What about the women in SAC?"

"He told me he had a threesome with Jamie and Justine. They were on acid, and the whole thing disintegrated into a mud-wrestling match in the backyard. Other than that, I can't think of anybody. That doesn't mean he didn't. I was busy with classes and assignments. My parents drove down to the campus once a month to take me to dinner and grill me about extracurricular activities. Had they known the truth, they would have dragged me home and locked me in my bedroom."

"Tuck didn't always confide in you?"

"Sometimes, but not always. His social skills weren't stellar, and I gave him advice." She squeezed her eyes closed. "Around the time of the demonstration, there was somebody he was interested in, but he didn't say who it was. She could have been a member of SAC, but her name wasn't Tricia or anything like that."

"Find the newspaper photo of the demonstration."

After some fumbling, she located the photo and spread it out. "I can barely recognize myself. I'm not even sure that's Tuck. These two women are in the shadows. One's Justine, I think. The other one might be Laura, but there were several women with dark hair. I don't remember the woman standing behind Abel, but it's been a while. I'd help if I could, Claire."

I needed a recent photograph of Tricia to see if Sarah recognized her, but I had no idea how to acquire one. I couldn't take Sarah on a field trip to an apartment complex, presuming I could get the address. Which I could, I realized in a flash of astuteness, by asking Will Lund. A deacon had access to the church files. Or, as a first resort, by looking her name up in a telephone directory. It was an endangered species, unfamiliar to the current technology prodigies. Caron lets her fingers do the walking across a keyboard.

"What about this campout at Flat Rock?" Sarah continued. "If that woman was there, maybe Tuck planned to meet her. It's a five-minute walk through Will's blueberry field. We used to go there to swim." She put her hand to her mouth and stared at me. "Do you think she . . . ?"

"I don't know," I admitted. "Whatever happened could have taken place anytime after dark. The campers would have been asleep well before midnight, freeing Tricia to sneak away to meet Tuck. That doesn't explain why they were in the barn — with a shotgun." Or why Colonel Mustard was in the billiards room with a lead pipe when Miss Scarlet was in the ballroom with a wrench. Or why Sarah didn't hear the shotgun discharge.

"No," she said, "it doesn't. Can't you make this woman talk?"

"Evan can subpoena her. It's sheer speculation, unless someone saw her in the field or at your house. I did my best to get the teenagers to tell me what took place, but they were threatened with eternal damnation if they said a word."

"Evan can subpoena them."

"I don't think Judge Priestly will allow that blatant a fishing trip. There's no evidence to link the two incidents." I leaned forward, my elbows on the table, and gave her a hard look. "I have another question for you, and I want the truth. Did Tuck tell you that he wanted to turn himself in to the

FBI so he could see his family before he died?"

"Who told you that?"

"That's irrelevant. Answer the question."

"If he did, I ignored it." She tried to look at me, but her eyes shifted away. "He was always saying crazy things. I stopped paying attention to him years ago."

"You weren't worried that after he turned himself in, you'd end up in prison, too? That should have caught your attention in the same way a semi thundering down the highway toward you would. Once the FBI had your assumed identity, they'd hunt you down. How long do you think you'd last without access to your bank account and credit cards? You couldn't get a decent job without a Social Security number."

"Okay, so we talked about it. He promised not to do anything until I made plans. I had to trust him."

"What kind of plans?"

"Going back underground. There are still communal farms run by gray-haired hippies." She gave me a rueful smile. "It didn't sound all that bad after forty years of living with Tuck."

"It might have been simpler to kill him," I said.

"Don't be silly. If I were going to murder

him, I would have done a much better job. Do you know how many poisonous plants grow in a hundred-foot radius of my house? Larkspurs, belladonna, lupines, mushrooms, and dozens more. His death would have been attributed to heart failure."

An experience at the beginning of the summer confirmed that. In that instance, the medical examiner and the state lab had failed to identify the cause of death until I brought it to their attention. Accolades had not showered upon me like the gentle rain from heaven, alas.

"Don't share that with the jury," I said. "Take this stuff back to your cell and read it carefully. There may be phrases in the letters that sound oddly familiar. See if any faces pop into your mind."

"Darn, I made plans to go on a picnic in the park this afternoon and catch a movie this evening." She gathered up the clippings and letters. "Reading letters from my husband's lover while in a cell doesn't sound nearly as pleasant. Maybe I can do some editing and come up with a bestseller titled *Fifty Shades of Icky*. I'll drop your name in the acknowledgments."

"Please don't," I said as rose. "I'll be back later."

"And I'll be here."

■ ■ ■ ■

After I walked back to Evan's office building, I debated going inside to tell him what
Sarah had said. It would be a symbolic
gesture, since she hadn't revealed anything.
I sat in my car and took out my cell phone.
I had no messages from my beloved husband or from Caron. Fuming, I called
Luanne. "What are you doing?" I demanded
when she answered.

"Fine, thank you."

"You're welcome. What are you doing?"

"Marinating steaks and watching game
shows. What are you doing, besides calling
me with unnecessary brusqueness?"

"Sorry," I said insincerely. "Can you leave
the steaks long enough to help me find an
escaped prisoner?"

"Did that woman break out of the county
jail?"

"Not unless she did so in the last five
minutes. I'll pick you up in front of your
store in the next five minutes." I cut off the
call and drove to Thurber Street. Because
the bars were closed, there were few cars
and scant pedestrian traffic. I pulled into a
parking space and honked. Luanne lives in
an apartment on the second floor and

claims to enjoy the loud music and nightlife. If I were forced to live there, I'd have been boiling oil at two o'clock in the morning.

Minutes later Luanne got in the passenger's side. "I wasn't sure what to wear for the occasion. It's been forever since I tracked down an escapee. Are we going to borrow bloodhounds from the state troopers? They're cute, but they drool."

"The state troopers?" I said as I headed for County 107.

"I have to be home by seven. Sweetie's coming for dinner and a movie."

I politely disregarded the nickname, although I did tuck it away in a corner of my already overloaded mind. "Let me tell you a story about an antiwar demonstration, false identities, a weasel, and other fancy things." During the next ten minutes I gave her a disjointed account of everything that I'd found out since Friday morning. When I described the prison breakout, I realized I should have kept the sketch of Roderick James, but I'd left it with Sarah. I asked Luanne if she could take a photo with her cell phone. She assured me that any idiot could. If Oliver Goldsmith was hanging out at Zachery's house, then I might be able to capture him, in a sense. Assuming he didn't drown us in the pond.

"That's Sarah Swift's house," I announced as we drove past it. "Will and Juniper Lund live across the unpaved road. These are their fields, and this is the river downstream from Flat Rock."

"Fascinating." Luanne took a nail file out of her purse.

"You're a worse assistant than Evan Toffle, and that's saying a lot. Okay, this is Pinkie Sheer Road. We're just going to stop at Zachery's shack and look for any indication that someone's living there."

"A southern-fried zombie?"

I swatted at her with my right hand. "This is serious. The trial begins Tuesday morning. Right now Evan has no alternative suspects, no mitigating circumstances, no witnesses. All he has is a client who refuses to cooperate with her own defense. Wessel will win, and Sarah will be in prison for the rest of her life."

"You know that Wessell's aware of your involvement, don't you? He's going to chortle from his high and mighty pulpit."

"Which is precisely why I have to find the killer."

"What if Sarah Swift turns out to be that person?" Luanne said quietly. "Are you going to move to Newport and sleep in the Rosen boathouse?"

I winced. "I wish you hadn't mentioned that. Remind me to tell you about the wedding present, which isn't present. Okay, that's the shack. Look for any kind of movement or anomaly. I'm convinced Oliver Goldsmith is staying in the vicinity. When I called out that I was a friend of Sarah's, he appeared within seconds."

The shack was as desolate as it had been earlier. No weeds had been trampled. Zachery's truck had not moved. A flock of cowbirds took flight in an amorphous cloud when I cut off the engine and opened the car door. I heard nothing but vehicles on the county road and chirps from the woods.

"Nobody's home," Luanne said.

"That doesn't mean Oliver isn't hiding in the outhouse."

"Our friendship does have its limits."

"I would never impinge on your common sense and refined sensibility," I said, putting a foot on the ground. "All I request is that when you hear my blood-curdling scream, you call the sheriff's department and report it."

"No problem."

I approached the shack with caution. The door was ajar. I rapped on it loudly and said, "Anybody home?"

"Mr. Goldsmith!" called Luanne, who was

287

right behind me. "We need to talk to you about Sarah Swift!" She lowered her voice. "It worked last time, right? I have my phone. If he looms in the doorway, I'll take a photo and then we'll bound away like cheetahs. I will, anyway; I was on the high school track team."

It was as good a plan as any. I rapped again, but no one loomed. I pushed open the door and looked inside. The front room had a worn, saggy sofa, a small TV set, and a kitchen area with an old refrigerator and a stove coated with grease. Empty whiskey bottles and beer cans were scattered on the floor and counters. Zachery's diet seemed to have consisted of canned beans, crackers, eggshells, and moldy bread. Beyond that room were a bedroom and bathroom. I was pondering my next move when Luanne shoved me into the room.

"Well?" she whispered.

"Are you asking me if there is one?" I whispered back. "If there is, it's outside." I tiptoed across the room and peered into the bedroom. The mattress on the floor was stained, the blanket of army surplus origin. Oddments of clothing were in piles on the floor. Based on the droppings along the baseboards, rodents had shared the room for years. I continued to the bathroom. The toilet and sink were filthy, and the bathtub was cracked. If there had been running water, it had not been utilized for personal hygiene.

"As I said, nobody's home," Luanne said cheerfully. "Let's get ice cream on the way back."

I bit back a shriek as leaves scuttled across the floor. "I don't have time for trivial indulgences," I said as I backed out of the bathroom. "Maybe he's hiding outside."

"You're going to beat the bushes for a prison escapee who was convicted of murder?"

"Any better ideas?"

"Caramel swirl with pecans."

"Did I mention what a lousy assistant you are?" I went outside and looked around, although I had no intention of beating bushes or anything else. Plastic garbage bags were piled behind the shed, and broken glass littered a faint path and glittered in the stark sunlight. I waded through the weeds to look inside the dubious structure. My eyes rounded when I saw a green van.

"Over here," I yelled at Luanne.

"If that's an oversized outhouse, forget it." She was texting as she walked to the car. "I'm letting Sweetie know where we are in case your fugitive lurches out of the woods with a machete. I do not intend to be carrion. I want a proper funeral with a horse-drawn hearse and the lonely wail of bagpipes from the distant moors."

I pulled open the door, alarming a variety of indigenous species, and waited for a moment before I went inside. The license plate was daubed with mud. I squatted down and scratched it until I could see the details. It had been issued in Arizona and had expired two years ago. I wiped the dust off the back window and made sure no one was crouched inside it, thus avoiding what might have been an ungainly scramble to my car. I opened the driver's door. The only incriminating evidence I saw was an empty soda bottle. The key was not in the ignition. I climbed into the driver's seat and discovered I could barely touch the pedals. Zachery Barnard was much shorter than I; he had not been the last driver. I leaned over to open the glove compartment. There was no packet with the obligatory registration and insurance papers. I pulled out a collection of maps, a crumpled cigarette pack, and matchbooks, and found myself staring at a handgun. It was hard to imagine that its owner was a member of a well-regulated militia. I searched the back of the van and found an eclectic array of paperback books, a sleeping bag, dirty clothes, and a disposable plastic bag with basic toiletries.

I went back to my car and took out my cell phone. Luanne glanced up but resumed texting. I called Peter. He had the decency to answer. "What's going on with Caron and Inez?" I asked.

"I liberated them from the dungeon and took them back to the theater to get Caron's car. They said they had to go by the grocery store but would be home soon."

"Did they explain?" I asked.

"Caron gave me some garbled story about the play and the props. Inez said she thought she'd left her purse there. Caron said it was all Inez's fault. Inez insisted that it was all Caron's fault because of the long line to use the ladies' room at intermission. Caron replied that she was not a plumber." Peter sighed. "They swore they'd gone back for Inez's purse and gotten locked in somehow. I have no inkling what they were actually doing there. Those two could have talked their way out of Abu Ghraib."

"Less than a year until college," I said, relieved they'd concocted a convoluted explanation that did not include the Ming Thing. "I need you to run a license plate, if it's not too much trouble."

"Why?"

"It's way too complicated to go into now. I need to know who owns a particular vehicle."

"Then enlighten me. I have all the time in the world."

I didn't, but I launched into an account of my encounter with the faux Zachery Barnard, the morgue, Tuck's clippings, and my theory about Roderick James, a.k.a. Oliver Goldsmith. Luanne was giggling by the time I told Peter why I wanted him to run the license plate. I had to admit it sounded fanciful.

"Where are you now?" Peter demanded. When I told him, he harrumphed and said, "Leave immediately, right this minute. Do you understand me?"

"Yes, dear, but you have to promise to call me back about the license plate." I started the engine. "Did you hear that? I am backing up as we speak. I'm not very good at it, so I'd better concentrate on avoiding the ditch. I'll be waiting for your call, dear." I dropped the cell phone in my purse.

Luanne finally stopped giggling. "Isn't it possible the van belongs to Zachery's brother or nephew, or he stole it from a tourist? He hasn't been driving his pickup in a long while."

"Yes, it's possible." I managed to get

turned around and drove to the county highway. "It's also possible that Sarah shot Tuck, Tricia Yates is a Wiccan and was dancing naked on the rocks, and the Weasel is madly in love with me but has poor communication skills. The possibilities are limitless. Peter's mother won't notice that her wedding gift isn't on the mantel. Evan Toffle will end up on the Supreme Court. Caron will get a Ph.D. in astrophysics, and Inez will own a chain of striptease joints."

"Are some of us feeling testy?"

"Some of us are in danger of being left on the side of the road," I muttered, "and it's a long walk back to Thurber Street. We can wait at Sarah's house until Peter calls. He'll have the information about the van within a matter of minutes."

"Didn't Deputy Dawg tell you to stay away?"

"I'm going to park in the yard. That doesn't count as trespassing," I said loftily. When I turned on the unpaved road, I spotted several vehicles in front of the house. "Deputy Dawg didn't waste any time notifying the FBI, darn it, and his car is by the barn. I don't have time to chat with them."

"Nor do I," Luanne said. "Take me home so I can poke the steaks and take a shower before Sweetie arrives. There's no reason for you to hang around for Peter to call. If the van's registered to Roderick James, the FBI will be on it like ticks on a warthog. If it's stolen, what are you going to do? The man has a gun in the glove compartment. That doesn't mean it's the only weapon he has. He could be lurking in the vicinity with a rifle or a big knife."

"True. Take my phone while I drive back to town. I can do it on autopilot by now, but I refuse to answer calls while I'm driving."

Once we were headed in the right direction, Luanne asked me about the wedding present. I related the sad story of my negligence. She found it much more amusing than I did, and was still snorting when I dumped her on the sidewalk in front of her store.

"Are we having hamburgers for dinner tomorrow night?" she asked. "Shall I add a splash of cognac to the baked beans and serve them *flambé*?"

I stuck out my lower lip, imitating Caron. "You are Not Funny."

"Call me when you can."

She disappeared into the store. I stared at the cell phone, puzzled that Peter hadn't yet called. From my limited knowledge gained by reading police procedurals, I knew the information was available on an easily accessed database. I stopped at a convenience store for a small bag of chips and a cup of iced tea. It was not my ideal menu for lunch. Of course, this reminded me that I would be serving lunch tomorrow to Peter's mother, and peanut butter sandwiches would not impress her, even if I cut off the crusts.

I made it to the parking lot in front of Evan's office before I embedded my fingernails in the steering wheel. I dug a tissue out of my purse and wiped my face. My reflection in the rearview mirror was not comforting. I resembled Billy's worst nightmare. I stuffed chips in my mouth and tried not to think about anything whatsoever. My blouse was covered with crumbs when the cell phone rang.

"What?" I said, spewing crumbs on the dashboard.

"Where are you?" asked Peter in a more dulcet tone.

"In front of the Legal Aid office. What did you find out about the van?"

"It belonged to a woman named Emma Peru, who resided in Tucson. She reported it stolen three years ago. She died two years ago."

"And?" I said as I wiped frantically at the

salty dandruff.

"The shed was empty."

I dropped my hand. "How long did it take the FBI to get there? Never mind, that's a dumb question. Oliver Goldsmith was hanging around, watching us, and as soon as we left, he did, too. Did they take fingerprints in the house?"

"They will, but they were sidetracked by a report of burglars in Sarah's house. Deputy Norton reported it earlier."

"Good for him. The FBI needs to be checking out Zachery's place. Oliver was there." Not that I would have touched anything without plastic gloves.

"I thought you said he was Roderick James."

"I think he is, but I'm not sure. I'm not sure about anything." I could hear the tremor in my voice. Before Peter could offer sympathy, which would send me flying over the edge of self-control, I managed to say, "But I haven't given up." I repeated the conversation I'd had with Sarah about Tricia Yates. "I need a current photo. After I catch up with Evan, I'll go back to the church and see if they have the equivalent of a yearbook or directory."

"You don't have to do this," Peter said. "Even if Tricia was a member of SAC and was having an affair with Tuck a year ago, it doesn't mean that she had anything to do with his death. Sarah is lying about that night. She has means and motive. The shotgun was replaced inside her house."

"But she's not stupid. She told me bluntly that if she'd intended to kill him, she would have done it in a way that would not implicate her. That I believe." I glanced up as a pizza delivery car pulled into the parking lot. "Chaperone with an eagle eye, darling. I'll be home eventually."

I trailed the aroma of pepperoni to the door, where Evan was counting dollars, and went to the restroom to wash my face with unnecessary vigor. When I entered his office, I nodded politely before grabbing a slice of pizza and settling in a chair. The poor lad was a worse mess than I. He'd started the day in a coat and tie, but now he looked as though he'd dressed in the dark and spent the day in a bar. We ate pizza in weary silence.

"Here's the update," I said at last. I told him about finding the green van and then learning that it had disappeared. We agreed that we needed to ascertain if Sarah could identify Tricia, although neither of us was optimistic. Evan said he'd been unable to get an appointment with Prosecutor Wessell until the next afternoon. I said boorish things. Evan's cherubic face began to resemble a cherry. Rather than watch to see if he imploded in pulp, I announced that I was going back to the Mount Zion Methodist Church to try to find a current photo of Tricia.

I had no reason to believe it wouldn't be locked, but I wasn't ready to give up. Breaking a window may have crossed my mind, albeit briefly, so I was heartened to see an unfamiliar car parked near the front door. I went inside and stopped at the back pew, listening for something more substantial than a church mouse. Nothing stirred. I went down the aisle and toward the office. As I prepared to barge in, Grady appeared in the hall. He was wearing his standard missionary garb: short-sleeved white shirt, dark trousers, bow tie. Miss Poppoy would have nailed him from a hundred feet.

"Ms. Malloy?" he said.

"I'm so glad I caught you. I was afraid that the building was locked."

"I have a key. Why are you here?"

It was a reasonable question. The answer would have required a run-on sentence to rival James Joyce's finest effort in *Ulysses*. "Looking for Tricia," I said mildly.

"She left after the service and won't be

back until tomorrow — no, Tuesday morning. Are you still snooping into the campout nonsense? It was typical teenage behavior."

"Then why did you and Tricia make such a big deal about it? The kids were terrified when I asked them." I prefer evasion and omission to straight-out prevarication, so I chose my words deliberately. "One of the kids talked."

"Yeah, which one?"

"I will share that with the prosecutor if it comes to that. I'm sure what I heard was an exaggeration born of postpubescent angst." I hadn't been on the track team in high school, but I'd played a mean game of Blind Man's Bluff. "Shall we sit down in the office and discuss it?"

"Nothing happened," Grady said.

"Then stick to your story. You might want to start sending out your résumé as soon as possible. Your reference will not glow in the dark. These kids are minors, and their parents are staunch conservatives."

"Okay, Ms. Malloy, let's talk. I'm not going to allow you to spread some crazy rumor about me."

Before I could respond, he took my arm, pulled me into the office, and locked the door.

13

"Was that necessary?" I said to Grady as I sat down behind Tricia's desk. "Do you anticipate a posse of parents barging in to demand the lurid details?" I opened a lower drawer and feigned surprise. "Would you look at that? Tricia left us a libation. I don't know about you, but I've had a long day. There's only one cup. Why don't you look in the kitchen for another one?" I took out the half-empty bourbon bottle and poured myself a wee shot, then sat back and smiled at him. I wasn't apprehensive. Even the mildest-mannered bookseller can take down a choir director in a bow tie.

Grady leaned against the door. "There's no one else in the building, and there won't be a service tonight because of the holiday, but it's a habit. Tricia always ordered me to lock the door so we wouldn't be interrupted if she . . ." He motioned at the bottle. "Dealing with teens is stressful. I only took this

300

job to get the paycheck. I'd like to end up with a large congregation with adults who can sing. My choir came up with a rap version of 'The Old Rugged Cross.' I almost let them do it so I could practice CPR on the elders, but I'm not very proficient."

"The Red Cross offers free classes. Now why don't you tell me what really happened at the campout so I can be on my way? If you can persuade me that this had nothing to do with Tuck's death, I may not feel compelled to demand a criminal investigation." I may have emphasized the word "criminal."

"Who's Tuck?"

"The man who was killed that night. Your turn, Grady."

"I think I'll go find a cup," he said, sounding as petulant as a trophy wife who hadn't been offered breakfast at Tiffany's.

As soon as he left, I yanked open the rest of the desk drawers in search of a glossy church directory filled with names, addresses, and lovely color photographs. Tricia had a fondness for sesame sticks, raisins, and chocolate drops. She had a remarkable variety of breath mints. Other drawers contained a ledger, folders, and typical bookkeeping paraphernalia. I was eying a cabinet when Grady returned.

He poured bourbon into a coffee mug and sat down across from me. "I'm going to tell you what happened, but I will deny every word of it if it leaves this room. If you persist, I'll claim that you came back here to seduce me and went berserk when I rebuffed you."

I was impressed with his display of assertiveness, although it wasn't going to save him. "Knock it off, Grady."

"Yeah, there were some problems that night. The boys knew we were going to Flat Rock, so the little bastards went there beforehand and hid their booze and pot on the other side of the river. Tricia was so proud of herself for thinking to search their backpacks and confiscate their pathetic little stashes. I knew better." He waited for me to coo in admiration, but I declined. "She ordered everyone into their assigned tents about ten o'clock. There were giggles, whispers, an attempted foray, that kind of crap, and then they quieted down. Tricia told me she wanted to make a private call and disappeared. I saw her wade across the water upstream. I was wondering about it when I saw several of our dear campers doing the same, only not so far away. It seemed wise to see what they were up to, so I gave them a few minutes and then followed them."

"And?" I asked, my eyebrows lifted. I was far more intrigued with Tricia's behavior, but I wasn't ready to pounce on it.

"I could smell the pot by midstream. Two of the girls had taken off their shirts and spread them on the stubble. Jason, Bianca, and Annie were cramming blueberries in their mouths like feral scavengers, the juice dripping down their chins. It was disgusting. I bawled them out, told them to pick up the evidence, and warned them that I'd tell their parents if they ever said one word." He stood up to splash the last of the bourbon into his mug. "So maybe I should have, but their parents are a bunch of self-righteous despots. Besides, if they'd all been grounded, I'd have lost my job."

I'd given him limited time to rehearse. His story was credible, and the superfluous details were colorful, but he was unable to control the faint quaver in his voice. "You'll have to do better than that," I said sternly. "Tricia was there when they were forced to take an oath on the Bible."

He seemed to find his chair uncomfortable. "Maybe, but that's pretty much it. Tricia returned and heard us. She demanded to know what happened, and was appalled because it could get her fired, too. By this time, the girls were crying and the boys were slobbering. Tricia sent me back for her Bible, and then we formed a circle and passed it around. I kept waiting for the firmament to blaze while the celestial choir belted out a fierce hymn of salvation."

I bought part of his story, but I had a feeling he had glossed over his involvement. He had twitched when I mentioned a criminal investigation. "What time was this?"

"Maybe eleven or so. We herded the kids back to their tents. Tricia wanted to seal the zippers with duct tape, but I talked her out of it. When you gotta go . . ."

"True. Did you ask Tricia why she'd taken a stroll in the blueberry field?"

"Everybody was really, really upset. If I'd seen her beamed up into an alien spaceship, I wouldn't have asked her if she enjoyed the ride. She was bitching and moaning worse than the kids. A couple of them had rashes on their hands and ankles and were carrying on like they had that flesh-eating bacteria. I was calculating whether I could pay the rent with a minimum-wage job."

"And nobody heard a loud noise from across the field?"

"Did I just say that everybody was really, really upset? An explosion might have caught my attention, but we're talking nuclear. I may have heard a car backfire shortly after we got back. I was more worried about surviving on discarded hamburgers and cold fries from a fast food waste bin."

"How well do you know Tricia?" I asked. "I gather the two of you hang out in here. Has she ever talked about her past?"

Grady put down the mug. "You wanted to know what happened at the campout, and I told you. This has nothing to do with Tricia. I don't know anything about her past beyond the basics. She doesn't have a college degree, and she never got married. She hates it here, but she can't move to a city until she can afford it. We are not friends; we are two survivors on a deserted island, forced to ferment the coconut milk to keep ourselves sane." He wobbled to his feet and did his best to point his finger at me. I did not need to duck. "You just tell Bianca to keep her mouth shut and we'll be okay. Got that, Ms. Malloy?"

He stomped out of the room, huffing and puffing with indignation. When I heard an exterior door bang closed, I began a systematic search of the office for any paperwork concerning Tricia's employment. Methodists were methodical, I assured myself as I took files out of the cabinet. I found Grady's file, which contained a résumé (bachelor's degrees in musicology and religious studies from a private college) and an earnest letter. He'd been born and raised in Indiana and had volunteered every free hour to his beloved hometown church. He currently lived in a rental house on a side street near the campus.

Tricia's file was no more enlightening. From Ohio, community college, bookkeeping jobs in small companies, a reference letter from her last position at a nonprofit declaring her to be honest and proficient. The photocopy of her driver's license was blurry. I copied down her address at a notorious apartment complex across from the Farber College dorms, and her telephone number. At the last second, I removed the page with the photocopy. I did not lock the door on my way out.

Grady's car was gone. I pondered my next move as I got in my car and took out my keys. Tricia was definitely involved in whatever happened that night. She'd taken a walk, most likely to meet Tuck in the moonlight. She'd dutifully returned and found her charges in disarray and disgrace, and the consequences had drowned out any random noises.

I decided to call Evan to tell him that we had something resembling a lead. Nothing worthy of euphoria, I had to admit, but promising. When he answered, I said, "I just had a conversation with Grady, the choir director, and he told me that —"

"I can't talk," the ingrate said curtly. "I'm on my way to a motel to follow up on an anonymous tip. I'm not at my office, so don't go there." He ended the call.

I gazed at my cell phone, perplexed. He was on his way to a motel, he'd had a tip, and he didn't want to discuss it. If I'd had one of Tricia's breath mints, I would have popped it in my mouth on the off-chance he'd caught a whiff of bourbon via his cell phone. I have been known to underestimate the sophistication of twenty-first-century innovations. I used my forefinger to erase the tiny wrinkle between my eyebrows and called Peter.

"How's the party?" I asked when he answered with a grunt.

"You don't need to come home to chaperone," he said. "I have everything under control. I'll talk to you later."

"What's going on?"

After a pause, he said, "There are some people who would like to talk to you. I told them I have no idea where you are, and I don't want to know. Don't use a credit card." He, like Evan, terminated the call without a cheery good-bye.

I dropped the cell phone as if it were melting. I seemed to be the Wicked Witch, however. There were no flying monkeys in the trees or storm troopers on the roof of the church. "Some people" sounded ominous. Wessell did not qualify, nor did Deputy Norton, leaving the FBI in the forefront. Peter and Evan were afraid their phones were tapped. I snatched up the cell phone and almost hurled it out the window before I caught myself. I squeezed buttons until it blinked and went black. It did not seem prudent to remain where I was, but I'd been warned to stay away from the office and my house.

It seemed like a good time to go fishing.

Larry Lippet and the unseen but vaguely ominous Marie were not outside among the menagerie. This was encouraging, since Deputy Norton was likely to be on my trail and might have asked them to watch for me. I parked by the trash bin, briefly considered piling branches on my car, noted there weren't any handy branches, and climbed over the stile. When I arrived at Flat Rock, I saw Billy on the far bank. Instead of fishing, he was flipping over stones and poking whatever he saw with a stick.

I waved. "Any luck?"

"Not yet. I'm looking for dragon eggs."

"Mind if I join you?"

"You got to bring your own stick," he said before hunkering down to tug at a large stone.

William appeared behind him as I waded across the water, my shoes in my hand. "Claire? Is everything okay?"

Not exactly, I thought as I beamed at him. "I have a few more questions, that's all. I remembered that you and Billy were coming here to fish."

"And search for dragon eggs," Billy called as he dropped the stone and moved down the gravel bar. "When I find one, I'm going to put it in a shoe box with a lightbulb to keep it warm. After it hatches, I'm going to take it to show-and-tell. Nobody's ever brought a baby dragon to school."

"I believe that," I said as I stepped onto the gravel bar and wobbled on each foot until my shoes were where they belonged. I joined Will. "I finally found out what happened the night the church choir was here. The night Tuck was killed."

William scratched his head. "I didn't know anything happened. I mean, besides the . . ."

He gestured at a fallen tree trunk. "Sit down and tell me. Is this going to help Sarah? I was convinced that she shot Tuck, but you've got me wondering. It seemed so straightforward. Now I don't know what to think."

Billy put his fists on his hips. "You said you were gonna help me, lady."

"I am, after you help me," I said. "What's more, I can appoint you an honorary detective for the Farberville Police Department. You'll get a citation."

"I'd rather have a dragon."

So would I, especially one that could be trained to attack on my command. "A citation is pretty cool. No one at your school will have one. Can you take a break and tell me again what you saw that night? You weren't lying about seeing what you believed were zombies. I confirmed this with some of them."

William frowned at me. "I wish you wouldn't encourage this. His imagination runs wild as it is. His mother and Junie are worried about him."

"When my daughter was four, she decided she lived on a planet called Frittata. She demanded that we take all of the furniture out of her room, and wore nothing but pink thermal pajamas and red rubber boots for a month. She got bored and moved on. So will Billy."

Said child threw his stick in the water and came across the gravel bar. "You talked to zombies? Cool!"

I leaned forward. "They were pretending to be zombies to fool everybody. You said you saw flashlights. Do you recall how many?"

I could tell he was not pleased. "You mean the zombies were pretending to be zombies. They didn't fool me. They had two or three flashlights. What's more, they were yelling and hitting at each other. That's how I knew they were for real zombies, not pretend zombies."

William laughed. "Good luck with this."

Billy was not going to make a good witness, I warned myself with a sigh. "The bang woke you up, right? You went to the window and saw one of them behind the barn."

"Stealing vegetables," Billy said adamantly. "Like carrots and squash." He gave me a disgusted look and stalked back to the gravel bar to continue his search.

The timeline was getting increasingly muddled. Grady had told me that the confrontation with the wayward teenagers had taken place shortly after ten, which meant the Bible had gone from hand to hand no later than eleven. I looked at William. "Is there any way you could have been wrong about when you heard the shotgun? Maybe you forgot to set back your clocks for daylight savings time?"

"In August?" he said. "We would have noticed if we were off for six months."

"What time did you see lights at the house?"

He sat down next to me. "This was over a year ago, you know. Before the movie came on at ten o'clock. I'd gone outside to have a cigarette. Junie goes to bed before nine every night and gets up at dawn. So do I, but I had a lot on my mind back then. A big company had offered a contract for my entire blueberry crop, but there were a lot of clauses written in legal jargon. Licensing, certification, government inspections, quantity and control, immigrant workers, and a bunch of crap. It took my lawyer three months to okay it."

"Legalese can be daunting," I said with engaging sympathy. "Tuck came home before ten, but he was not in the house when Sarah arrived. Is there any chance you went outside for another cigarette?"

William tugged on his chin as he gazed at the far bank. "Sorry, but no. I settled down

312

on the sofa with a beer and a piece of Junie's peach cobbler. At one point I thought I heard Billy's voice, so I went upstairs to check on him. He was sound asleep. His windows look out on the backyard and the field."

"You heard a voice?"

"What I most likely heard was an owl going after some critter, maybe a possum or a coon. Nature's noisy, Claire."

Presuming nature included teenagers. "Do you remember what time?" I asked. He shook his head. "I learned earlier this afternoon that Tricia Yates abandoned her post as chaperone at Flat Rock and came over to this side of the river. I believe she was meeting Tuck."

"That sly dog," William murmured. "I don't really know Tricia, but she's pleasant. It's damn hard to imagine Tuck in . . . an intimate relationship with anyone. Did Sarah know?"

"If she did, she's not admitting it. From what I was told, Tricia crossed the river shortly after ten. You might have heard her voice." I stopped as I considered a screeching inconsistency in Grady's story. In his version, the teenagers had snuck away a few minutes later, and he had followed them. Yet by the time he confronted them, they were stoned, drunk, and semiclad. Although I do not indulge in the first two frivolities, and in the last only in my bedroom, I doubted they could have achieved all of this in a manner of minutes. Furthermore, they were all there when Tricia appeared. Had Grady lectured them for the better part of an hour?

"Who told you this?" William asked.

"That doesn't matter. It does mean that Billy was telling the truth, with a minor embellishment. He did see figures in this area, lurching about, some with flashlights. It gives credence to his story about seeing someone by your barn, too."

"I didn't see anyone. I'd like to think I would have noticed zombies, or even mere mortals, trespassing on my property. The sound of the shotgun blast alarmed me, as well as the livestock."

"Did you go into your barn?"

"Yes," he said, sounding a bit surly, "but only for a minute. The lights were off at Sarah and Tuck's house. That kind of surprised me. I didn't see or hear anything going on over here."

"Billy could from the second story." I looked at the neophyte archaeologist, who had taken a break to throw rocks at insolent squirrels in the trees. "The deputy who interviewed everybody said that Billy claimed to have evidence. Do you have any idea about that?"

"A chunk of rotting flesh? An eyeball? The kid has enough imagination to write scripts for action comic books or swindle millions of dollars. He could even grow up to be a politician. Today he's after dragon eggs. Last week he was digging a bunker in anticipation of a Martian invasion; the week before, he was building a raft to float from here to New Orleans. Any evidence he claimed to have found was in his mind."

"Did the sheriff's men search the area?" I asked.

"For what? They had a solid case against Sarah, based on her own admission that she was home at eleven. They had witnesses who said that Sarah was angry at Tuck and had threatened to kill him. She'd been drinking. She lied about the nonexistent fishing trip."

"No, he lied about it." I paused to think. "He thought she was having an affair and intended to catch her in the act."

"Then why was he there before ten o'clock, with the lights on? Wouldn't he have waited until she and this supposed lover were inside the house?"

A reasonable question. Rather than brood,

I waved at Billy. "Can I ask you something else?"

He came grudgingly, stopping several times to hurl rocks in the water. "Ask me what?" he demanded.

"You told the deputy that you had evidence from that night. What was it?"

"It wasn't from that night. Grandma made me go back to bed. I'm getting hungry, Gramps."

I realize I'd betrayed him by my failure to support his zombie theory. Bribery did not seem appropriate in front of his grandfather. Squeezing an answer out of him was even less so. My maternal stare would be met with cynicism, if not derision. I waited until he glanced at me. "What you found may be very important, Billy. It may solve a complicated case and help Miss Sarah. Please tell me what you found."

"A red bandana," he said. "It was in the ditch by the driveway, all stinky and dirty. I knew it was an important clue, but that old deputy snorted when he wrote it down. The other deputy laughed when I told him it belonged to one of the zombies. They wear bandanas so they can tell each other apart."

I nodded. "So I've been told. Do you have it?"

"I wear it when I'm a cowboy. Today I'm

a dinosaur hunter."

"Is there a chance I might borrow it?" I said, trying to remain calm. It was the first tangible clue, unless it was merely a dirty bandana that had been in a ditch for weeks or months. The latter was more probable.

"Will you give it back?"

"Wouldn't you rather have a new one? I know you're leaving for home tomorrow, but I should have time to bring one out to you. It's red, right?"

"I already said that," Billy retorted. "Yeah, you can take it. Are you gonna be a cowboy?"

William was chuckling. "I can hardly wait to see you in a cowboy hat and boots, Claire. Which color cowboy hat will you be wearing?"

"White, of course," I said. It would have been lovely to sit on the riverbank and mindlessly throw rocks into the water, but the clock loomed overhead. "I need to track down Tricia Yates and get her version of what happened here." I smiled at Billy. "She may have seen the zombies, too." I took off my shoes and braced myself for water, mud, and stones. "If you hear a dog barking, feel free to come to my rescue. If not, I'll be at your house in the morning."

"I don't have my gun," Billy said sadly.

I made my way back to the other side, put on my shoes, and waved at the two before heading for the stile. With a thick stick, I might add. I arrived at my car without encountering any hounds from hell, snakes, or carnivorous animals. I'd started to drive toward County 102 when I remembered that I had incurred the wrath (or at least the interest) of the FBI. Not only would they know the make, model, and license plate of my car, they might have requested assistance from the Farberville Police Department. I wondered how that had played out. Much merriment would have ensued as the dispatcher put out a BOLO for the wife of the deputy chief of police.

It seemed prudent to assess the situation while outside the city limits. I lacked the nerve to take sanctuary in Sarah's house, which was apt to be under surveillance by sheriff's deputies or federal agents. I'd heard the door of the Mount Zion Methodist Church lock when I'd exited. Zachery Barnard's house lacked amenities. I finally decided to pay a visit to Miss Poppoy. If Geronimo's vehicle was there, I would continue to the next convenience store to avail myself of the facilities and use the pay phone.

I resisted the impulse to drive by Zach-

318

ery's shack. The primary reason the FBI wanted to talk to me had to be that they had identified Roderick James's fingerprints on the green van. I did not want to drive into their clutches. I continued past the road and turned into Miss Poppoy's driveway. There was only one car parked in front of her house. Feeling better about my chances of remaining on the lam, I went to the porch and knocked on the door.

Miss Poppoy was wearing a housedress and was wig-free. "I know you," she said as she gestured for me to come inside. "You're not a missionary. Would you like some tea and cookies?"

"I'd love some," I admitted, "and if it's not a problem, I need to use your phone."

She gave me a beady look. "Long distance?"

"No, Farberville. I need to speak to my husband."

"I reckon that's okay. You can freshen up down the hall, second door on the right. I'll put on the kettle."

Once in the bathroom, I sat down on the edge of the bathtub and forced my neck and shoulder muscles to relax. I was unable to convince my brain to stop flitting like a hummingbird from one bit of information to the next. After a few minutes, I washed my face and hands, ran my fingers through my untidy hair, and plastered on a socially acceptable smile.

As I came into the hall, I heard Miss Poppoy's voice. "These blasted missionaries think they have the right to interrupt me in the middle of *Top Chef*. They bang on the door like Mongolians."

I faltered, but only for seconds, and went into the living room. It was uninhabited, so I headed to the kitchen. Miss Poppoy was in front of the stove, still talking blithely about the intrusion of missionaries, but I had no idea what she was saying.

Seated at a small table was a familiar figure.

14

I may have staggered backward as I gaped in an unbecoming fashion. I knew he couldn't be Zachery Barnard, since he was tucked in a drawer in the morgue. Oliver Goldsmith was out; he'd died in the latter part of the eighteenth century. The man at the table bore a keen resemblance to the sketch from the trial, if one added forty years, wrinkles, and gray hair. The aggressive chin and asymmetrical nose had not been softened by age.

"You look pale," Miss Poppoy chirped. "Why don't you sit down? Would you prefer something stronger than tea?"

I remained in the doorway, uncertain how he would react. He wore an unbuttoned flannel shirt with chopped sleeves over a T-shirt and jeans; if he had a gun, it wasn't visible. "Mr. James, I presume?" I said.

"Call me Rod," he said genially. "You know, Poppy, I do feel a need for something

321

stronger. Can you spare a beer?"

"Of course, dearie." She put her hand on his shoulder in an unsettlingly intimate way. "Would you like another bologna and cheese sandwich?"

I was so bewildered that I expected to see the Cheshire Cat peering down from atop the refrigerator. "What are you doing here?"

He put his hand over Miss Poppoy's and squeezed it. "You're too kind. Just a beer." He gave me a level look. "After you and your friend left Zach's place, I decided it might not be wise to drive my van. I parked it in the pond. I was going to hitchhike out of state, but this delightful woman stopped and picked me up. My angel of mercy."

Miss Poppoy blushed. "I felt so sorry for him, on foot and broke, so I offered to fix him lunch before he resumed his journey. We've been chatting ever since. Roddy majored in British literature in college. I have a passion for Jane Austen, the Brontë gals, and that rascal Mr. Dickens. We've been having a lovely time." She giggled as she slid her hand down his chest. "I'm going to teach him to play mahjongg this evening."

I felt a stab of sympathy for him, then reminded myself that he had killed an undercover agent at the demonstration and subsequently escaped from Folsom Prison. I suspected his history would not daunt Miss Poppoy. I sucked in a breath and sat down at the table. "I reported the location of the van. The FBI is looking for me, which implies they found your fingerprints and ran them through the system."

"I expected no less," Roderick said. "You claimed to be a friend of Sarah's. Is that true?"

I saw no reason to explain why I was attempting to help her. "Her trial starts Tuesday morning. The prosecutor has a strong case. Her lawyer, on the other hand, is inexperienced and floundering like a beached fish. Sarah has been lying to both of us." I stopped to let him consider what I'd said, then continued. "She insists that she was home and fast asleep when Tuck was killed with a shotgun. The sound woke the neighbors, and was heard by campers on the far side of the field. Nobody's buying her story."

Miss Poppoy joined us at the table. "I feel sorry for the woman. Tuck was a sumbitch from start to finish. He growled at me at the farmers' market when I commented on his bruised tomatoes. It was all I could do not to slap him upside the head."

"What if she has an alibi?" Roderick asked me.

"She said she came straight home from her book club meeting and went to bed," I said, meeting his gaze. "That's her story. Does she have an alibi?"

"I do hope so," said Miss Poppoy. "She brought me chicken soup and homemade bread when I had bronchitis. Whole wheat, and fresh from the oven. No one that kindhearted would kill somebody, even a nasty piece of work like her husband. I know a bruised tomato when I see one."

Roderick got up and went to the refrigerator. He returned with a beer, but set it down unopened. "She wasn't home at midnight."

Miss Poppoy deftly opened his beer and handed it to him. "Sarah's not a liar. If she says she was home, she was home. I am very sensitive about people. I knew the minute I met her that she was as honest as the day is long."

"Do you have any scotch?" I asked our hostess, who was beginning to remind me of Billy. This was not a compliment. After she'd disappeared into the living room, I turned to him. "Where was she? Silly question. She was with you, wasn't she? She refused to say so because the authorities are still looking for you after all these years. If you were to step forward, you'd be sent back to Folsom to finish your sentence plus whatever is added for escaping."

"Yeah," he murmured.

"How did you find her?"

"There's a network. I made inquiries, and after years of searching, someone in the underground community traced Tuck via Facebook. He was stupid enough to drop a few clues about his real identity. Maybe he thought the feds had lost interest. That's the problem with amateurs — they underestimate the power of the opposition. The government has been scanning mail, planting bugs, and eavesdropping on phone calls for decades. Internet security's a joke. Only recently has this been made public and become a scandal. Hell, my phone was tapped in 1967, and a nondescript white car was always parked across the street. I used to take the agents tea on cold mornings and tell them my plans for the day. I offered to find out if they could audit my classes, but they declined. Guess they weren't into liberal arts."

Miss Poppoy returned with bottles of scotch, gin, and vermouth. "I do believe I'll have a martini. What about you, Roddy?"

He smiled at her. "I'd better stick to beer. Claire may be planning to call the FBI. I'll need a clear head if I have to flee out the back door."

She gasped. "She most certainly will not! I will not allow a guest in my home to be dragged away in handcuffs."

I held up my palms. "I'm not going to call anyone except my husband. The FBI is after me, too." I waited to see if Miss Poppoy realized that she was entertaining fugitives in her kitchen. In her situation, I might have been uneasy, or perhaps significantly alarmed. As I fled out the back door.

"Well, then," she said, "I'll bake some cookies." She began opening cabinets and yanking out various ingredients. "I'm afraid I don't have any chocolate chips. I fed them to Larry Lippet's nasty dog, but he survived. You simply cannot believe everything you read on the Internet. I hope you have a fondness for gingersnaps."

I must admit I was still dazed by Roderick's presence, as well as a trifle pleased about my deductive prowess. "When did you come to Farberville?" I asked him quietly.

"Two years ago. After I . . . departed an untenable locale, I was unable to acquire a fake identity, so I had to take crappy jobs. I worked alongside undocumented migrant workers picking everything from artichokes to zucchinis. I transported drugs from Mexico and Colombia. I picked up a few dollars selling blood. Most of the time, I stayed in the South because it's easier to be homeless when you don't have to deal with freezing temperatures and sleet."

"Did you know that Sarah and Tuck were together?"

"No," he said, "but it was the only lead I had. I wouldn't have wasted fifteen seconds worrying about Tuck. He was a pain in the ass when I met him in '69. He was convinced that if he spent one night in the local jail, he'd be beaten and raped."

"Roddy," Miss Poppoy trilled, "have you seen the molasses?"

He winced but stood up, twinkling as if she were his beloved grandmother. "Let me help you look, Poppy."

While the two of them searched through cabinets, I poured scotch into a jelly glass and took a sip. I had no doubt that Peter would be less than pleased that I was sitting across the table from a convicted murderer, and he would feel compelled to go into great detail about my imprudent, reckless, irresponsible behavior. It was best, I told myself, not to mention Roderick's whereabouts when I called home. I planned to do so only when I was prepared to leave Miss

Poppoy's house, since the FBI could trace the call in less time than it takes to flush a toilet. Being a fugitive was a major annoyance. Sarah, Tuck, and Roderick would agree, although they'd had forty years to practice. I was a novice.

Roderick found a bottle of molasses on a top shelf. Miss Poppoy squealed in admiration and returned to her mixing bowl.

"Shall I assume you felt more kindly toward Sarah back then?" I asked him as he sat down.

"We had a relationship. Nobody talked about marriage. Societal shackles, the degradation of women, the imposition of artificial constraints on sexual freedom, and so on. We had dreams of an idyllic farmhouse, children allowed to express themselves freely, and a macrobiotic diet from our organic garden." His fist hit the table hard enough to rattle the bottles. Miss Poppoy yelped. I held back an uncouth response despite a tingle of panic. "Damn that war!" he went on in a bitter voice. "Tricky Dick sent more than half a million young men to Vietnam to be killed in a swampy jungle. My cousin came home with one leg and a fatal addiction to heroin. One of my best friends from high school died at Danang;

another one survived but committed suicide in '68."

"How did you avoid it?"

"Luck of the lottery. I was ready to go to Canada if I had to. Tuck, I seem to recall, starved himself to get a 4-F. To celebrate, he ate a bucket of fried chicken, and then spent the next forty-eight hours in the can."

"Let's go back to Sarah," I said hastily. "You tracked her here two years ago and rekindled the relationship, right?"

Miss Poppoy closed the oven door and sat down with us. "I do enjoy a good love story. Don't think for an instant that I read those books with bare-chested swashbucklers and raven-haired damsels with excessive cleavage. The damsels, not the swashbucklers. Well, mostly."

Roderick bit his lip for a moment. "I hope I don't disappoint you, Poppy. I had the name of the town, and I knew Tuck had an organic blueberry farm. I asked around, found out where they lived, and watched the house. When Sarah drove off by herself, I followed her to the diner where she worked. It took me a week to get up my courage —"

"You swashbuckler!" shrieked Miss Poppoy, her eyelashes fluttering. "Do you have a scar?"

"Not one that I could show to a lady," he said, glancing at me as if I could constrain her. In his dreams. "When I finally waited for her in the diner's parking lot, I was as nervous as a freshman at his first mixer. My hands were sweaty, and my mouth was so dry I could barely speak. She was stunned. I had to help her to her car. We had a long talk about the last forty years — her life with Tuck, mine as a convict and a vagrant. What happened after that is private."

"You had sex in the backseat?" Miss Poppoy said. She held up her hand until Roderick gave her an unenthusiastic high five. "How absolutely romantic! The neon lights from the diner, customers coming and going, car doors slamming, the danger of being caught! You must join me in a martini, Roddy. We shall toast your daring!" She went to the refrigerator and peered inside it. "Blast it, Geronimo finished off the olives. We'll have to make do with radishes. Now what did I do with the martini glasses?"

I would have handed over all my cash for a roll of duct tape. "How did you end up at Zachery Barnard's house?" I asked him.

"I couldn't afford the Hilton." He accepted a jelly glass from Miss Poppoy, eyed the radish with distaste, and took a cautious sip. "I ran into him at a bar on Thurber Street. Well, on the sidewalk, since he'd been thrown out. He told me I could park the van in his shed for a small fee. After some negotiations, I followed him home and pitched a tent in the woods. I slept in the van when it was cold. I found enough work to buy him a bottle of rotgut whiskey every week and keep both of us in bread and beans. He had a secret fishing hole that was good for catfish and crappie. I shot a squirrel or a rabbit every once in a while."

"Were you there when he drowned?" I did my best to sound curious rather than accusatory.

"You don't think I . . . ?"

Miss Poppoy's eyes widened. "Did you push poor Zachery in the pond? That was very bad of you, Roddy. I cannot condone that sort of behavior. You must leave at once!"

"Of course not, Poppy," he said soothingly, putting his hand on hers. "I was clearing brush for some guy I met at the co-op. He lives on the other side of the county. After Claire's appearance at Zach's place, it seemed like a good idea to split for a couple of days. When I got back last night, I thought he'd gone to Thurber Street and gotten himself arrested for drunk and disorderly. I didn't know what happened to him until you told me."

I did not inquire how he thought Zachery had gone anywhere without a means of transportation. He could explain his reasoning to Deputy Norton or the FBI. "Are you willing to come forward to give Sarah an alibi?"

He gazed at the floor while he considered his answer. His voice was barely audible as he said, "If it comes down to it, I will. The consequences don't much appeal, though. She didn't kill Tuck, and neither did I. That means someone else did. Do you have any leads?"

Miss Poppoy had remained silent for all of one minute, which seemed to be her limit. "We must uncover the identity of the murderer so that Sarah and Roddy can fulfill their dreams." She eyed him critically. "You two are too old to have children. Perhaps you can have grandchildren instead. You can name them Vera, Chuck, and Dave."

"When I'm sixty-four," Roderick said, grinning at her.

We all cringed when the telephone rang. Miss Poppoy put down her glass and waggled a finger at us. "No talking until I get back. I don't want to miss a single word.

This is so much more stimulating than those novels I never read." She scurried into the living room.

"I do have a lead," I admitted, "but it's based on a dubious assumption. You might be able to help me, Roderick."

"I don't know how, but I'll do what I can to help Sarah. She was miserable with Tuck. The last few years were especially awful. He prowled around the house like a manic cat, convinced the mice were plotting against him. He made her eat before he did in case she'd poisoned the food. She and I talked about splitting, but she was afraid he might kill himself — or come after us."

"Naughty, naughty," Miss Poppoy said as she came back into the kitchen. "You were supposed to wait for me. That was Geronimo. He was coming to visit when he saw two cars from the sheriff's department parked alongside the highway less than a quarter of a mile from here. Because of a wee problem with them in the past, some nonsense about his mother, ferrets, and a meth lab, he drove past the driveway and saw another car. Is that what's called a stakeout?"

"Geronimo?" said Roderick, clearly bewildered.

"He blames it on the ferrets."

I put my elbows on the table and cradled my face. "Did anyone drive by while you were picking up Roderick?" I asked Miss Poppoy.

"Quite a few people, come to think of it. Larry and Marie honked and waved. They go to the movies on Sunday afternoon, come hell or high water. Oh, and a state trooper with sunglasses. He stared, but he didn't wave. That tacky woman who lives by the turnoff to Pinkie Sheer Road was in her front yard, jabbering on her cell phone. When she saw us, her cheeks expanded like a puffer fish."

I sighed. "Yes, it's a stakeout. The deputies must be waiting for the FBI agents before they descend on us. I estimate no more than five or ten minutes. Miss Poppoy, you need to get in your car right now and leave. If they stop you, tell them that I dropped by with a friend and we discussed the weather. Please don't mention any references to Sarah or Tuck."

She bristled. "I will not be forced out of my home by a bunch of deputies. Shall we have another round of martinis?"

"I don't want you to get hurt," Roderick said. "As long as you stick to Claire's story, you won't be accused of harboring fugitives."

"Harboring fugitives? I am harboring my dear friends."

I lifted my head. "When the deputies arrive, they'll be anticipating trouble. Their guns will be drawn, and they'll be nervous. You need to leave — now. Otherwise, we'll have to tie you to a chair and put tape over your mouth, just like those intruders did last year."

"You'll do no such thing! If both of you insist on leaving, you can hide in my backseat." She clapped her hands and laughed. "I know where we'll go. There's a wonderful bar and grill in Maggody, about thirty miles from here. We can have dinner there, and dance afterwards. You do like to dance, don't you, Roddy? I've been told there's a motel out back with beds that vibrate." Her eyebrows, drawn with an unsteady hand, wiggled.

"The deputies will search your car," I said. "You need to go have dinner in Maggody on your own. Roderick and I will wait here."

"I have cookies in the oven."

"We'll share them with the deputies and the feds," I said. I did not bring up the probability of tear gas canisters and assault weapons. Miss Poppoy might be testy when she returned to find shattered windows, broken doors, and bullet holes, along with bloodstains on the carpet. "I need to call my husband," I said in a small voice, very close to tears. Or hysterics, as I envisioned Caron's grief and Peter's devastation.

She gave me a dishcloth and waited while I dabbed my eyes. "You don't have time. There's a riding lawn mower behind the garage. Geronimo bought it because he and I like to cruise the back roads on moonlit nights. It doesn't go fast, but it can go down narrow, rocky paths. If you keep going in a westerly direction, you should be safe."

Before I could come up with a response, Roderick gripped my wrist. "Let's go, Claire. Poppy, go in the living room and watch for figures moving toward the house. When they get within a hundred feet, go out on the porch with your hands up. Tell them — I don't know what, but you'll come up with something. Offer them cookies. Hell, make them martinis with radishes. Does the riding mower have a key?"

"It's in the ignition," she said. "Are they allowed to drink on duty? I don't want to waste perfectly good gin if they aren't going to drink it."

Roderick yanked me to my feet, although it took little effort on his part. I went around the table to hug Miss Poppoy and then allowed Roderick to escort me out the back door.

In *The Great Escape*, one of my favorite movies, Steve McQueen masterminds the unexcused departure of more than seventy POWs from a high-security stalag in Germany via a tunnel. The men, dressed in civilian attire, disperse in different directions. Most of them are recaptured and executed. Captain Hilts, our star, takes down a Nazi on a motorcycle, changes into his uniform, and roars across a meadow in a futile attempt to jump a barbed-wire fence into Switzerland. I may have gotten a few details wrong, but it's been a long time since I'd seen it.

Roderick and I chugged across a meadow at no more than five miles per hour. He drove, while I perched on the back rim of the seat, my arms wrapped around him. My derriere protested each and every bump, but riding mowers are not designed for two. The noise seemed louder than one of General Sherman's tanks. I wished that the sun would sink, allowing us sheltering darkness, but I had little control over the matter. When we reached the edge of the woods, he veered sharply until he saw a path between the pine trees.

The mower lurched as we went down a steep incline. Miss Poppoy had said the path was narrow and rocky. I would have described it as two feet wide and strewn with embedded boulders — and perilous. I'd never before wondered if riding mowers had brakes as we bounced along, branches slapping at us, but it seemed to be a relevant issue. Roderick used his feet to keep us upright. I helped by yapping each time the mower threatened to topple. When we arrived at a riverbank, I whacked him on the shoulder and shouted, "Stop!"

Obligingly, he did. When he cut off the engine, the silence was almost as confounding as the noise had been. I climbed off and tried not to grimace as I took a step. "I need a minute."

"Who the hell is Geronimo?"

"This is hardly the time to analyze Miss Poppoy's social life," I said grumpily. I discreetly massaged my gluteus maximus while I studied our locale. "Or her idea of a romantic ride under the stars."

"More of a suicide pact," he said. "Too bad this Geronimo didn't go for an ATV. He must be a masochistic dude."

"In more ways than I care to imagine. It looks as though we can follow the river until we find a place to cross it."

"And then?"

I picked up a pinecone and threw it at him. It was not a playful gesture. "How should I know? You're the one who escaped from prison by slithering through a drain-pipe. I'm a bookseller, a mother, and the wife of the deputy chief of police. My daughter and her friend were arrested for trespassing this morning. My mother-in-law is arriving tomorrow. The Ming Thing is in the local landfill." I picked up another pinecone. "Furthermore, if we're captured, I'll be charged with aiding and abetting or some silly thing, and end up in court facing Prosecuting Attorney Wessell, who is a despicable weasel! How dare you ask me what to do?" I gripped the pinecone so fiercely that it crumbled in my hand.

He caught my arm before I could hurl the bits at him. "The path is flatter now. Let's put a few more miles between the cops and us before we figure out our next move."

"Take off your shirt."

"Here? This is not a good idea, Claire."

I held out my hand. "Your shirt, please."

He gave me an odd look as he complied. I folded it into a long rectangle and felt its thickness, saddened that he hadn't been wearing a sweater or jacket. "This will have to do," I said as I glanced up. He was fumbling with the zipper on his jeans. "What on earth are you doing? Is this really the time to go for a swim? You're the one who suggested that we plunge further into the wilderness. If the feds figure out where we've gone, they'll come after us with ATVs and bloodhounds." I abruptly realized what he was thinking. "This is going to serve as a cushion for the rim of the seat, not as a pillow. Sheese, Roderick!"

"Yeah, right," he said, his face as red as I suspected mine was. "Westward ho, ho, ho . . ."

After he sat down on the riding mower, I climbed on behind him and tucked the cushion where it would do the most good. The path was level and less rocky, so we were able to chug along at a decent speed. There were still occasional jolts and joggles, but I was no longer terrified that the mower would flip over and crush us. Thorny vines left oozing scratches on my legs and ankles. Unmindful insects flew into my hair. Roderick turned his head and spoke, but I couldn't hear him over the raucous engine. I would have preferred a Cadillac, a Jeep, or a carriage. There were no dealerships in the area.

We failed to encounter dragons in the ensuing half hour. The river was on our left, woods on our right. I was about to ask for a break when we came to a barbed-wire fence. Roderick turned off the engine, and once again silence engulfed us. Beyond the fence was a pasture with a scattering of cows. Those nearby raised their heads to regard us somberly. None of them looked mad.

I eased off the seat. My first step was a stumble, but I kept my balance. I was more concerned about my composure, which was less substantial than a cobweb. "What now?" I said as I stared at the cows. "If Steve McQueen couldn't jump a fence on a motorcycle, our chance of success on a riding lawn mower is slight."

"Nonexistent," Roderick responded distractedly. "I didn't see any place we could get across the river on this contraption. We have less than three hours of daylight. It's gonna get hairy after that."

"Unless these are feral cows, there has to be a farm around here. I'm afraid to use my cell, but I might be able to persuade the farmer to let me use his." I had no doubt that my charming demeanor would overcome anyone's reservations about admitting a stranger inside his house. The problem was whom to call. Not Peter or Evan. I contemplated calling the local taxicab company, but I'd have to use my credit card to pay the fare. Once my card was swiped, the information would be in the system and the feds would be chortling at my naiveté. Luanne was my best hope. I did not look forward to the conversation. "Any better ideas?" I asked the cows.

Roderick snorted. "Our faces may already be on the local channels. I'll be described as armed and dangerous. We may find ourselves on the porch, staring at the barrel of a gun."

"So stay out of sight," I said with a modicum of irritation. "I'm only wanted for questioning — or I was, anyway. My rap sheet is growing an inch every hour I spend with you. For all I know, I've been accused of being your accomplice when you escaped from Folsom."

"When you were a teenager? Don't get carried away, Claire. When we're in the vicinity of the house, I'll disappear. I've had plenty of practice."

"Leave the key in the ignition," I said as I gingerly eased through the strands of barbed wire. I had accumulated more than enough scratches without adding one across my sore derriere. "Geronimo will know where to find it."

"Who the hell is Geronimo?" Roderick asked again as he followed me. "I keep picturing a seven-foot-tall guy in war paint."

I told him what Miss Poppoy had said as we followed the fence. The cows shifted away from us. I am not a student of bovine psychology, nor do I aspire to be one, but I assumed we made them nervous. I dearly hoped it was a celibate herd, lacking an ill-tempered bull. I was not in the mood for a taurine confrontation.

The farmhouse was rustic but tidy. I was encouraged by the satellite dish on the roof. Anyone with access to six hundred channels surely had a telephone. "Find a place to hide near the road," I told Roderick.

He gave me a snarky salute and crawled through the fence. I went through a gate and walked around the house to the porch. I brushed leaves and twigs out of my hair, pasted on a civilized smile, and pushed the doorbell.

"Coming!" called a raspy voice from within. I maintained the smile when a stout, dark-haired woman opened the door. She was holding a spatula rather than a gun. "Hey," she said, "are you here for the baby shower? I'm Abbie Benton, Olivia's sister-in-law. Come on in and make yourself comfortable. As soon as I finish plating the lemon bars, I'll get you a cup of coffee. Your name is . . . ?"

"Claire," I said. "You cannot believe how much I would prefer to be here for the baby shower, but I'm not. Please give Olivia my best wishes for a healthy baby. I'm in a spot of trouble. I need to make a call, but my cell is at the bottom of the river."

She studied me. "You look like you've been dragged through the woods by your hair. I won't ask what happened to you because it's none of my business, but if there's a man involved, you need to dump him. You're welcome to use my phone, long as you're not calling overseas."

"Farberville. Thank you so much, Abbie."

She ushered me into a living room decorated with ceramic figurines, posters of puppies and kittens, multicolored throw pillows, and a TV only slightly smaller than the mural of the Last Supper. "Phone's in the kitchen," she said. "How about a glass of iced tea?"

"That would be lovely." I sat down on a stool and tried to remember Luanne's number. It was on speed dial on both my landline and my cell; I didn't remember when I had last dialed it. Abbie gave me a pitying look as she set a glass of iced tea within reach. I was still frowning when she slid over a plate with a lemon bar.

"You poor thing," she said.

I couldn't quibble with her assessment. No one could feel sorrier for me than I did. I was scratched, sore, hungry, in the company of a killer, unable to go home to my husband, and wanted by the FBI. I willed myself not to fling my arms around Abbie's neck and bawl, and concentrated on Luanne's elusive telephone number. It occurred to me that it might be on the cell phone that Peter had grudgingly given me. Regrettably, I'd declared that said phone was at the bottom of the river, so pulling it out of my purse (yes, I'd clung to my purse despite everything) would not be politic.

I politely inquired if I might freshen up, and was given directions to the bathroom. I did not have time to sit on the edge of the bathtub as I'd done at Miss Poppoy's house. I found the phone, hit the appropriate button to access contacts, and softly crowed when I found Luanne's name and number. I repeated the number until I'd etched it into my mind. I kept muttering it while I washed my face, carefully avoiding the mirror above the sink.

"Thank you," I said as I came into the kitchen. Abbie nodded as she poured a bottle of fruit juice into a punch bowl. I dialed Luanne's number, mindful that what I said would be overheard, and tried to think how best to present my dilemma tactfully.

"Hey," I said when she answered. "I need a bit of help."

"Now what?" Luanne said. "Sweetie's going to be here in an hour. I need to bathe and decide what to wear. I'm torn between the black negligee and the red teddy."

"That man you and I were looking for earlier today . . . I found him, but it did not go well. Can you pick me up?"

"Where's your car?"

I glanced at Abbie, who pretended she wasn't listening. "Unavailable. I really need you to pick me up, Luanne. I wouldn't ask if it weren't important."

"Are you in trouble?"

"More than you can begin to imagine. Please?"

"All right," she said, "but I may be wearing the negligee. Where are you?"

I asked Abbie for her address and directions to her house, then said to Luanne, "I'm at 1450 North Anger Road. 'Anger' rhymes with 'danger.' Take the first left after the E-Z convenience store and go about three miles. I'll be out by the road."

"Alone?"

"No, I'm fine," I said, smiling at Abbie. "A very kind woman took me in and gave me iced tea and a lemon bar. I'll see you shortly." I hung up before I had to field more questions. "My friend should be here in fifteen or twenty minutes. I see you're busy getting ready for the baby shower, so I'll wait outside." I picked up the lemon bar and took a bite. "This is delicious. When my life is calmer, I may call and ask for your recipe."

"Are you in some kind of trouble with the law?"

"Me?" I scoffed. "I own the Book Depot on Thurber Street. The most heinous crime I commit is selling those yellow study guides to students who can't be bothered to read *War and Peace.* Thank you so much for letting me use your phone."

"You're welcome," she said, eying me suspiciously.

I went through the living room, across the porch, and along the road until I came to the fence. Roderick was nowhere to be seen. I wasn't feeling overly fond of him, but he was Sarah's alibi. He also might be able to identify Tricia Yates as one of the members of SAC. The photo on her driver's license was difficult to discern.

If I could find him and borrow Luanne's car, it might be time for an unannounced visit to the notorious apartment complex.

15

I looked back at the farmhouse to make sure Abbie wasn't watching from her porch before I said, "Roderick?"

He appeared at the edge of the woods. "Any luck?"

"I called a friend who's on her way to pick us up. As much as I'd like to leave you here, I need you to see if you can identify someone. Tuck was having an affair with a woman using the name Tricia Yates. I believe she was a member of SAC. She could have escaped, or she could have served out her sentence and been released."

"Did she kill Tuck?" he asked as he crawled through the strands of barbed wire. He remained at a prudent distance from the road. "Does Sarah's lawyer know this?"

"I called to tell him, but he was worried that his phone was tapped. He said he'd received an anonymous tip about a motel." I stopped to think about it. "Did you and

Sarah rent a room that night?"

"At a cheap motel on the highway. She was afraid that if we went to her house, Tuck might come home because he'd been bitten by a mosquito and needed medicine for malaria. He was a sorry mess."

So was I, although I wasn't about to admit it. "What time did you leave the motel?"

"Sarah left around midnight. I stayed the rest of the night, watching TV and drinking wine. The mattress was lumpy, but it beat a sleeping bag on the ground. I split at seven the next morning. There were cop cars and a news van at her place. I got this crazy idea that the feds were onto her and Tuck, so I went on to Zach's place and packed my crap in case I needed to run. When I drove to a gas station, I heard about the shooting on a local radio station. No details, just that the sheriff was investigating the homicide at their house and the victim was male."

A car came down the road, driven by a woman with pink cotton-candy hair. We exchanged cheery waves. I glanced over my shoulder, noting that Roderick had re-treated, and waved again as another car packed with baby shower guests drove by. Feeling conspicuous, I started walking toward County 102. Roderick's muttered curses suggested that he was having a more difficult time in the brush line. Two more cars passed me, their drivers and passengers gaping at me like guppies in their air-conditioned aquariums. I could only hope that Abbie was too occupied serving punch to call the sheriff's office.

Luanne finally appeared in her silver Jaguar. She's never offered any information about her financial situation, but Second-hand Rose was not the pride and joy of the local chamber of commerce. I knew she'd gone to boarding school in Switzerland and to a women's college that charged tuition equal to the gross national product of a small country.

She pulled up next to me and put down the window. "I'm Butch Cassidy, you're the Sundance Kid. Get in the car before the posse arrives."

"Our ride's here," I yelled as I opened the car door.

Luanne gave me a perplexed and not especially friendly look. "Please don't tell me that you're with that guy who escaped from prison."

I shrugged as "that guy" came out of the woods and once again crawled through the barbed-wire strands. "I'm not going to tell you anything, okay? The less you know, the better. The only thing we're going to talk about is the weather."

Roderick looked distinctly scruffy as he traversed the ditch, but he was not salivating copiously, rolling his eyes, reciting religious scriptures, or scratching his privates. I waited until he got in the backseat, then sat in the passenger's seat and said, "Let's get out of here."

Luanne made maneuvers worthy of a trained professional, and within seconds we were racing down the road as if we were being pursued by the Batmobile. She seemed disinclined for conversation, as was I. When we reached the county road, she whipped out without so much as glancing at the stop sign. She navigated through the minimal traffic, and we arrived at her apartment in a matter of minutes. I exhaled.

"Now what?" she demanded.

"Go upstairs, flip the steaks in the marinade, take a shower, and douse yourself with seductive perfume," I said. "I need to borrow your car. If anyone calls to inquire about me, respond in French and hang up."

"As in Peter?"

I got out of the car and waited while Roderick squeezed himself out of the backseat. "Peter won't call you. I'm in trouble with the FBI. They want to speak to me, but I'm not ready to speak to them."

Luanne looked at me. "Are you going to be okay, Claire?"

I went around the car and hugged her. "Yes, eventually. Have a lovely evening with Sweetie."

"Should I bring the baked beans to the county jail?"

"I'll let you know, but it's not unthinkable. We need to leave, so run along. I promise to drive carefully."

"Do you think I care about my car?"

I shooed her away before I became teary. Once I was in the driver's seat and Roderick was beside me, I said, "Let's drop in on Tricia Yates."

He did not respond. I pulled onto Thurber Street and drove by the campus to the apartment complex. Its official name was Skull Creek, and it lived up to its seedy reputation. Although it was late Sunday afternoon, parties were in progress, some on balconies and others around the pool. Music blared in a cacophony of atonal screeches. Shirts and shoes were not required. I stopped and searched my purse for the piece of paper I'd taken — well, stolen — from the church files. "We're looking for 221-B."

Roderick was staring at the students as if he were at a zoo (and on the preferred side of the bars). "Wow, this is a blast. Maybe I shouldn't have wasted my time at protests and demonstrations, trying to bully the Pentagon into noticing to us. I could have hung loose by the pool with semiclad women, smoking pot and guzzling brew."

"Really?" I said grimly, searching the buildings for signs.

"No, not really. We were vehemently opposed to a senseless war in an obscure country seven thousand miles away. Kennedy, Johnson, and Nixon spewed out propaganda about saving the world from communism." His voice rose. "Do you think the five million people who died during the Vietnam War cared about politics? What about Laos and —"

"Calm down. It was a long time ago, and you did everything you could. We need to find Tricia's apartment." I spotted a *B* on one of the buildings and parked as close as I could. "Look at this photocopy of her driver's license. Is there anything familiar about her?"

He was still breathing heavily as he took the paper. "I don't know. Maybe, maybe not. She looks like someone is tossing a grenade at her."

"The DMV camera is programmed to capture that expression. If I'm right about

Tricia, you haven't seen her in forty years. Her car's parked over there, so she's home. Try to be inconspicuous, okay?"

"As I get out of a silver Jaguar that costs eighty grand? People are already staring."

"See if there are sunglasses in the glove compartment," I said.

"That'll fool 'em."

I put the car keys in my purse and opened the car door. Roderick was wearing a pair of Luanne's designer sunglasses when he came around to the front of the car. It was not an effective disguise. He kept his face lowered as we climbed the exterior staircase and walked along the balcony to Tricia's apartment. Two boys with their feet on a cooler blocked our way but politely moved their feet.

"Whassup?" one of them said without interest. The other was too busy chugging a beer to ask much of anything.

"Yo, dudes," muttered Roderick.

I knocked on Tricia's door, waited a minute, and knocked again. "She has to be here," I said. "I'm sure that's her car."

"She could be out by the pool," he suggested, looking over the rims of the sunglasses at the fifty or so students surrounding it.

"She has short silver hair. I don't see her.

She's not fond of her neighbors, so she wouldn't be partying with them. Poisoning the water in the pool or stalking them with an assault weapon is —" I stared more carefully at the partygoers, then leapt behind Roderick and said in a low, urgent voice, "Give me the sunglasses."

He held them over his shoulder. "What's going on, Claire?"

"I thought I saw Frank Norton cuddling up with the brunette in the orange bikini. Could this be a setup?"

"Who's Norton?"

I muttered an expletive as I peeked around his arm. "He's a deputy in the sheriff's department. He's been popping up at inconvenient times and places for the last three days. He must be following me."

"He's damn quick if he is," Roderick said. "In the time it took us to walk up the stairs, he changed into his swimming trunks, dashed to the pool, and picked up a hot girl. Did his badge come with superpowers?"

"It didn't even come with average powers. I don't see him now, so I guess I was mistaken. Tuck's paranoia must be contagious." I banged my fist on the door and shouted, "Tricia!"

"She may not want to talk to you."

"Then she's out of luck." This time I

banged like a jackhammer ripping through concrete. I noticed that the two beer drinkers were watching us, and smiled at them. "Have you seen Tricia Yates this afternoon?"

The more talkative one said, "I saw her go inside when we went out for food at about one. Haven't seen her since then, but we don't exactly hang out together."

"Hell no," mumbled his cohort. "Be like getting drunk with my grandmother."

During the exchange, Roderick had nudged me away from the door. "It's not locked," he whispered. "Now what?"

The two boys continued to watch us. They may not have been physics or math majors, but they might find our behavior suspicious if we simply opened the door and went inside. I turned my head and looked intently at the door. "It's Claire and . . . Oliver, Tricia. Sure, we'd love to have some iced tea." I looked at Roderick. "She says she was in the shower and has to get dressed, but wants us come on in."

I grabbed Roderick's arm and pulled him inside the apartment. "For a prison escapee, you're not very quick-witted. Haven't you ever had to improvise?" Without waiting for a rebuttal, I called Tricia's name. There was no response. With the blinds closed, the living room was as shadowy as a basement.

There were liquor bottles on the counter of the kitchenette and pans haphazardly piled in the sink. A card table supported a computer and piles of books and papers. The door to the bathroom was open; the square footage inside it was minimal.

"Creepy," Roderick said in a low voice. "I'm expecting someone or something to leap out at us."

"Try not to swoon." I moved cautiously toward the bedroom door. "Tricia, it's okay. I just want to ask you a few questions. There's no reason to hide. I'm not going to leave until we talk, and I mean it. Please don't make me search for you."

I pushed open the door — and clamped my hand across my mouth to muffle a hysterical squeal. Tricia was draped across the bed, a large knife protruding from her chest. Her shirt and the bedspread were soaked in blood. Her eyes were open, glazed and unseeing. I backed out of the doorway and stumbled to the nearest seat. "She's dead," I said hoarsely.

Roderick took a quick look. "Oh, yeah. Not cool. Not cool at all. Let's get out of here fast." He retreated so quickly that he tripped over a footstool and fell backward in a tangle of arms and legs.

I closed my eyes and took several deep

breaths to fight off a wave of nausea. I concentrated on an image of my handsome husband's face, his molasses eyes gazing into mine, his hand on my shoulder, his forehead creased as he opened his mouth to lecture me about my rashness and inflated sense of civic duty. He was in the middle of pointing out that I could face prison when I erased him with one fell swoop of my equally imaginary eraser.

"Stop wiggling on the floor and find a place to sit," I said sternly. "We don't have time to panic. If you want to grab a liquor bottle, I won't object. This is beyond not cool. This is very, very bad." The last three words seemed to echo in the room.

Roderick got to his feet and went to the counter. A minute later he put a glass in my hand. "Drink this. We can't go racing out the door without those college boys noticing us. As implausible as it may be, they might decide to investigate. If the door's unlocked, they find the body. If the door's locked, they get suspicious and call the manager, who finds the body. We're screwed either way. They'll claim the woman was alive when we arrived because you spoke to her through the door."

"Why would I kill her? I don't have a wisp of a motive." I took a swallow of something that scalded my throat. Tricia's budget had precluded all but the cheapest brands of booze, obviously. This was not the opportune moment to complain to the maître d'. "We have to think. Go take a careful look at her face and decide whether or not she might have been one of the SAC demonstrators."

"Shouldn't I make some gingersnaps first?"

"Funny, Roderick. Go see if you recognize her." I forced down another swallow of 90 proof swamp water. I couldn't tell if it was marketed as wine or whiskey.

He puckered his lips and glared at me as if I'd snatched away his favorite toy. "All right, but I'm doing this under protest. You've made up this fantasy about her. She was likely to be whoever she said she was, an old lady working as a church secretary and plotting to burn down the church if she had the chance. What are we going to do when I don't recognize her?"

"Stop stalling."

"I'm not stalling," he said huffily. "I'm merely considering the possibility that you're wrong. Has no one ever done that before?"

I aimed my finger at him. "You are the most cowardly killer I've ever met. You shot an undercover FBI agent, and later escaped from prison. Now I feel as though I should hold your hand while you determine if you've ever met the woman. For pity's sake, didn't they teach you anything at Folsom Prison? Did you guys sit around all day and sing Johnny Cash songs?" I could hear the pitch of my voice rising to a height perilous to fine crystal. I forced down another mouthful of whatever it was. "Sorry, I'm a little bit upset. Please look at her, Roderick. Once you've done that, we'll have to figure out what to do. This may be the only place the FBI isn't watching, but I'm not willing to hide out here."

He went into the bedroom. I walked to the counter and put down my glass before my brain turned to 90 proof sludge. The refrigerator contained condiments, leftovers covered in plastic wrap, limp lettuce, and an empty pickle jar. I opened a cabinet and stepped back as tiny moths fluttered out. I was picking at a dried fleck on the stovetop when Roderick returned to the living room.

"I'm pretty sure that's Laura. I don't remember her last name, but she was one of the five who made it out of the student union and disappeared," he said, shaking his head. "This is too weird. Everybody was supposed to stay underground and never have any contact. Sarah and Tuck moved here, followed by Laura and me. It's like we scheduled a fortieth class reunion in Farberville. Maybe the entire membership's here, posing as librarians and mechanics." He sank down in a chair. "Or the FBI set up a sting to bring us together. All the artful clues on Facebook were posted by a dweeb in a cubicle at Quantico."

I would have congratulated myself on my keen observation, had Tricia not been dead in the next room. "She hasn't gone into rigor mortis yet, which means she can't have been killed more than two or three hours ago. I saw her leave the church at half past twelve. What time is it?"

"I'd guess around six o'clock," Roderick said from behind the counter. "Any chance it was suicide?"

"Not a Popsicle's chance in hell. If she'd slit her wrists or her carotid artery, maybe. Samurai warriors reputedly fell on their swords, but it takes single-minded strength to plunge a knife through one's rib cage. Our credibility may not be high, but we can alibi each other. Sarah can't be accused of this, although the Weasel would love to pin it on her. It wasn't a perverted love triangle. You were having an affair with Sarah, and Tuck was having an affair with Tricia. The four of you should have sat down and had a civilized conversation about new arrangements. The house has two bedrooms, after all. If that wasn't acceptable, you'd flip a coin."

"Except Tuck had other ideas, so she killed him."

"That's possible," I said, "but impossible to prove. I'm pretty sure that Tuck and Tricia met that night. He might have told her that he'd decided to turn himself in so he could see his family before he died of whatever disease he thought he had. Tricia was either heartbroken or terrified she might be caught." I rubbed my temples while I tried to concoct a feasible scenario that put them in the barn with the shotgun. "Tuck lied about the fishing trip so he could catch the two of you together. If he followed Sarah when she left the diner, he would have seen her go to the motel. It was reasonable to assume she would stay there all night. He went home for his scheduled tryst with Tricia."

"Who convinced him to take his shotgun out to the barn? That's not my idea of foreplay," Roderick said as he took a swig from a bottle. "Yuck. Pretend I never said that. Maybe he planned to hide in the barn until Sarah showed up the next morning.

When Tricia — a.k.a. Laura — showed up, he beckoned her in there."

"The timing's messed up. Tricia was back with the campers at eleven, and the neighbors are certain they heard the shotgun at midnight." I went to the window and peeked between the slats of the blinds. There were no vehicles from the sheriff's department forming a barricade in the parking lot. If the feds were out there, they were lurking with admirable professionalism. I reminded myself that my car was at Miss Poppoy's house. By now, Roderick's van would have been pulled out of the pond and towed to a fenced compound so the forensics squad could examine every slimy inch of it. Luanne's car wasn't nondescript by any means, but I wouldn't have gotten this far if the FBI was monitoring her phone calls.

"So what do we do?" asked Roderick. "This place is giving me hives. How long do you plan to stay here?"

I spun around. "You were in prison. Did I miss the part about the electroshock therapy that turned you into Mary's little lamb? For pity's sake, stop whining and help me think. We can't stay here indefinitely, but I don't want to tempt fate by driving around town. Traffic cops love to hassle people in luxury cars. Want to speculate on what will happen if I have to show my driver's license? What are the odds the police officer will tell you to run along while he handcuffs the felonious Ms. Malloy?"

"I didn't kill the undercover FBI agent. It was an accident."

"I don't have time to hear about your avowed innocence," I said, as angry at myself as I was at him. Perspiration was forming on my face and back, and my armpits were damp. My stomach was calmer, but my mind was buzzing like an enraged hornet, zigzagging from one unanswerable question to another. "Did you call Evan Toffle's office and tip him off about the motel?"

"No," he said. "It's the kind of place that doesn't waste money on maid service. My fingerprints are likely to still be there after a year. My DNA could be on the sheets. Who did call? The only person who knew we were there was Tuck, if our theory's right."

"And he was dead within hours. The only person he could have told was Tricia when they met that night. She suddenly decided to tell Evan, and she was dead within hours, too. That's an extraordinary coincidence."

"Did she have any close friends that she might have told?"

I shrugged. "I have no idea. See if you can

access her e-mail while I try to find her address book." The clutter was daunting, especially in the dimness. I turned on a lamp and tackled one of the piles on the card table. Roderick fiddled with the keyboard. The computer screen lit up in a promising way. I moved a stack of notebooks and correspondence to the coffee table and examined it. All the unopened envelopes contained bills. A bank statement showed a balance of less than five hundred dollars. Her dentist had sent a reminder that she was overdue for a visit. A card with a depiction of balloons and confetti was an invitation to a baby shower on North Anger Road. Tricia was missing it.

"Awesome," Roderick said, chuckling. "She must have been online earlier, and didn't bother to sign off. She has no e-mails or spam." He continued to click. "Her address book is limited to doctors, a car repair service, two discount shopping sites, Mount Zion Church, and a Chinese carryout. I didn't find any addresses for people who might be family or friends."

"No luck here," I said. "I suppose she was too haunted by her status as a fugitive to risk personal relationships. Too much tippling and she might spill her secret. What a sad life." After a nanosecond of sympathy, I recovered nicely. "The one person she might have confided in is the choir director at the church. Misery loves company, when accompanied by whiskey. His name's Grady Nichols. He's the one who told me that Tricia went for a stroll through the blueberries the night of the murder. There was a lot more going on than he admitted." I took a sip of the whiskey and shuddered. "Why does everything have to be so damn complicated? I am sick and tired of people with fake identities — like you, Sarah Tuck, and Tricia. Maybe William and Junie changed their names from Bonnie and Clyde, and Grady is Charles Manson's eldest son."

"Don't freak out. Let's find out if Mount Zion has a Web page." He mumbled under his breath as he hunched over the keyboard. "Mount Zion seems to be popular with the religious groups. What denomination?"

"Methodist, on County 102."

"Got it!" he said. "In case you're interested, it was founded in the forties in an abandoned schoolhouse built in —"

"I'm not interested."

"Grady Nichols. He believes that music is a spiritual path to heaven, and is filled with awe by the youthful enthusiasm of his choir. He coaches soccer in the middle school league and enjoys cooking, reading, and playing the piano at a senior center. Guys like him used to proselytize outside the student union. They were more worried about Armageddon than Vietnam."

"Look him up in the online telephone directory. I need to know exactly what happened that night. I'm too frazzled to listen to his glib version, and I'm prepared to sit on him until he tells the truth."

"You think he killed Tricia?"

"If I were sure, I'd make an anonymous call to the police. All I know is that something significant happened, and he underplayed it. The teenagers may have been drinking, smoking pot, and behaving like horny monkeys, but . . ." I leaned against the edge of the counter and replayed the conversation with Grady. "He told me that he saw them wading across the river and followed them. Unless he stopped to catch tadpoles, he should have been no more than a minute or two behind them. The ringleaders had to find their cache before the mischief started. Grady claimed they were already stoned when he caught them."

"He was lying. The weed around here is crap. I've got his address. It'll take more time to get his telephone number, if he has a landline. Young people usually don't these days."

"I don't intend to call and tell him I'm on my way," I said, offended by his remark that implied Peter and I were on the verge of dotage. Cell phones were handy, but it was nice to call home. Tears welled in my eyes for the hundredth time. I swallowed and said, "We can't leave Tricia like this. Maybe the college boys wandered down to the pool or went inside. We saunter out to Luanne's car and drive to the nearest pay phone to call nine-one-one and report the body."

Roderick stood up. " 'Death's truer name is 'Onward,' no discordance in the roll and march of that eternal harmony whereto the world beats time.' "

"Don't make me beat time on you or Tennyson," I said. I went to the window and lifted a slat. I couldn't see outstretched legs or a cooler. "Onward, as in out to the balcony and down to the parking lot. Try to look as though you've been having tea. If you so much as stumble, I'll push you down the stairs and leap over your body on my way to the car. Good luck in the emergency room."

"What's with this bitchiness? I'm trying to help, you know."

"You're trying to keep yourself out of prison. I understand that you want to save Sarah, but you haven't made any noble gestures. That's okay. I'm going to exonerate Sarah before Wessell tears her into shreds and spits out her bones. Grady's the best lead now. You can go down to the pool and try to charm one of the sexy coeds. Maybe she'll let you stay with her until she wakes up one morning and realizes that you're her grandfather's age. Just give me Grady's address and we'll part ways in the parking lot. You've had many years to perfect the art of staying underground. The Missouri border's half an hour away."

"I love Sarah. I'm not going anywhere." He snorted as he realized what he'd said. "Except back to prison. Will you still need me, will you still feed me, when I'm ninety-four? Let's shake the truth out of Grady Nichols. I'm right behind you, Claire."

"Lucky me," I said as I opened the apartment door and stepped onto the balcony. I was not greeted by bells and whistles, whoops, sirens, alarms, or more ominously, bullets. The college boys were gone. The party by the pool was beginning to break up as the participants picked up towels, coolers, and other possessions. None of them looked remotely like Deputy Norton. "Come on," I said to Roderick, "and put on the sunglasses. Your photo may have made the local news."

369

"I was wiping off our fingerprints."

"I'm glad to hear prison wasn't a total waste of time. Let's go."

We hurried down the steps and into Luanne's car. I drove out of the apartment and headed for the nearest cluster of fast-food restaurants and stores. There were no pay phones. A convenience store across the road lacked one, too. If I used my cell phone, the FBI would utilize GPS to pinpoint my location; I preferred for them to keep searching the woods behind Miss Poppoy's house. When they inevitably tracked us to Abbie's house, they would liven up the baby shower. The call I'd made to Luanne would be traced. Her flawless French might delay them, but they were as inexorable as a glacier.

"There are pay phones at the student union," Roderick said, "or there used to be. Not many people around on a Sunday evening."

I turned toward the campus and entered the labyrinth. The streets were mostly empty, as were the sidewalks. Parking places were plentiful, to my relief. The student union was old and tired, almost hidden by massive magnolia trees and overgrown shrubs. I parked as a couple came out the front door. They stopped when they saw the silver Jaguar, then resumed walking across the grass in the direction of the dorms.

"Wish me luck," I said as I grabbed my purse. After a hesitation, I took the keys out of the ignition. "If I'm not back in five minutes, I suggest you relocate to an adjoining state. Hitchhiking may be hazardous to your health."

"After all we've been through, you don't trust me?" he said in a wounded voice. "I risked my freedom to haul you away on a friggin' lawn mower. I identified Laura. I could have split at any time, but no — I stayed with you in case you needed help. Now you think I'd steal your friend's car?"

"It crossed my mind," I said, too weary to snap at him. Hoping he hadn't taken a class in hot-wiring cars while in prison, I went into the student union and looked around. The information desk was unoccupied. I peered down hallways until I saw a glorious line of pay phones, none of them in use. I did not want to be overheard. It had been a long while since I'd used one, possibly predating Caron's birth. I read an instruction card and learned that I could call 911 without inserting a quarter. I took a tissue out of my purse and used it to pick up the receiver, and used my knuckle to punch the buttons.

371

"This is nine-one-one," said a bored female voice. "What's your emergency?"

I opted for a French accent. "A woman was stabbed in the Skull Creek apartment complex, 221-B. *Je pense qu'elle est mort.*"

"Your name?"

I replaced the receiver, wiped the buttons with the tissue in case the FBI kept knuckle prints, and walked out of the building at a seemly rate. Roderick was slumped in the front seat, brooding over my lack of faith in him. "Done. What's Grady's address?"

"I wouldn't have stolen the car, Claire. We're in this together because we want to save Sarah from being wrongfully imprisoned. I've had nightmares since the day she was arrested." He swiped at a tear. "She's my soul mate, the only woman I've ever loved."

"I'm touched," I said, untouched. "What's Grady's address?"

He told me without further ploys for sympathy. I recognized the name of the street and started the car. It purred with pleasure as I left the campus and turned on a side street. I missed the house number the first time, but caught my mistake and turned around. Roderick had gone into such a deep funk that I had to poke him after I'd pulled as far as possible into the driveway of a small frame house. We dragged two trash cans and a disabled bicycle behind the car, and then spread the grungy remains of a hammock across the trunk. The camouflage was imperfect but adequate.

"Your role is to rumble if he gets evasive," I told him. "I may have to fabricate a story as we go along, so don't contradict me. Okay?"

"Whatever you say."

I poked him more vigorously. "This is our only lead. If you want to save Sarah, you have to do your part. Grady won't be intimidated if you snuffle and whine." I had never envisioned myself giving a pep talk to a convicted murderer. Caron and Inez might find it cool. Peter would not. I wonder if his mother would shake my hand through the bars when we were introduced.

Roderick followed me to the front door. I knocked, and then stepped back. I had no idea what to do if he wasn't home.

Grady opened the door.

16

Grady stared at us. "What do you want?" he said, his bow tie fluttering madly as he swallowed. Had it not been clipped on, it might have taken flight.

"To talk to you, obviously." I veered around him into the living room, which was decorated in curbside salvage chic. "We're going to have a lengthy, uncomfortable conversation about what happened at Flat Rock. This time you're going to tell me the true story."

Roderick shoved him aside with unnecessary vigor as he followed, rumbling like a petulant bear. He grinned at me, but I frowned and shook my head.

"I don't have anything else to say to you," Grady said. "I screwed up as a chaperone, but nobody was hurt. There may have been some hangovers the next morning, and a couple of kids were scratching like flea-bitten hounds. The incident was Tricia's topic at the sunrise service the next morning, and she laid it on thick. 'But now having been freed from sin and enslaved to God, you derive your benefit, resulting in sanctification, and the outcome, eternal life. For the wages of sin is death . . .' Romans 6:23. Scared 'em shitless, so maybe some good came out of it."

"Including Bianca?" I asked sweetly. "Was she shivering in her panties?"

"Who said anything about Bianca?"

I glanced at Roderick, who obligingly rumbled. "I know all about it," I said. "Statutory rape, sexual assault, booze, drugs, endangering a minor — all serious stuff. When you get out of prison, you'll be on the sex offenders list for the rest of your life. That'll make it hard to get a job as a choir leader at the Church of the Almighty Millionaires." I gestured at Roderick. "He can give you some hints how to find seasonal employment as a migrant farmworker. You should listen. Once you're on that notorious list, you won't be able to find a job or rent an apartment. You'll be run out of town wherever you go."

"That's ridiculous!" he sputtered. "I told you what happened."

"You gave me the sanitized version, in which you saved the teenagers from drunkenness and debauchery. You instigated it, Grady." Roderick rumbled without a prompt. I narrowed my eyes and allowed my forehead to crease fleetingly. "You didn't plan on the level of participation, did you? You issued a discreet invitation to Bianca to join you on the opposite bank. At least I'd like to think you invited only one of the girls, but I may be wrong. Once the other kids figured out that Tricia had left, they waded across the river. Did they catch you in the midst of licentious behavior?"

This time Roderick's rumble sounded like the purr of a male lion gazing at his next meal. He seemed to have an extensive repertoire.

"No," Grady insisted, his voice beginning to quiver. "I caught them and put a stop to it."

"I'm more interested in figuring out where Tricia went and how long she was gone than I am in your sleazy sexual behavior," I said mildly, "but if you continue to stick to your story, I'll call the city prosecutor in the morning. She's the mother of two teenaged girls, and rumored to be relentless when prosecuting sexual misconduct."

Grady crumpled into a chair, sobbing. Roderick went into the kitchen and returned with a beer. Across the street, car doors banged and a voice called out for help with grocery bags. A motorcycle roared down the street. I contemplated how to organize an elegant luncheon at my house from a holding cell. My allotted phone call might need to be made to a caterer, if I could find one on short notice.

"Please don't turn me in," Grady said in a raspy voice. "I'm begging you. The sex was consensual, I swear it. It was just so . . . god-awful. Most of the kids pulled off their clothes. Someone forced me to take a couple of hits of pot, and it turned into a bizarre reverie. I tried to make them stop or at least get away, but there were so many hands grasping me." He gulped as if he were drowning in our ill-disguised contempt. "They wouldn't listen to me. I tried, I really did."

"A love fest," Roderick drawled. "Also known as a group grope or an orgy. They were teenagers. Jeez, don't you have any friends your own age?"

"It wasn't my fault," he bleated.

That was one of Caron's pet mantras. It had been used often with little success, and I was not impressed. "That's when Tricia showed up, right?" I asked Grady. "She must have been appalled."

He wiped his nose ineffectively. "I expected her to go ballistic and screech all kinds of sanctimonious shit at us, but she just stared. I told everybody to get dressed, sit down, and shut up. Tricia was weird, like she was overmedicated. I was starting to worry about her when she pulled herself together and launched into a lecture. The part about swearing on the Bible was true."

"What time was it?"

"More like midnight," he admitted. "Once I started telling you about it, I had to make it sound like it happened fast. I'm so sorry I lied to you."

Roderick rumbled, but less ominously. "You got anything to eat, man?"

It occurred to me that I might have been hearing his stomach rumbling. "I have money. Shall we order a pizza?"

"I'll do it," Grady said eagerly. "I think I have a coupon. Pepperoni okay with you?" He got up and started toward the kitchen.

I asked Roderick to follow him, then flopped back in the chair to ascertain if I was capable of thought. I felt as if the day had begun Thursday afternoon, seventy-two hours previously. Peter's manly prowess had diverted (and delighted) me, but I'd not slept well afterward. And might not in the future, unless I was issued a decent mattress and considerate cellmates. It was getting dark outside. I couldn't go home or to Luanne's apartment. What cash I had would cover the cost of a motel — if I dared drive the only silver Jaguar in town and park it outside the room. The FBI surely had traced the call I'd made from Abbie's house. Luanne might have been able to deflect them in French on the telephone, but not after they appeared at her front door in black suits and sunglasses, with a *traducteur français.*

The two men came back into the living room and sat down. Roderick looked cheerful; Grady looked as if he'd interrupted his own funeral. They sat down on the sofa as far apart from each other as possible.

Grady jabbed his thumb at Roderick. "Who's this guy?"

"Oliver's an old friend of Tricia's," I said, pleased to have a neat opening for my next question. "Have you seen or talked to her since you left the church earlier today?"

"Why would I?"

"To tell her she needs to replenish her liquor cabinet?" I suggested, hoping Roderick would lay off the rumbling.

"She'll discover that Tuesday morning. We don't socialize outside of church. I'd rather watch cooking shows than listen to her whine about her salary, her apartment building, her car, her hair, and everything else. She used to be tolerable, but a while back she mutated into a harpy."

"After the campout," I said, nodding. "She saw you at your worst and was disgusted. I'm surprised she let you share her bourbon." I considered this for a moment. "Was she blackmailing you, Grady? All she had to do was a little research online to find out you committed a handful of misdemeanors and a truckload of felonies."

"She writes the checks, and she knows I make less than she does. During the week, I coach soccer and give piano and voice lessons for grocery money. I sing at weddings so I can hang around for the buffet. All my credit cards are maxed out."

"Maybe she wanted private lessons," said Roderick, emphasizing the word "private" with a leer.

Grady's eyeballs bulged. "You've got to be kidding! There's no way I'd ever do that! The idea of touching her makes me want to puke. No blackmail, no nothing! We never talked about that night."

I believed that much. It would have been a very awkward conversation for both participants. "All was forgotten until I came along and started poking the hornet's nest. Were you worried that she'd blurt out the whole story? She didn't have anything to lose, but you do."

He smirked. "But then she'll have to explain where she was. The guy that got shot lived across the field. We saw the police cars and TV vans when we drove past the house the next morning. He wasn't a member of the church, but she could have known him. Her behavior was suspicious, and it wouldn't help that the teenagers and I would have to say that she was acting real strange when she came back from that direction. Tricia and I had what you might call a mutual agreement not to elaborate on the events that night."

Roderick rumbled, indicating skepticism.

I was formulating a response when the doorbell rang. I took out a twenty-dollar bill and was about to hand it to Grady when I was seized with an epiphany of blinding brilliance. Despite my innate modesty, there is no other way to describe it. I pulled back my hand and said, "I'll get it."

I opened the front door and assessed the delivery boy. He was no more than seventeen or eighteen years old and had the cheeks of a chipmunk. His hair was pulled back in a ponytail. I was delighted to see headphones hanging around his neck, with a wire that went to a device in his shirt pocket.

"Pizza Pizzazz," he chirped. "One large pepperoni with green peppers and onions. That'll be sixteen dollars and fifty-three cents, ma'am."

I took the box from his hands and set it down on a nearby table. "I'll be back shortly," I said to Roderick and Grady, and then gently propelled the boy out onto the porch, waving the twenty-dollar bill like bait. "How many more deliveries on your run?"

"Uh, like two," he said, mesmerized by the bill as I wafted it under his nose.

"Would you be interested in a fifty-dollar tip?"

"Yes, ma'am."

"Allow me to explain how you're going to earn it."

Minutes later I was in the passenger's seat of his subcompact as he drove past the stadium. As per our arrangement, he was wearing the headphones and singing along with whatever was eroding his hearing and endangering him with a future of tinnitus. I pulled out my cell phone, fiddled with it until it came to life, and called Peter.

"Hey," I said, "I wanted to let you know

I'm safe. Had any more visitors?"

"Two of them haven't left. They know what you're driving."

"Not at the moment. Did Wessell stage another press conference?"

"He's getting national media coverage. He made an announcement about Roderick James, which added to the reporters' frenzy. Your name was tossed into the fray. CNN and MSNBC reporters are camped on our road. Jorgeson sent a patrol car to block the driveway. Turn yourself in before it gets worse, Claire." When his voice broke, so did my heart. "I love you, even when you're on one of these fanatical crusades. We'll confront this together, I promise. I have our lawyer on standby, but she can't help until you're in custody and charges have been filed. Caron's handling it as best she can. She said to tell you that she's got your back. You need to go to the PD."

"I will tomorrow. Got to go. I love you." I hung up as the delivery boy pulled into a driveway. He gave me a fuzzy smile as he retrieved a pizza box from the backseat and went to the door. I struggled not to lose what little self-control I had. I'd heard the extreme anxiety in Peter's voice, which was very dear of him but not constructive. If I were to turn myself in, Wessell would have me in a stockade in front of the courthouse. My jail jumpsuit would have a scarlet *M* for meddlesome. Or murder, I glumly amended, if he found a way to charge me with Tricia's death.

The delivery boy returned. "Cheap bastards. A two-dollar tip? Give me a break!"

"My tip will ease your pain." I waited until he'd replaced the headphones and backed out of the driveway, and then called Luanne.

"Guess who?" I said, although I doubted she was in the mood for games. I can be very perceptive.

"Do you know how much trouble you've gotten me in? Why did you take my car to a murder scene at a skanky apartment building? If Sweetie hadn't come early and provided me with an alibi, I'd be at the jail in some hideous orange outfit, waiting for my lawyer to drive back from his lake house at five hundred dollars per hour! Have you lost your mind? The news anchor said that Wessell accused you of aiding and abetting a fugitive, who happens to be armed and dangerous. They don't know that I —"

"Was kind enough to pick me up a few hours ago," I cut in before she incriminated herself. "That's what friends do. Your phone is tapped by now, and mine as well. I can't tell you any more. I'm okay. Good-bye."

The delivery boy arrived at his last designated address, which turned out to be a motel. He found the room number and parked. He gave me the same smile as he took the pizza box and climbed out of the car. I calculated that my final call could last no more than five minutes. I wondered if the FBI agents were having a jolly time trying to locate me via cell towers. I rolled down the window and stuck out my head to listen for a helicopter flying above the area while its copilots peered down for silver Jaguars. No spotlights swept across the parking lot, which was for the best since the couple in the pool were skinny-dipping in the muted light of a pink neon sign. Their version of Marco Polo was X-rated.

Once the delivery boy returned and put on his headphones, I called Evan. "How's it going?" I asked brightly when he answered.

"Holy shit," he yelped. "You shouldn't be calling me."

"Deal with it. I know about the motel room. The man who was with her will give her an alibi if we get down to that."

"Unless it was Roderick James, the notorious felon who broke out of prison and now has every law officer in the county and dozens of FBI agents searching for him. Not the most credible witness. He could have killed Tuck because of some forty-year-old grudge. How convenient that his story gives both of them an alibi."

"You're rather peevish," I said. "Another member of the SAC group is involved, too, although there's a small problem putting her on the stand. She was there and may have killed Tuck."

"Give me her name. The FBI might as well go after her, too."

"You don't want to know. Any idea who gave you the tip about the motel?"

"Muffled voice, female. You seem to know a lot more than I do. I did learn something significant, however. Sarah used her credit card at the motel. No one from the sheriff's office bothered to request her credit card activity. I'm going to use that to undermine their case."

"Very sloppy of them." I frowned as I realized there was another possible clue the investigators had ignored. If I told Evan, I might as well be broadcasting it on the radio. I needed to have it in my possession first. "Did the night clerk see her leave?"

"No, and he didn't notice anyone with her. He gets paid to keep his eyes on the TV behind the desk. The only reason he remembers her is that she seemed too old to be fooling around. He's used to older men and younger women."

"I have to go, Evan. I'll try to check in with you when I can." I ended the call as my temporary chauffeur got in the car, and I powered off the phone when we were more than a mile from Grady's house. I dug out my wallet and removed some bills. When we arrived, I waited until my young friend took off the headphones before saying, "I promised you fifty dollars to let me ride with you. I'm adding another fifty so that you'll forget it ever happened. If you go back to your pizza place and start bragging about this, you'll find yourself in court facing a judge. Trust me on this." He reached for the bills, but I held them out of reach. "Say it," I commanded him in my steeliest maternal voice.

"Never happened. I delivered the pizzas and now I'm reporting in to pick up the next bunch of pizzas. You know, we can do this again anytime you want. Just call Pizza Pizzazz and ask for Darcy. The telephone number's on the receipt."

I gave him the money. "Thanks, I'll keep it in mind."

"Have a nice evening," he called as I walked toward the house. Yeah, right.

Roderick and Grady were watching TV, the empty pizza box on a stool. The former gave me an inquisitive look; the latter ignored me. I went into the kitchen and opened the refrigerator. The contents were not promising, but I found a package of sliced cheese and made myself a sandwich with the last of his bread. I took it and a glass of ice water out to the backyard and sat down on a dubious webbed aluminum chair. I was not surprised when Roderick joined me.

"Where've you been?" he asked as he opened a beer.

"Delivering pizzas. I know the FBI can trace the location of my cell phone, so I provided them with a little excitement. It's incapacitated now. The police followed up on my nine-one-one call and found Tricia's body. A helpful resident told them about the silver Jag. We're not implicated yet, but the detectives will question her neighbors. Unless the boys on the balcony went to the movies, they've already described us."

"Bummer."

"I agree. I did learn one curious thing. Sarah's lawyer told me that the anonymous tip about the motel came from a woman. It had to have been Tricia. She was either trying to help Sarah or alerting the feds about you. Are you sure you never encountered her?"

He scratched his chin. "Not that I recall, but I wouldn't have paid any attention. I don't study people's faces in the grocery store or on the sidewalk. When you made me look at her, I was able to recognize her because I was focused on the SAC members. I had her in context."

"Could Tuck have recognized you and told Tricia?"

"No way. Sarah and I were very careful not to be seen together. She's positive that he had no clue about our liaisons. I never went to the farmers' market, the co-op, the library, the convenience store, or anywhere he frequented. The only reason he started following her after work came from his home-grown paranoia."

"What about your green van?" I asked. "He might have noticed it on the county highway, caught a brief glimpse of your face, and begun to suspect he recognized you."

Roderick snickered. "Maybe, but even if he'd found a way to trace the license plate, all he'd have learned is that it's registered in Arizona. When the plate expires, I peel a sticker off a parked car and glue it on mine. Been driving it for three years."

I gazed at the shadowy trees that hid the stars. Music and voices from various locales in the neighborhood drifted in and out of my consciousness. Too many people with aliases and a shared past, I thought bleakly. Three anonymous tips, so far. One from me, doing my civic duty. One from Tricia, motive undetermined. The third had been made to Wessell's office, at a most opportune time — unless he'd been saving it for maximum impact. A single TV van had shown up to cover his first grandiose press conference on the steps of the courthouse. Peter had said that the national media had swooped in like turkey buzzards for Wessell's subsequent theatrics. I winced as I envisioned him in court, his weasel face damp with excitement as he pointed at Sarah and elaborated on her heinous crimes in the past. How could she not be guilty of murder? She'd been on the FBI's most-wanted list for forty years! Would the honest, law-abiding residents of Stump County allow her to get away with yet another murder? The courthouse was his bully pulpit. "Bully" was the operative word.

"Let's construct a scenario," I said, discarding the last few bites of the sandwich. "Everything was cruising along. You and Sarah had found each other, and Tuck and Tricia had done the same. Infidelity wasn't an issue for at least a year. Then, out of nowhere, Tuck decided to turn himself in to the FBI so he could reunite with his family before he died of an outlandish disease he learned about from watching reruns of *House*."

"He freaked out," Roderick said, "but he may have been right. He was having headaches, sore muscles, fever, and fatigue. Sarah told me that she saw brief moments of facial palsy, like he was having a stroke. I researched his symptoms online and came up with Lyme disease. Bad news when it's gone untreated for a long time."

For the very first time since I'd heard Tuck's name, I felt a glimmer of sympathy. He was a notorious hypochondriac, dismissed by his doctors and the emergency room staff. Anything short of a visible splintered bone would have been treated with two aspirin and a condescending pat on the back. On top of that, he was paranoid. On a scale of one to ten, his credibility fell below zero.

"Let's stick to the scenario," I said. "Tuck told Sarah about his intentions. What was her response?"

"She made him promise to wait until she had a plan, and he agreed. She and I talked about where to go. Her identity would be blown, but we'd have enough time to locate a safe haven. The underground network is vaster than you might believe. Once upon a time, it was operated by hippies, antiwar protesters, draft-card burners, and dudes on their way to Canada. You showed up, contributed as best you could, and moved on. Some of these places were for peaceniks, others for the proviolence faction. Back in the seventies, I stayed in communes from California to Vermont. It's harder now to find a place to stay and regroup, but we figured we could."

I had no urge to grasp his hand and hum an antiwar hymn. "Maybe after Tuck follows Sarah to the motel, he loses it. When he gets home and Tricia's there, he tells her that he's going to call the FBI right then. She tries to talk him out of it, but he won't budge and they end up having a bitter fight. Now she's incensed because he's dumping her after she'd made sacrifices to be with him — or because she's liable to be arrested along with Sarah. Life without Tuck, or life without parole. She convinces him to take the shotgun out to the barn. Blam."

Roderick nodded. "I can buy that. Tuck was hysterical, and therefore easy to manipulate. Once it was done, Tricia put the shotgun back in the closet, turned off the lights, and walked back to the campsite. Turned out she couldn't crawl into her

392

sleeping bag straightaway, thanks to Grady's transgressions, and was berating them at midnight. Sarah didn't leave the motel until after twelve, so she didn't get home until twelve thirty at the earliest."

"How ironic that the only way Sarah can save herself is to send you back to prison. She and Tricia had more in common than they thought, although Sarah has an alibi." I recalled what Evan had said regarding the alibi and found myself with a second scenario, an unnerving and unwelcome one. Was it possible that Sarah and Roderick had decided to choose fight over flight? If she was found innocent, the two of them could continue their affair with a mere modicum of discretion for the foreseeable future. He would ditch the van in another state, and then move into Sarah's house. He'd be introduced to William and Junie as an old friend from college or a distant cousin. My breathing quickened as I envisioned Sarah in the barn with Tuck. Sarah or Roderick, or both of them.

"Something wrong?" he said.

"I'm worried Grady might watch the news and find out about Tricia's death," I said with commendable glibness, considering his proximity. Sarah decapitated chickens for dinner. Roderick had gone to prison for murder. My only weapon was a glass of water.

"Not gonna happen. He has forty-three episodes of *Law & Order* on his DVR, and he's determined to watch them all in a mindless marathon. He's mastered the art of fast-forwarding through commercials. Are you old enough to remember when you had to walk across the room to change channels? After I escaped from prison and moved in with a woman I met at a bar, the remote control was the first technology that blew my mind. The bulls at Folsom decided what we watched. Changing the channel without permission cost a week in solitary." He leaned back, his hands hooked behind his head. "I was so damned bored that I played with the bugs. I was known as 'the Roach Man of Folsom.' Not my favorite sobriquet, I have to say."

I was exhausted, and my blood sugar level was on a roller coaster. I was in desperate need of Peter's arms around me, his voice assuring me that it would all go away. I was battered, and a particular part of my anatomy had not yet recovered from the excruciating escape on a riding lawn mower. But more than anything, I wanted to convince myself that Roderick had not been lying to me since our encounter in Miss Pop-

394

poy's kitchen, that he was not a calculating killer. "Tell me the truth about the demonstration," I said. "I need to hear it."

"Yeah, okay, but it was forty years ago, so the details are mushy. When I joined up with SAC, I found out that all they did was stage pathetic little antiwar protests in front of the student union — if the weather was nice. They held up their signs and chanted the same ol' slogans. The campus cops walked right past them. I'd been at Berkeley, was a member of SNCC, and stood alongside the Black Panthers. We staged sit-ins and occupied buildings, and took beatings from the pigs." He groaned. "Sorry, Claire, I know your husband's a cop."

"He has no porcine proclivities," I replied tartly.

"Of course not. I convinced this SAC chapter to make themselves a true nuisance to the campus administration. We gathered in front of the ballroom, symbolically chained the doors, and plunked our butts on the floor. We refused to respond to the campus cops when they ordered us to leave. Nothing should have happened, even after the local cops arrived. I'd warned everybody to expect to be arrested and dragged to jail. The rich kids, like Sarah, were ready to bail us out via American Express. We were having a fine time singing the anthem from Country Joe and the Fish — you know, 'and it's one, two, three, what are we fighting for?' — when this new guy, Abel, jumps up with a knife and grabs hold of a scrawny boy cop. The cop pulls his gun. It turns into a shoving match, the spectators panicking, everybody yelling. Abel yanks the gun away from the campus cop and thrusts it at me. By now, it's looking like a full-fledged football brawl, with fists flying and cops bellowing. Abel knocks me down and we're wrestling on the floor. The gun goes off, which scares everybody shitless. To this day, I don't know if I pulled the trigger. The jury decided that I did. End of story."

"Hardly the end of the story," I said, "or we wouldn't be here."

"True. If the demonstration had simply wound down, Sarah and I'd be teaching literature courses at a community college, planning our retirement, and watching our grandchildren play soccer."

"Vera, Chuck, and Dave?"

"Or something like that." He finished the beer and crumpled the can in his hand. After a long moment, he said, "If you're thinking that Sarah and I conspired to shoot Tuck, say so and I'll be blowin' in the wind. You can tell the FBI that I took you hostage and had a gun at your back the entire time. Maybe I threatened to harm your daughter if you didn't cooperate. After all, you're highly skilled in the art of improvisation. You don't even bat an eye when you dish out bullshit."

"You're not bad at rumbling," I said. I was aware I might be making a mistake, perhaps a fatal one, but I could not believe he was capable of cold-blooded murder. Or Sarah, unless I'd seriously misjudged this gray-haired, sexagenarian version of *Romeo and Juliet*.

"Can your husband rumble?" Roderick asked.

"I hear him now. Picture an incredibly handsome man with dark hair, an authoritarian nose, soft brown eyes, glittering white teeth, and molten lava coming out of his ears. I almost feel sorry for the FBI agents assigned to babysit him." I smiled, albeit sadly. "Okay, you and Sarah weren't responsible for Tuck's murder. I think Billy saw Tricia on her way back to the campsite — and that was after he'd been awakened by the blast. He swore he saw zombies across the field. Someday his parents will have to explain what his zombies were doing, and I don't want to be within a hundred miles of that conversation."

"Billy?"

"The Lunds' grandson. He's four and endowed with a flamboyant imagination. The deputies from the sheriff's department basically ignored him."

"Because he saw a couple of zombies? Very pedestrian of them."

"I reared a child like that," I said in defense of my disparaged witness. "There was always a mote of truth in her dust storm; the trick was to spot it. I talked to him and William before I went to Miss Poppoy's house. Oh, dear, do you think she's all right? I can picture her on the front porch, waving a gun at the deputies and agents as they charge up the driveway." I covered my face with my hands. "I'll live with guilt for the rest of my life if she . . ."

"What she did was feed them fresh gingersnaps and send them away, thoroughly bewildered. Who in the hell is Geronimo?"

"He was an Apache chief who instigated attacks on the Spanish when they invaded his territory, wherever that was, back in the early nineteenth century. These days he has something to do with jumping out of airplanes. I don't know, Roderick, and I truly don't care. All I want to do is tidy up this mess and go home."

"You sure he was an Apache?"

I dumped the last of the water in my glass onto his lap. "It's time to talk to Grady. Rumble your heart out."

17

Grady sat on the edge on the sofa, intently watching as the jury forewoman said, "We're unable to arrive at a verdict, Your Honor. We've debated for three days, and we're deadlocked."

The avuncular judge sighed. "I have no other choice than to declare this a mistrial. Ladies and gentlemen of the jury, the court thanks you for your time. You are dismissed."

I stepped in front of the TV screen. "Now it's time for a reality show, Grady."

He reached for the remote control, but Roderick was quicker. I remained where I was until Grady sank back with a martyred moan.

"Let's talk about Tricia," I said.

"Let's not," he said. "I told you every damn thing that occurred that night, as best I remember. Sex and drugs, but no rock and roll. No blackmail, either. You want the salient details? Do you want me to draw a picture? Are you some kind of voyeur?"

Roderick planted himself next to Grady. "Shut up and listen."

"No! I've had it! I want you both to leave my house. Call the prosecutor and tell her the whole story. I'll be tried, sentenced, and sent to prison, where I'll be beaten and sodomized. Is that what you want?" He tried to get up, but Roderick had him pinned against the arm of the sofa. "Beat me now if it'll make you happy. I don't care!" He raised his knees and folded himself into what appeared to be a very uncomfortable yoga position. With his head between his thighs, his sobs were muffled.

I studied him for a long moment, unable to decide if I'd overestimated him and he truly was a pitiful wimp, or if I'd underestimated him and he was a liar — and a killer. I glanced at Roderick, whose puzzled expression mirrored my own. "Pull yourself together, Grady," I said coldly. "You need to read the local morning newspaper. There are a lot worse perverts than you who end up with probation, community service, and compulsory therapy. On the other hand, you can never get off the sex offenders list."

"I knew a guy in prison," Roderick commented, "who had a thing for a pretty little heifer. He was doing life for first degree murder. The farmer sold Elinor to a meat-packing plant, and the guy went berserk with a shovel. His cellmates said he mooed in his sleep all night. I always think of the poor jerk when I order veal scallopini."

I clamped my hand on my mouth before I laughed. Grady's sobs grew louder, and his body was twitching as if he'd been poked with a cattle prod. "I think what Roderick is trying to say," I said, still struggling to remain solemn, "is murder is a serious crime."

"So?" Grady squeaked.

"You told us you were here all afternoon. Can you prove it?"

He looked up through watery red eyes. "Why?"

Roderick rumbled. "Answer the lady's question."

"Yeah, I can prove it. I had company. What does this have to do with the campout? That was a year ago."

I crossed my arms. "I need to know the names of your visitors. We'll use your cell to call them and confirm your alibi."

"Alibi? I don't need an alibi. Why do you care what I did this afternoon?" He blinked as he began to assimilate what I'd said. "Did somebody get killed? Tricia? Is that why you asked me if I'd seen her? What the hell happened to her?"

"Why don't you tell me," I suggested.

"I don't know!"

"Tricia was stabbed to death in her apartment. My working theory is that you were afraid she'd expose you. You went there to talk her out of it, but she wouldn't listen to you. The ensuing argument escalated until she was screaming at you. You grabbed the nearest weapon, a large knife, and chased her into her bedroom. The police found her body two or three hours ago."

Grady squirmed free and stumbled to his feet. "You're crazy! You're both crazy! I was here all afternoon with a friend. I'm not going to give you her name because I'm not a suspect!" His arms were waving so frantically that he might find himself under siege by Don Quixote. Merely watching him made my shoulders ache.

Roderick chuckled. "But you are a suspect, my man. Skull Creek is a five-minute drive from here. There was no sign of a break-in, which means Tricia opened the door for her assailant, someone she knew. Five minutes to kill her, five minutes to drive home. That adds up to all of fifteen minutes."

"And another fifteen minutes," I said, "to

bundle your bloody clothes in a plastic bag, shower, and cram the bag into someone else's trash bin. The CSI will find minute traces of blood, no matter how much you scrubbed the bathroom."

"But I didn't do it!" Grady howled, stomping his bare feet, spittle spewing in a most repulsive manner. "Tricia wasn't going to do anything that would incriminate herself. We've gone over this a dozen times. Even if she wasn't involved with the murder, she'd lose her job. She'd already lost her so-called soul mate." He squeezed his lips together as he realized what he'd said. "She committed suicide," he added lamely. "Menopause was messing with her mind. All those hormones. She was depressed, drinking more, showing up late for work. She told me that at a board meeting in May, she came close to punching Deacon Wentworth in the nose."

"So Tricia confided in you about her relationship with Tuck. Did she tell you that he was going to turn himself in?"

"Turn himself into what?"

"Sheesh!" Roderick said, exasperated.

My head began to pound in an arrhythmic tribal war chant. I sat down and tried to think, but no more than a dozen neurons fired. "I need to get some sleep," I announced. "I'll take the bedroom. Roderick, you and Grady figure out something." I pointed my finger at Grady, but my aim was wobbly. "Call the police, run away, or watch reruns until the sun rises. Keep in mind you're in so far over your head that your best bet is to start tunneling for China."

I went into the bedroom and closed the door.

When the alarm went off at six, I rolled out of bed. My outer clothes lay in a circular heap not unlike poop from a very large dog. I found a pair of jeans, a belt, and a long-sleeved white shirt in Grady's closet. I felt no remorse; he would not require an extensive wardrobe in prison. I took a short shower and dressed in clean clothes. I ran my fingers through my hair but once again avoided the mirror.

Roderick was sprawled on the sofa, snoring. Grady squatted in his bare feet on a chair in yet another bizarre yoga pose. Rather than meditating, he was absorbed in an alley scene on the TV. Captain Cragen and Detective Logan were somber as the body of a young woman was placed on a gurney. "It's the fiancé," Grady whispered helpfully.

I went into the kitchen and started the coffeemaker. After searching the cabinets, I set out a box of crackers, the package of sliced cheese, a can of tuna fish, and three small cans of chopped green chilies. Bacon and eggs were not on the menu. I poured myself a cup of coffee and ate a cracker while I reflected on the cast, the crew, the sets, and the script of Tuck's murder a year ago and Tricia's the previous day. Sarah's trial would start in slightly more than twenty-four hours. Wessell was armed with a cannon; Evan had a water pistol. I didn't even have fingernail clippers. What I did have was every law enforcement agent within a hundred miles searching for me. My mother-in-law was on a private jet over Virginia or Tennessee. The pilot might comment as they flew over the Blue Ridge Mountains, while the butler served fresh croissants. I hoped she ate heartily, since my luncheon menu was nonexistent.

I went back into the living room and whacked Roderick's foot. "Wake up, and for pity's sake, put on your pants. I don't have all day to deal with this nightmare." I whacked his foot again, and then swooped in on Grady and snatched the remote control. "Go have some coffee and something to eat. We're leaving in half an hour."

"Can't leave," he panted. "Briscoe is about to inform the girl's parents. They don't know she was paying her tuition at Hudson University by pole-dancing at a strip club. The fiancé went there for his best friend's bachelor party. He was enraged." He held out his hand. "I need the clicker. A commercial's coming. I never watch commercials. Got to fast-forward through 'em."

I turned my back on him and hit the power button. As the TV screen faded into darkness, Grady whimpered. I looked at him and said, "We're down to twenty-eight minutes. You can shower and change clothes if you wish. We will not be stopping at a café for waffles, so make do with what's on the table. You, too, Roderick."

Roderick sat up. "Where are we going?"

I was no longer a mild-mannered bookseller motivated by a desire to do my civic duty. Hell hath no fury like a woman meeting her mother-in-law for the first time. Attila the Hun would step aside as I approached him. Genghis Khan would cower. Harvey Dorfer, the sheriff of Stump County and presumably supervising heavily armed barricades on every county road, would weep when Election Day rolled around. As for County Prosecutor Edwin Wessell, I was prepared to grind his case under my boot heel and walk all over him, figuratively. Literally, if I could figure out how to do it.

"Coffee's ready. Do whatever you have to do, but be ready to leave when I say so." I glared at them but opted not to rumble.

Half an hour later, Roderick was in the backseat of Grady's car, complaining steadily about the close quarters. "Drive out toward the church," I ordered Grady, who was still mumbling hints to the *Law & Order* detectives. Had I not been in his presence for the previous twelve hours, I'd have suspected him of being high on drugs or alcohol. I wondered if there was a twelve-step program for rerun addiction.

Grady emerged from his fantasy precinct long enough to say, "There's a cop car behind us. What do you want me to do?"

I ducked. "Don't run any stop signs, and obey the speed limit. It's just a coincidence."

"Use your turn signals," volunteered a voice from the backseat.

"Thanks for the advice," Grady said in a sarcastic falsetto. "I thought I should slam on the brakes and let the cop rear-end us."

"Don't count on us to visit you in prison," Roderick said. "Don't worry, though. You'll make lots of new friends."

His hands tightened around the steering wheel. "I have an alibi for yesterday afternoon. She's a soccer player on my team and old enough to consent. How do I know that the two of you didn't kill Tricia? You pin Tuck's death on Tricia, and then silence her before she can defend herself."

"What did Tricia say to you after the teenagers were back in their tents?" I asked as I lifted my face to peek in the side mirror. There was no official vehicle behind us. Grady was disintegrating under pressure. I wished I could withdraw my question before he drove into a brick wall. There were many brick walls in Farberville.

"We sat on a rock, smoking dope. I salvaged two half-empty bottles and we finished them. She was crying. Tuck told her that he was calling the FBI the next morning. He said he was sorry about the repercussions, but he had to see his family before he died. She couldn't believe how cold he was. It'd taken her decades to find him, and she believed they'd spend the rest of their lives together, that happily-ever-after shit. Then he said that he saved all her letters, but he didn't remember where he stored them. If the kids in the tents hadn't been close by, Tricia would have been ranting so loudly the mosquitoes wouldn't dare approach us. I was afraid she'd start frothing at the mouth."

"Did she say how they ended the conversation?" I asked.

Grady frowned. "Parting wasn't sweet sorrow, if that's what you mean. Here's the church, here's the steeple. Oops, no people! Now what?"

"I'll tell you when to turn." I realized that I'd promised to bring Billy a new bandana. The only businesses open were convenience stores and coffee shops. "Do you have a bandana in your trunk?"

"Why would I?"

Not an unreasonable response, I conceded. "Because you dressed up as a cowboy for Halloween?"

Grady turned his head to stare at me. "No, I did not dress up as a cowboy for Halloween. I was a chaperone at the church party, and I went as Martin Luther."

"Eyes on the road!" Roderick barked.

Grady's head snapped back into its former position. "You know, I did have a bandana. A while back the seniors in the congregation rented a hall from the VFW and sponsored a community square dance. I was assigned to oversee the refreshment table, and told to dress in clean jeans, one of those polyester shirts with snaps, and a bandana tied around my neck. Someone loaned me cowboy boots. Hee haw and hallleluah! I felt like an extra in that musical set in

410

Oklahoma. I can't recall the name of it, but it has lots of dancing cowboys."

"Turn here," I said, "and drive carefully. Sarah's house is likely to be under surveillance. Park in the first driveway on the right." After he'd done so, I said, "Did Tricia attend the square dance?"

"Involuntarily, like me. She carried platters of food from the kitchen and bussed tables. She was pissed because she had to buy a denim skirt and a bandana. Neither of us got paid for overtime."

I took the key out of the ignition, eliciting a snicker from the backseat. "Here's the plan," I said confidently, fooling neither of them. "Roderick, you need to stay out of sight. The Lunds watch the local news. Grady, come with me." We started walking across the lawn. Most of the toys had been put away, but the tricycle was parked under a tree. "Have you met their grandson, Billy?"

"Too bad Methodists don't believe in exorcism."

I took that as a yes. It was seven o'clock, but William had told me that they woke up early. I knocked on the front door. When Juniper appeared in an apron, her hands dusted with flour, I said, "I apologize for interrupting you while you're making breakfast, but I'd like to speak to Billy."

She looked over my shoulder. "Grady Nichols, what on earth are you doin' here? Are you two friends?" I sensed from her hesitation that she wasn't casting us as drinking buddies or bridge partners.

"My car broke down," I said before he could respond, "and Grady offered me a lift out here. Is Billy awake?"

"He's at the kitchen table, working through a stack of pancakes layered with ice cream and blueberries. He gets to choose his final breakfast before he goes home. If my daughter finds out, she'll tear into me about all that nutrition nonsense." She grinned. "Grandmas don't worry about sugar and carbs. They make cookies."

"We'll wait out here," Grady said. He took my arm and tugged me toward the porch chairs.

"He's almost done," Juniper said as she closed the door.

"Let go of me!" I said in a low voice. "You just blew our chance for pancakes, with or without ice cream and blueberries. Do you know how long it's been since I've had a decent meal? Did you and Roderick even think about saving a slice of pizza for me?"

"You went off with the pizza guy." Despite his sanctimonious if senseless defense, he

412

had enough wits left to back away from me. It was a wise decision.

I sat down and gazed at the trees surrounding the yard. Sarah's house was partially visible. I hadn't seen any cars parked in the driveway or by the barn. Tuck had believed that FBI agents perched in trees to watch his every move. I understood his paranoia. Juniper could have gone inside to call the sheriff's department. Deputy Norton, who seemed attuned to my inner GPS, would show up shortly, a gun in one hand and a pair of handcuffs in the other.

William and Billy came out to the porch, saving me from an elaborate vision of my life behind bars.

"Hey, Claire," William said. "We weren't expecting you so early."

Billy the Kid, dressed in rubber boots, shorts, a holster, and a red felt cowboy hat, put his hands on his hips. "You aimin' to rustle cattle, lady? I'm the law around these parts, and I ain't puttin' up with thieving, 'specially my grandpa's cows. You just unhitch your horse and ride out of here peaceful like."

I held up my hands. "I'm unarmed and not at all dangerous. I came to borrow your red bandana, remember?"

William bent down. "I don't trust her,

Sheriff. I saw her picture on a wanted poster in the general store." He looked up at me, smiling without warmth. "She and her partner are outlaws."

Grady came around the corner of the porch. "I'm no outlaw," he said to Billy. "You know me. I'm the choir director at your grandparents' church. You met me at the Fourth of July picnic."

Billy grinned. "Yeah, I threw a firecracker at you and you spilled potato salad all over Mizz Morland. Wow, was she mad! You chased me all over the park, but you never caught me." The tip of his tongue slipped out for a second.

"About the bandana?" I said to him.

He felt around his neck, made a face, and hurried inside. I had no clue what to say to William. He'd seen the news and knew that I was a fugitive. Grady's presence must have perplexed him.

"It's a long shot," I finally said, "but the bandana could contain DNA evidence. The lab will find Tuck's blood and Tricia's sweat."

"Did you confront her?"

"No, there was a little problem. Anyway, I believe she met Tuck sometime before midnight. They ended up in the barn, arguing. She shot him, wiped the blood off her face and hands with the bandana, and inadvertently dropped it when she hurried back to the campsite. Billy saw her as she made her way back to Flat Rock, but it was dark."

"Or some good ol' boy tossed the bandana out of his truck as he drove by," William said.

"That's possible, but it qualifies as Brady material. The prosecution is required to turn over all evidence to the defense. The deputies who investigated ridiculed everything Billy said, threw away their notes, and refused to take the bandana for testing in the state lab. Evan, Sarah's lawyer, will insist on entering it into evidence. That's enough to put the trial on hold, or at least provide grounds for an appeal."

"If you say so," he said doubtfully.

Billy bounded through the front door. He wore a bandana around his neck. It was bright red and pristine. "Grandpa got me this when I couldn't find my old one. We looked everywhere, even under the bed and in the closet. He had to make a special trip to the store yesterday so you wouldn't be upset. Do you still want it?" His fingers fumbled with the knot at the back of his neck.

I put my hand in my purse and retrieved

my wallet. "No thanks, Billy, I wanted the dirty one. You don't need another new one, so why don't I give you enough money to buy a shiny badge?" My smile was superficial, the best I could produce as I discounted my previous scenarios. I was bemused when my legs began to itch, since I'd always scorned the premise of psychosomatic maladies. I came to what might be described as a rash decision.

Billy tugged my hand. "Made out of real silver?"

"Absolutely." I turned to face William. "How much do you think a silver badge costs?"

"A hundred dollars!" Billy shrieked as he yanked his cap pistols out of his holster. He fired a round of shots at Grady, who crumpled to his knees and clutched his chest. Billy moved in for the kill.

"I'll have to write an IOU," I said.

"You're safe. Billy will have forgotten all about this by the time his parents arrive to pick him up. If you're besotted with guilt, you can find one at the discount store for less than a dollar."

"Would that be a good place to buy ointment for a rash?"

William's smile faded. "If you got into poison ivy, you can apply any kind of medicinal cream for fourteen days and it'll clear up. Otherwise, you can tough it out for two weeks."

I sat down on a chair and pretended to examine my ankle. "No, I'm okay except for scratches. Tricia developed a painful rash the night Tuck was killed. So did a couple of the teenagers on the campout, after they'd come across the river to frolic in the blueberry bushes."

"It's my fault I didn't put up an eight-foot-high wall topped with bits of broken glass? The last time I put up a NO TRESPASSING sign, I found the charred remains in a campfire circle. I write off a small percentage of the crop to theft. It's hard to pick blueberries in the dark."

"Tricia had to walk between the rows of bushes on her way to and from Tuck's house. Why do you think she developed a rash? Your crop is certified organic. She couldn't have come in contact with a pesticide."

"Not in my fields," William said firmly. "I abide by all the regulations from the National Organic Program Standards Office and the Organic Trade Association. I use bone meal and an approved insecticide made from chrysanthemums."

"So you say," I murmured. "You told me

that you have a contract with a company that makes organic products. It requires you to produce a large quantity of berries every season. Ever discover any very hungry caterpillars on the bushes? If you can't meet your quota, you'll lose the contract."

"That's none of your business."

Juniper came out onto the porch, a mug of coffee in each hand. "I thought you and Grady might like something to drink."

"Thank you," I said. I didn't know the extent of her participation in what I believed was organic fraud (and I claim credit for inventing the phrase). "And thank you for calling Sarah's lawyer with the tip about the motel. He's already had an interesting conversation with the clerk, who remembers Sarah."

She glanced at William. "I hope it helps. Billy, we need to go upstairs and pack your suitcase."

"In a minute, Grandma. I don't want this bad guy to escape."

Grady raised his head. "I swear I won't move. I'm deader than a doornail."

Billy pondered this. "No, I'm gonna have to tie you up till the posse gets here. There's some rope in the barn." He dashed down the stairs and around the corner of the house. Juniper shrugged and went inside.

418

"How did she know about the motel?" I asked William.

"What motel? I don't know what you're talking about, Claire. Sarah must have told Junie something about a motel. Ask her, not me."

Grady, who was on his back, began to inch toward the corner of the porch. If he intended to flee, it was going to take him a very long time.

"Sarah hasn't told anyone about the motel, including her lawyer," I said. "Even though she has an alibi, she refuses to name the person who was with her."

"Roderick something, one of the demonstrators who broke out of prison and tracked down Tuck and Sarah? I caught the evening news. If I was the prosecutor, I'd be wondering which one of them left the motel and killed Tuck. Co-conspirators can't alibi each other."

"True," Grady called from behind a large pot of geraniums. "Ask Jack McCoy."

"They don't need to," I said, ignoring Grady, "because neither of them is guilty. You weren't watching a movie that night. You were out in the field, spraying whatever pesticide you use to ensure a bountiful crop. When Tricia came by, you hid and then tailed her to Tuck's house. You had to find out if she saw you and told Tuck. He had a lot of knowledge about pesticides and regulations, didn't he? The only reason you'd be in the field at night was not to be seen."

He was struggling to maintain an amiable expression, but his face was waxy. "This is gibberish."

"As soon as Tricia stormed away, you went across the road and confronted Tuck. Did you take the shotgun from the closet and march him out to the barn?"

"He was already there, planning to shoot Sarah when she came home," William said, "or so I surmise. I was watching a movie."

"Was Tricia watching a movie yesterday afternoon when you went to her apartment?" I noticed Grady had wiggled himself off the porch and out of view. Roderick was broiling in the backseat of the car. Neither of them could rush to my defense within minutes. Seconds were out of the question.

"I drove into Farberville to buy a bandana. While I was there, I bought detergent, paper towels, three pairs of socks, and a copy of the Sunday paper. I got home in time to watch Billy climb a tree out back before supper." He leaned back, stretched out his legs, and crossed his ankles. "Had no call to go by Tricia's place. I avoid her when I can."

I mimicked his pose, although his legs stuck out a foot farther than mine. "Well, I think you did. You were content to let Sarah take the blame for Tuck's murder. When I started pricking holes in that version, you decided to shift the blame to Tricia. Roderick would have been a better candidate, but you were unaware of his true identity. You persuaded Juniper to call Sarah's lawyer. You knew I'd tell Evan about the affair, and what I'd learned about the campout at Flat Rock. *Voilà!* Sarah has an alibi and Tricia's at the scene of the crime — with a motive."

"She was furious when she came back across the field, or so I surmise. I was watching a movie." He gave me a smug grin.

"Then you knew that Tuck was going to turn himself in," I said. "Who knows what else he was going to blurt out to the FBI? His identity, obviously, and Sarah's. His affair with Tricia. Your violations of the organic policy. A terminal disease provides one with the ultimate safety net. A life sentence doesn't have much impact when it translates to a year."

William stood up. "Even if what you say is true, you don't have any evidence. Tuck and Tricia aren't going to testify against me, and Sarah doesn't know what took place. The bandana is a heap of ashes. I did happen to buy some clothes at the discount store, some khakis and a T-shirt like I always wear. Junie didn't notice when I came in. My old clothes are in one of the many trash bins in Farberville. I'll deny every syllable of this conversation, should you go whining to the sheriff."

Billy came racing into the front yard, his cap pistols drawn. "Grandpa, there are a bunch of guys getting out of cars in the driveway! They may be zombies in disguise!"

I took the cell phone out of my purse. "They're more likely to be FBI agents. Not only have they been listening to my calls, they've been tracking me via the GPS device. Our conversation's been recorded." I gave him my brightest smile. "As for evidence, there are a hundred acres of it."

The ensuing three hours were dreadful. I gave a lengthy statement to the agents. They were bewildered, but I stuck to the truth. By the tenth time, I resorted to words of one syllable. Grady was found in the woods, clutching a box turtle that he insisted was Captain Anita Van Buren. Roderick had managed to extricate himself from the car and vanish. I found myself crossing my fingers that he could locate Miss Poppoy's riding lawn mower and chug merrily to Missouri.

Between interrogations, I called Evan and told him everything. When he regained his composure after an interminable bout of hyperventilation and silly questions, he assured me that he would be filing a motion to have the charges against Sarah dropped. One of the senior lawyers at Legal Aid had cut short his weekend in order to seek fame by tackling the indictment from the 1970 trial. Evan seemed a bit disappointed that he would not be arguing First Amendment rights in front of the Supreme Court. I assured him that he would be second chair.

I was about to call Peter when Deputy Frank Norton swaggered onto the porch. "Mizz Malloy," he said, "you do keep showing up. As much as I'd like to arrest you, these boys have priority. Sheriff Dorfer sends his regards, by the way. He guffawed when I told him about how you kept meddling."

"Just doing my civic duty." I tilted my head. "Why, Deputy Norton, are you blushing? Do you have a little crush on me?"

"I do not, ma'am!"

"No, it's a sunburn. Was yesterday your day off?" I waited until he gave me a faint nod. "Do you always hang out at the Skull

423

Creek pool, or do you stalk young women at other apartment complexes?"

"I don't stalk anybody!" He turned sharply and retreated to the back of the house. Sick puppy.

Peter's phone went to voice mail. I was calling Caron when a thirty-something young man in a black suit came out of the house and gestured at me. I'd learned the drill by now: I was wanted in the living room to reiterate the entire story in minute detail. The same questions would be answered with the same explanations. I'd be asked to clarify and elaborate. I'd do my best.

"One minute," I said to the agent. "I need to assure my daughter that I'm unharmed." He obligingly stepped back. I punched a button, and to my relief, Caron picked up. I hurriedly said, "I wanted to let you know that I'll be home in an hour, dear. Where's Peter?"

"What on earth have you been doing, Mother? You and that convict are all over the news. My Facebook page is swamped with snide comments. Rhonda Maguire insinuated that you're having an affair with him. Carrie wants to know if I'm still going to the senior picnic this afternoon. I am So Humiliated."

"Where's Peter?"

"He went to pick up pizza. His mother insisted on olives and anchovies. Inez is allergic to olives. I loathe anchovies."

"She's there?" I said, forcing myself to breathe. "Never mind, of course she is."

"Inez is keeping her company on the terrace. I came inside to get the pitcher of tea."

"Did you find the Ming Thing?"

"In a way. Inez and I learned that some man from the drama department at the college had bought the stupid thing, along with other stuff for a set. We looked him up on the Internet. It turned out he's a bigwig in the community theater, and they were opening a new play Friday night. We went to the theater in the afternoon, but there were people all over the place."

The FBI agent harrumphed softly.

"I only have a minute," I said.

"So I persuaded Joel to take me, and Inez happened to show up. That icky thing was on a shelf on the stage. During the final act, I told Joel that I was sick and Inez was taking me home. We hid in the wardrobe room until the play was over."

The FBI agent harrumphed less softly.

"Hurry, please," I whispered.

"As soon as everybody was gone and the lights were off, we went onto the stage and grabbed the thing. How were we supposed to know all the doors had dead bolts? We decided to wait until someone showed up in the morning, but that didn't happen. Finally, we just opened the emergency exit and ran. A security cop grabbed us and called the police."

The FBI agent harrumphed loudly.

"And?" I said.

"I dropped it." Her sigh was masterful, filled with angst and anguish. "We scooped up all the pieces and spent last night gluing it back together. It's on the mantel, even uglier, if you can imagine."

"What did Peter's mother say when she saw it?"

"She laughed and admitted it was a cheap souvenir that she bought as a joke. You're going to die when you see the turquoise silk robe she brought you. Mine's a gorgeous jade green. She gave Peter a set of antique porcelain temple lions. I put them on either side of the fireplace to protect us from evil spirits."

The FBI agent harrumphed like a tiger with a hairball.

"See you soon," I said as I turned off the cell phone.

It took more than an hour before I was

dismissed with stern orders to remain available and to not so much as stick my little toe beyond the city limits. Peter had called in favors from his enigmatic connections at Quantico. Chief Panzer had vouched for my impeccable character. Sheriff Dorfer had agreed that I was not yet a menace to society.

An FBI agent drove me to the police impound lot and oversaw the release of my car. I'd solved the case, but I certainly had not solved everyone's problems. Sarah was in custody. Roderick was headed for parts unknown. Grady would need a lawyer from Legal Aid. Evan, if forced to represent him, would be blushing throughout trial.

On a much cheerier note (worthy of fireworks and champagne), Prosecutor Wessell had made a fool of himself. He'd been adamant about Sarah's guilt. He'd proclaimed it from the courthouse steps, in front of the national media. Martin Luther had made less of a fuss over his ninety-five theses. The Weasel's previous prosecutions were fair game for scrutiny. I looked forward to listening to him bleat on the nightly news.

When I arrived home, I cautiously opened the front door and made sure everyone was on the terrace. My mood improved a bit when I spotted empty wine bottles on the kitchen island. I scurried into the bedroom and changed clothes. One should not meet one's mother-in-law dressed in a random man's shirt and jeans, I thought with only a twinge of hysteria. I did what I could with my hair, put on minimum makeup, and emerged from the bedroom with a sense of foreboding.

Caron and Inez were sitting on the tile floor, towels draped over their bathing suits. My beloved husband was lying in a chaise longue.

A female voice came from the chaise longue beside him. "Okay, so a priest, a rabbi, and a giant frog walk into a bar."

For the first time, it occurred to me that I might like Peter's mother.

ABOUT THE AUTHOR

Joan Hess is the author of both the Claire Malloy and the Maggody mystery series, a winner of the American Mystery Award, and a former president of the American Crime Writers League. A member of Sisters in Crime, she was recently recognized with a Lifetime Achievement Award from Malice Domestic. A long-time resident of Fayetteville, Arkansas, she now lives in Austin, Texas.